The Bartender Between Worlds

HERMAN STEUERNAGEL

THE BARTENDER BETWEEN WORLDS

Copyright © 2024 by Herman Steuernagel

First Edition

This is a work of fiction. Names, characters, places, and incidents either are the product of the author's imagination or are used fictitiously. Any resemblance to actual persons, living or dead, events or locales is entirely coincidental.

All international rights reserved. No part of this publication may be reproduced, stored or transmitted in any form or by any means, electronic, mechanical, photocopying, recording, scanning, or otherwise without written permission from the publisher. It is illegal to copy this book, post it to a website, or distribute it by any other means whether digital or printed without permission in writing from the copyright owner.

ISBN: 978-1-990505-20-1 (hardback)

ISBN: 978-1-990505-19-5 (paperback)

ISBN: 978-1-990505-17-1 (ebook)

Cover by MiblArt

Illustrations by Nettie Steuernagel

Edited by Natalie Cammaratta & Aime Sund

https://www.hermansteuernagel.com

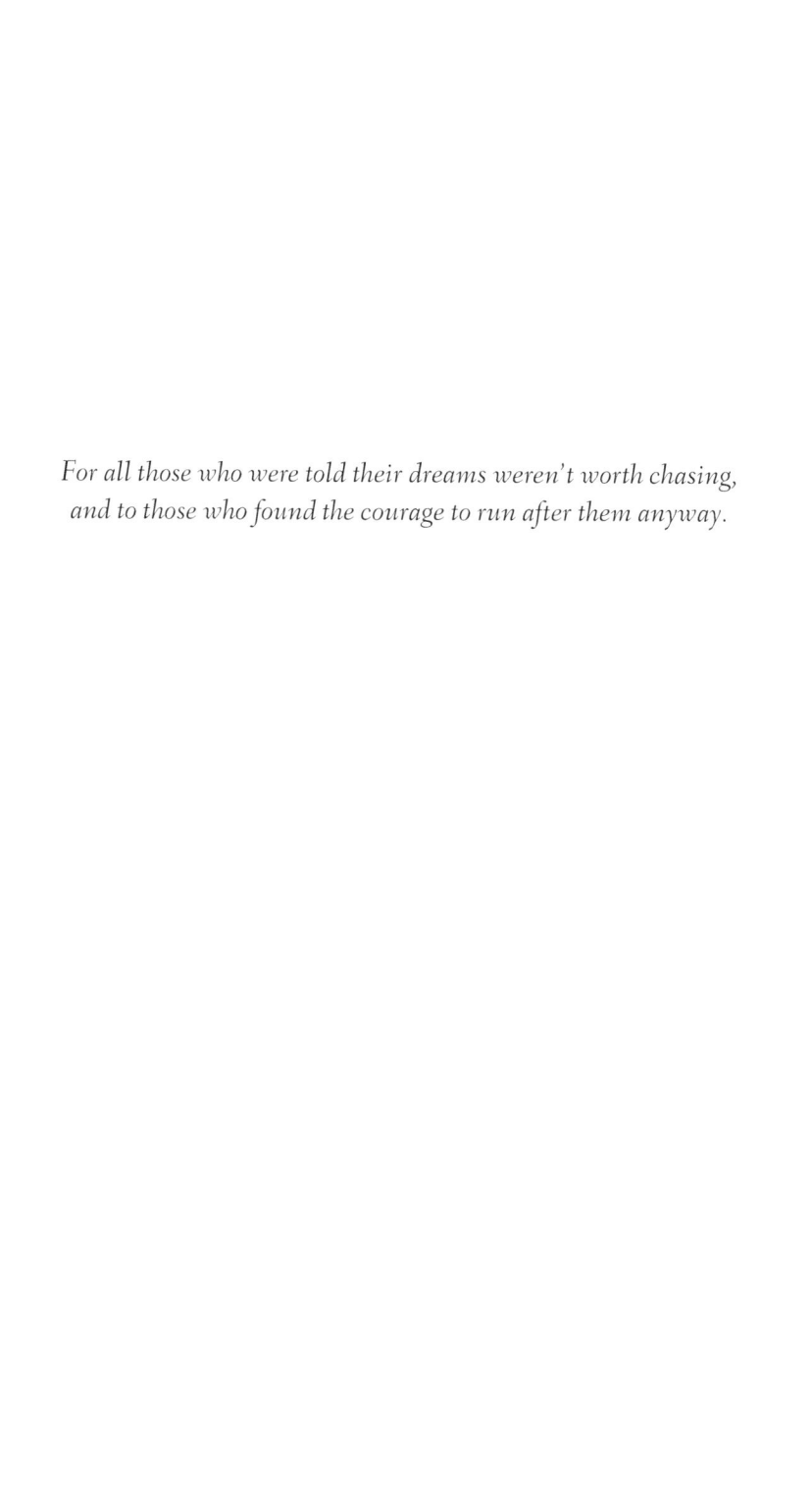

*For all those who were told their dreams weren't worth chasing,
and to those who found the courage to run after them anyway.*

A Pint of Ale

Chapter One

All Emma Corvus wanted was a pint of ale and a month's worth of rest.

The ale would come soon enough. But rest? That would come when she was dead if she were lucky. More likely she'd be overwhelmed by the heaviness of the souls who had left this realm because of her.

Above the village square, the sky darkened as though it held no appreciation for the work she and her partner, Liam Connor, had conducted over the past several months in this backwoods corner of Kalmar. The province was northeast of London, across the North Sea, along the Kingdom of Lancastria's northern shores. It was a typical town for the region, but for some reason filled with more magical creatures and dark beasts than Emma had ever encountered.

Both of them were Hunters of the Cursed, raised under the watch of the king's special forces for one purpose and one purpose only—to rid the world of magic.

Along with a handful of soldiers, they had traveled throughout the region, fighting relentlessly against the threat of monsters, warlocks, witches, and other magical creatures. None of them had gotten much rest. This edge of the kingdom was thick with the Curse, and though Emma had been named among the best of the Hunters, even she was exhausted.

What she wouldn't give for a pint of ale and a warm bed, a crackling fire in the corner of a room, and a nice book. How many nights had she dreamed of nothing more than a break? How many mornings had she woken to the cards of the harsh reality fate had dealt her? After a long and grueling winter of hunting creatures night after night, even the most unassuming magic wielder was a millstone threatening to drown her in a sea of duty.

Emma slammed the door of the cage wagon, wrestled the massive iron lock through the shackle hole, and clicked it shut before wiping the sweat from her brow. She and Liam dealt with the monsters themselves, but Cursed men and women were hauled back to London for trial.

A few gasps escaped from those in the town square who now encircled the two Hunters and their captives. The soldiers kept the inquisitive far enough back that they wouldn't interfere. There was nothing to be done now at any rate.

The woman inside, her blonde wavy hair pulled behind her ears, looked up at Emma in mock fear. Those blue eyes might have enchanted the men and women of Grenaa village, but she and Liam wouldn't be swayed so easily.

The crowd was a mix of those whose lives had been upended by the woman's magic, and those who knew the woman as part of their community: a seamstress, a mother, a friend. Experience had taught her that even those who had once loved this woman would be happy to see her detained.

This was hardly the worst monster she and Liam had faced. In fact, this witch, comparatively, was barely an inconvenience. Though Lewis, the village baker, who was now scurrying around the bakery in the form of a mouse, might not have seen it that way. When villagers began turning up as animals, it's understandable that fear ran rampant through the community. And a witch, no matter how beautiful and charming, was still one of the Cursed and needed to be brought to trial before the King's Court.

Magic—any form of magic—had to be eradicated from Lancastria at all costs.

"What was I supposed to do?" the witch pleaded. "I couldn't control it. Nobody would help me and—"

"You turned the grocer into a cat!" Liam spat. "He's been chasing the baker out of his own shop all evening! And the blacksmith is now a horse."

It took days for anyone to realize there was an extra stallion in his stable.

Not to mention their guardsman whom she'd turned into a pig before they clasped the iron into place, nor the one who'd discovered her blending potions the day before and was turned into a game hen.

Liam continued. "Intentional or not, King Brampton has demanded a cleansing of all Cursed from the kingdom. That includes you, witch."

"My name is Mona!" the witch hissed, emphasizing each word. Then she spat right back at Liam. "And your damned king can take that lock and shove it up his arse! My son was only a boy. Barely fourteen, and the army took him to fight in these never-ending expansionist wars! And for what purpose? The king's greed will never be satisfied."

Liam waved dismissively before turning back to Emma. "I can't listen to any more of this. Let's head to the pub."

She couldn't argue with that. As she turned, Emma's eyes met Mona's. Despite the relative ease of capture, these were the assignments she hated the most. This woman was not a true monster like those who haunted the forests of Lancastria —beings fiercer than animals, with magic aiding their horrors. They'd chill one's spine, both literally and metaphorically.

Mona was simply a woman—one who had somehow invited the Curse into her heart. Many like her had made deals with darkness to seek peace or revenge. Others swore they'd made no such pact, and it was those who worried the Hunters the most. If someone could become Cursed unintentionally, then the plague of magic needed to be stopped before its evil tendrils overturned the kingdom itself.

In this case, however, Emma wouldn't be surprised if Mona had made a pact with the devil himself to exact revenge for her son's conscription. But that would be for the Court to decide.

Lightning streaked through the clouds overhead. An ominous sign for an already dastardly evening. "Is that the last of them here, then?" Emma asked.

Liam nodded. "At least the last reported. We stop here for a few days, then make our way back west."

Emma allowed herself to sigh in relief. Perhaps they'd get a break after all.

The crowd behind them was unnervingly quiet, though it was not an unusual reaction from townsfolk when one of the Cursed walked among them. Each of them waited for her signal—for acknowledgment that the blight of magic had been removed from among them.

She'd smile, but she was too tired even for that. She'd give them the bare minimum effort, for that was all she had left within her.

Oddly, this part of the work bore her no satisfaction—she'd been hunting long enough to know that, much like her, these townsfolk might get a brief respite from the Cursed, but soon there'd be others. More creatures appearing on their doorsteps, more men and women developing strange habits and abilities, more monsters stalking the perimeters of their homes.

It kept her employed, she supposed.

She stepped on a small wooden crate that had been turned over near the cage wagon and amplified her voice so those surrounding could hear her. "The Cursed will no longer bother the town of Grenaa!"

There was only a slight pause before a round of enthusiastic applause erupted.

When she and Liam had arrived, these villagers barely wanted to leave their homes. Emma couldn't say she blamed them. If at any moment the wrong word could cause her to turn into a frog or a bird, she'd hesitate to step outdoors as well. But tonight, they'd be celebrating in the streets. For a few hours, or maybe days, they'd forget the terror that had descended on their village.

Then they'd go back to their daily lives. Maybe for months, perhaps years, but eventually something new would arrive at the city gates, and Emma, or another Hunter like her, would be back to take care of it.

Mona had deflated, sunk to the bottom of the cage wagon with her head on her knees, her emerald skirts pooled around her. Who had she been before all this began? Had she celebrated with them the last time Hunters visited Grenaa?

Emma shook off thoughts of the witch and pushed through the crowd. This reaction, this fanfare, it was the same every time. They arrived at a village, investigated reports of witches, sorcerers, or monsters plaguing them, then dealt with the problem. The townsfolk were grateful for their help, and the Hunters moved on to repeat the process elsewhere.

"Enjoy the evening, friends!" Liam shouted above the applause.

This, of course, cued a parade of villagers who diligently lined up to shake their hands and shower them with unwanted hugs and unneeded praise. Another village was freed from the grasp of the Curse. It should have been something worth celebrating, but Emma was tired of it all.

The crowd eventually dissipated. Many returned to their homes, likely anticipating a restful sleep for the first time in months. Others, including Liam and Emma, went to the local pub to celebrate.

The Cursed will no longer bother the town of Grenaa.

The words still rattled in Emma's head as she sat at the bar beside Liam. How many people had she shipped back to London? How many more would kiss the flames of death?

She'd witnessed enough trials to know the procedure was nothing more than ceremony at best, interrogation at worst. There was no redemption for those accused of bearing the Curse.

Piss-poor ale sloshed in her mug as the bartender pulled the tap and allowed the yellowish liquid to bubble over. It cascaded over the side of the mug and foamed onto the counter before the blond-haired man deftly wiped it away with a rag.

She didn't even have to take a sip to know that what had made it into the glass could barely pass for ale.

These small-town pubs were always hit or miss, and she longed for a quality drink.

"For someone who has an entire town worshiping at her feet, you sure have a sour look." Liam playfully punched her shoulder.

He'd pulled his red hood down, revealing his thick crop of black hair. The hood was meant more for ceremony than functionality. During a hunt in the woods, the brightly colored garb was a beacon for monsters to either run or attack. Neither were beneficial. But a red-hooded Hunter made for a better impression, he'd always said. And on a night like tonight, where the stakes were lowered and there were witnesses, her friend enjoyed a little showmanship.

Indeed, from under his cloak, he'd pulled out the medallion that had hung around his neck since he found it as a boy. It was one of the rare talismans the Hunters had approved of. The sigil warded against magic. It wasn't the perfect defense—he could still be bitten, stabbed, or bludgeoned to death—but it did provide an enviable amount of protection against enchantments.

Emma adjusted her own forest green hood behind her. She had no interest in standing out this night; there was enough attention on her already.

Liam's mug was filled with a dark stout that, somehow, Emma knew was better than her own ale. It was a strange understanding she'd developed of late, and she had to shake off the sensation. She truly was overtired.

"You're not still upset about the werewolves in Nordmark, are you?" Liam pried when she didn't respond to his jest. "Come on, Em, it all ended well. And look at everything we've done here." He lifted his mug to the room. "Liam and Emma have saved the day once again."

Emma sighed. The werewolves had been a particularly harrowing experience. But that was a week ago, and it wasn't as if they hadn't suffered worse in the past. "I'm just tired of this, Liam."

Liam's expression went slack, then he shook his head slightly. "Tired? Of what? Being the hero? Being the salvation of the kingdom?"

Emma deflated, allowing her weight to rest on the bar in front of her. "Yes. That's exactly it."

Liam set his mug down. "You're serious? I realize we need

a rest, but you know we're lucky to be in this role. We're living an adventure that most only dream of. What could be more fulfilling than rescuing these poor souls from the creatures that haunt them?" He swung his mug out toward the rest of the bar again for emphasis, nearly hitting a distressed barmaid in the process. "This is a life that songs are written about. Hell, there's probably some storyteller in a room upstairs weaving together lyrics about us right now!"

Emma sighed again. Liam wasn't wrong. Everything they wanted or needed was provided for them by the king. She also enjoyed that they got to travel and see the kingdom, a privilege very few were fortunate enough to have, but still . . .

"Something's missing, Liam. I have a hard time putting it into words. There's a piece of me left . . . unfulfilled."

Liam smirked and rested a hand on her forearm. "I think I know what that piece is, and uh . . . you know I'm always happy to help."

Emma rolled her eyes and batted his hand away. "Knock it off. I'm being serious."

She had always found Liam attractive—what wasn't there to find attractive? Dark eyes, square shoulders, boyish charm. Hell, there were at least a half dozen Grenaa girls eyeing him up right now as they spoke. But they had tried to start a relationship once, and it ended messily. Their world was one of monsters and bloodshed. They were better off if they could remain undistracted by their feelings. Though Emma hadn't entirely written off the idea that it could happen one day.

She knew he was jesting, but now was certainly not the time.

Liam laughed and held up his hands in protest. "All right! All right! But seriously, what else could you want, Emma?"

Emma took another sip of her ale. It might have been her

imagination, but the taste had improved since the first sip. She tried to focus on what Liam was asking. What *was* she after?

"I don't know," she said. "I've never had a choice about what to do with my life. From the moment we were pulled off the streets and into the king's service, they told us we were to be Cursed Hunters. Trained us for what they decided then sent us to do their bidding. Don't you ever get the feeling there's something more out there?"

"Never." Liam grabbed Emma's arm again, this time as a more sincere gesture. "Who the hell is here by choice? You think any of these men or women decided to live in this backwoods town and go about their days the way they do? We do what we must to get by and make the best of what we're given. The sooner you accept that, the happier you'll be."

Emma surveyed her surroundings, taking another sip of her ale. The beer *had* gotten better—she was sure it wasn't just her imagination.

"Besides," Liam continued, "what else would you do?"

Behind the bar, the bartender pulled on a tap, and the same golden ale poured into another glass. Except she could tell the ale that flowed wasn't as good as what was currently in her mug. The intuition interrupted her thoughts fully. She couldn't explain how, but somehow, she *knew* the ale flowing from the keg was bitter with a slight sour smell and a rough finish.

Her glass held ale that was smoother with a sweet, hoppy quality that was growing on her.

She shook herself out of the thought to answer Liam's question. She knew exactly what she'd rather do. Ever since they'd begun traveling through the kingdom as Hunters, there was only one thing she'd dreamed of becoming.

"Who knows, maybe I'll become a bartender."

"A bartender?" Liam pressed his lips tightly together, a

faint smile breaking through, betraying the laugh he was struggling to contain. "What the hell would you want to be a bartender for? Pulling drinks all night for a bunch of sad drunks? What purpose would your life hold?"

Emma thought for a moment, studying her own glass. She didn't believe Liam was wrong, necessarily. But he wouldn't understand the appeal. There was something magical about turning simple ingredients into laughter and camaraderie. Not real magic, of course. But a power that wasn't tainted by the Curse. One that came from within her.

"Come on, Liam. I grow weary of the hunt. There would be something relaxing about pouring drinks," she said. "The way the ale flows into the glass, the head of foam that spills over it. But it's more than that. I'd be helping people, just in a different way."

Liam rolled his eyes. "How does pouring beers help anyone?"

"Look around you," she said. "Everyone here is enjoying themselves. They're having a laugh with friends, doing what they can to forget that life in the kingdom is hard. And every person the bartender meets is another chance to offer a listening ear. This is where friendships are formed, and weary travelers find solace."

She stopped short of confessing she'd always felt it to be her true calling. She knew Liam wouldn't understand that. Already his face was contorted with incredulity.

The pop of a cork signaled that the bartender had opened a bottle of wine. To the south, on the mainland, viticulture had become all the rage. That the trend had made it as far north as Kalmar province was surprising. There were no vineyards that stretched up onto the peninsula.

From where she sat at the end of the bar, she could tell the wine was bad. Much like the ale, it had soured somewhere along the long route to its destination. Her presumption was confirmed by the bartender's face, which puckered as he tried it.

"Damn." The light-eyed man's voice was gruff, as though he'd spent his evenings smoking cigars and his nights drinking brandy. He lifted the bottle to pour it into the drain.

"Wait a minute!" Emma called to him. "Don't dump that."

She had no idea why she reacted in that manner and really no idea what she expected to do. The bartender raised an eyebrow, looked at the wine, then back at Emma.

"'Tis spoiled, miss," he grunted. "I wouldn't serve this to my mother-in-law, whom I hate. I certainly won't be givin' it to the woman who saved this village." That earned a chuckle from some of the beefy men who sat nearby.

"Let me try it," Emma pressed.

"I have to decline, ma'am, and I do so with the deepest respect. With all you two have done to help our village, I would be right embarrassed to give this to you. Plus, I saw how you worked that blade on the forest trolls last fortnight, and I'd hate to be on the receiving end of it."

Liam leaned in close and whispered harshly in her ear. "What the blazes are you doing?"

Emma raised her hand. If she were honest, she didn't truly know.

"I won't hold it against you," she promised. "Just a theory. If I'm wrong, we'll dump it. No harm done."

"Bloody Londoners," the bartender muttered as he reluctantly brought the bottle over and poured.

That's when it hit Emma—when she realized what the sensation was. The wine was *singing* to her, asking for her help. And without any control or conscious effort, she responded. She could feel *something* flow from her and into the bottle, into the glass. Whatever it was, it was flowing from within her to make the wine . . . better. She could sense the integrity of the wine shifting, bringing it back to a state of its full potential.

It was almost as if it were . . .

Magic.

The bartender slid the glass across the counter and gave her one final side-eye. "If ye go blind. Do not blame me." He nodded to Liam. "You're a witness; I tried to stop her."

"Trust me, friend," Liam said, "I don't know what she's about. If you ask me, the stress of the past few weeks has sent her into a breakdown."

"If I'm to go blind"—Emma cleared her throat, trying to gain some sense of composure—"it will be from the piercing stare of an umbrathraller and not a glass of bad wine."

The bartender didn't react, perhaps not knowing whether Emma was serious or not.

"And if I am having a breakdown"—it was her turn to give Liam a smirk—"it's only because I have to constantly put up with your shenanigans."

That earned another fit of laughter from the group of men along the bar.

Emma lifted the glass, her heart hammering against her ribs.

The liquid spun as she swirled her glass, leaving blood red legs streaking along the inside. Aromas wafted from its surface. Bright cherry, sandalwood, and thyme.

She held her breath and took a sip.

"What'd I tell you?" the barkeep said.

Emma cleared her throat again as she set the glass back down. Blood drained from her face, and she tried to keep despair from marking her voice, but the words sounded distant as they left her lips. "This seems to be a fine example of a

Gascon wine." Trying to calm herself, she added, "Perhaps you just needed to let it breathe."

The skepticism never left the bartender's face as he poured another glass and swirled it around. It was reminiscent of a vineyard sommelier instead of the barkeep of an outskirt village tavern.

He took a sip of the wine, and his face contorted. For a moment, Emma thought he might spit it back out. But instead, he swallowed and looked at the glass as though he wasn't sure how it had ended up in his hand.

"Blazes, you're right." He smacked his lips and took another sip. "This might be the finest wine I've ever shelved. How'd you know?"

"Yes, how *did* you know?" Liam's voice dripped with disbelief. Emma had never been much of a wine connoisseur. Sure, she was highly critical of the ale in these small villages, but to question a bartender about wine from the other side of the bar and be correct . . .

"Lucky guess." Her mind raced, clinging to a memory she'd believed to be buried. "Remember when we were hunting shroudlings in Gascony last year? The one maître d' told us that some of the best wine needed to breathe before it could be enjoyed. I recognized the label on that bottle and thought perhaps that was the case here."

She risked a look at Liam, who nodded with a considering frown. "I do remember that, now that you mention it . . ."

A single bead of sweat ran down her back. Surprisingly, she hadn't felt this much pressure since she'd been face-to-face with four dozen of those shroudlings. Monsters she could handle, but what she had done fell into the realm of magic. "I suppose I filed it in the back of my mind. And look!" She gestured to the bottle that the bartender continued to study intently. "It came in handy."

"Handy! I'll say! Do you know how much coin you've saved me?" He leaned in and lowered his voice so only Emma and Liam could hear. "I could charge premium for this!"

He turned to the rest of the bar and lifted his arms, glass in one hand and bottle in the other. "The Hunters drink for free!"

The patrons erupted in another round of excited cheers. It was customary that townsfolk would buy the Hunters drinks after a successful purge, so the beverages didn't mean as much to Emma and Liam as they would have to the folks who didn't have to shell out a few extra coins for their guests.

Liam roared as though he'd never been given a free drink in his life, lifting his half-empty glass above his head.

Emma lifted her glass as well, but her mind was miles away from the token of thanks.

Out of view in the back storage area, the rest of the innkeeper's stock sat in a crate Emma could feel every single bottle. They called to her. Each begged her to sing to them as she had to their brother; it was a siren's song she found irresistible. She was barely aware that she had allowed herself to become entranced by the energy. With little hesitation, she allowed a piece of herself to flow into the liquid encapsulated in each glass bottle. The structure within subtly shifted so it would no longer be sour and spoiled but as rich and flavorful as the one the bartender held.

When it was done, the patrons' cheers had died down. It had only taken a few moments, and as far as Emma could tell there had been no visible sign of her effort. But she *had* done it. She felt the weariness, the strain it put on her mind. It had been nearly as exhausting as hunting the fiercest of supernatural creatures.

She let out a faint, involuntary gasp as the implications sunk in.

Liam lightly put his hand on her shoulder and leaned in so only she could hear his words. "Is everything all right? You look like you're about to faint."

All Emma could do was nod. "I might." She forced a smile. "I'm going to go upstairs and lie down. It's been a long week."

Liam nodded with a vague expression of concern, but he didn't argue. The statement wasn't untrue, but it was unlike her to retire early without decompressing for a few hours in the company of those they'd saved.

She moved through the crowd, their faces a blur, navigating the gauntlet of congratulations and thanks, to the staircase that would bring her to her room above the bar.

One word circled her mind over and over.

Cursed.

Whatever had happened here tonight had sealed her fate.

Perhaps Liam was right; perhaps nobody really had the freedom to choose their fate. This night, hers had been decided for her. She couldn't stay. Could no longer hold the title of Hunter. By morning, Kalmar would be miles behind her, and she'd be on her way to a new life.

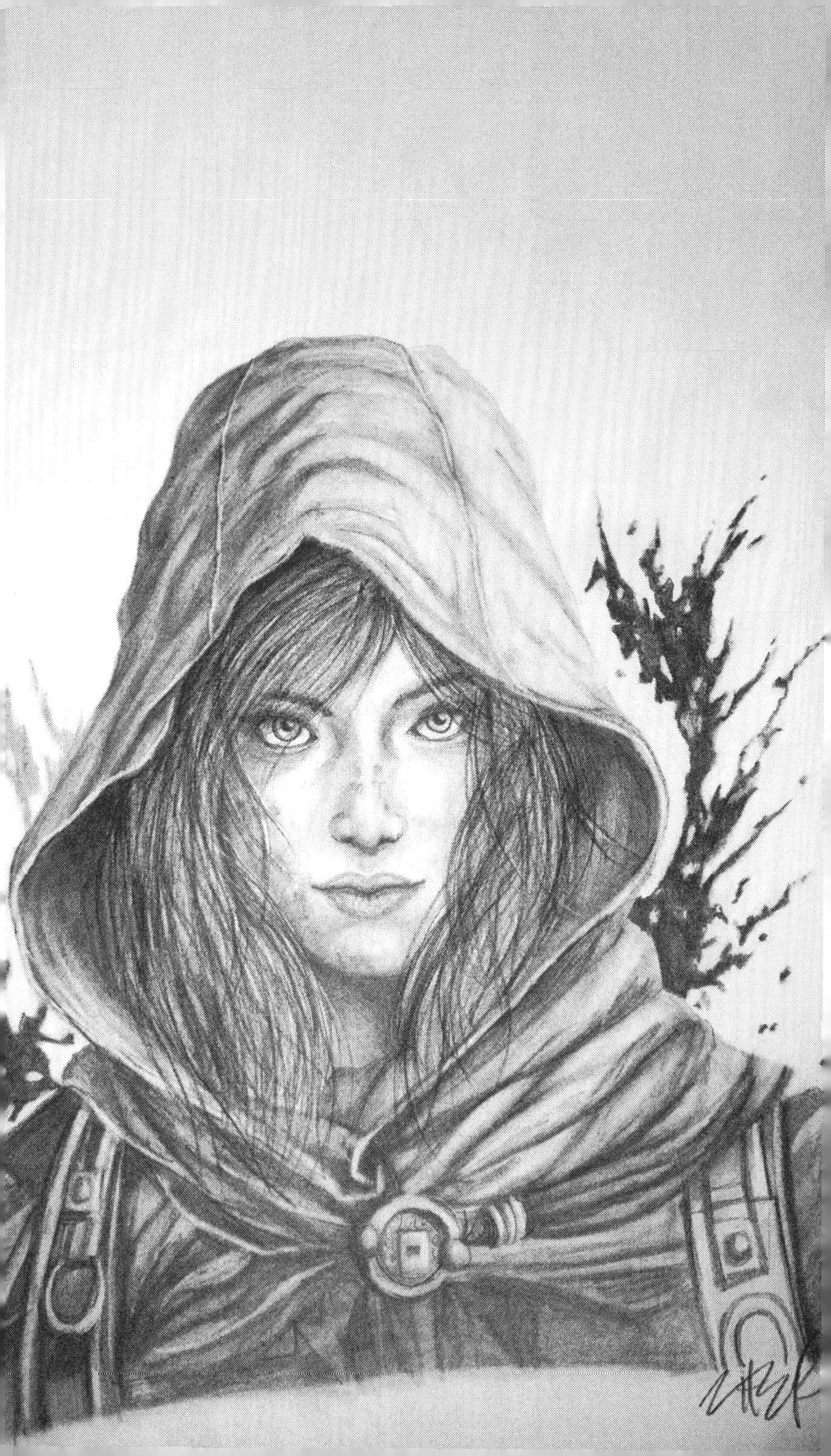

Runaway

Chapter Two

Emma Corvus was *not* running away.

She didn't run, didn't cower in fear, and she could certainly handle herself.

But she also wasn't stupid.

She'd left Liam and Kalmar behind nearly two months ago, and she concluded that she hadn't been fleeing as much as she'd been traveling—swiftly.

Even at an accelerated pace, it had taken that much time for her to travel undetected to what was typically considered the most remote village in Lancastria. She'd had to dodge authorities and anyone who might recognize her the entire way. It had been a journey over mountains, through streams, across the Channel, and the West Sea.

Traveling through the forested parts of Lancastria hadn't been easy. Especially on foot, but it was the only way for her to evade being tracked by the Hunters—not to mention the array of magical monsters that lurked the deepest part of the woods she was forced to traverse. It wasn't that she didn't know the terrain well, but her pursuers would as well. She had to ensure to cover her trail, and to do it well, or this plan would never work.

Cuanmore was as far removed as she'd ever felt from her life as a Hunter, and it still wasn't far enough.

As she entered the lowly pub, quaintly named The Cursed Dragon, the first thing to catch her eye was the lone musician standing in the corner. The young man bore a face full of freckles and a mop of hair that was more orange than red. Emma tucked a strand of her own bright red hair behind her ear self-consciously.

Haunting melodies drifted from his fiddle while somber-eyed patrons sipped at an amber ale which, based on the number of pints distributed throughout the bar, seemed to be the house specialty. The evening was still young, and she imagined this same fiddler would play more lively tunes as the night wore on.

The second person to catch her eye was a man who sat with his back turned to her, an ale on the table before him, nearly untouched. His salt-and-pepper hair grew in all directions like it had been styled by the sea breeze and had never known a comb. He wore a patterned vest overtop a collared shirt with white sleeves that seemed impossibly clean for a place like Cuanmore. Not that it was a dirty town, but the rest of the patrons appeared to be comprised of farmers, crafters, and builders—those who didn't mind getting their hands and trousers dirty.

Whoever this man was, he stood out from them all. In his hands, he worked some sort of small device. Gears and sprockets spread out before him in a chaotic display.

Surely, this was a sorcerer if Emma had ever seen one.

But that was no longer her problem.

Pressing deeper into the tavern, Emma allowed her mind to scan the bar, a skill she'd been able to develop and hone over the past few weeks along her journey. This could be the very tavern she'd find herself working in, and she had to know what libations she'd have to work with.

She might be Cursed, but she still needed coin to eat.

Besides a barrel of dank whiskey, it seemed ale was the only alcohol this local pub offered. Emma wrinkled her nose. Perhaps it was good enough for the lot of them, but she had to admit she'd hoped there'd be more to work with.

Emma pulled her hood back. Cuanmore was the last community the kingdom recognized as being within its borders. Located on the western shore of the island province of Hibernia, it was naturally segregated from the rest of the world. To the west was the endless sea. There were tales from sailors that insisted other lands existed to the west, but the appetite to spend the coin to explore seamen's tales was low. To the north lay barren lands of frigid cold and stone.

As Lancastria's final oasis and most northern port, Cuanmore nestled into a natural bay, protected from the harshest northern and western winds and storms. It was an access point for southern travel and the perfect location for seafaring merchants to offload goods for traders to transport farther into the island province. And even though the kingdom's flag waved above the town, the king and his armies rarely bothered with this remote outpost. As long as the people paid their taxes and didn't cause a fuss, they were on their own.

Hell, as far as she knew, these villagers took care of their own monsters and magic users.

Which, as far as Emma was concerned, was perfect.

Despite the chill of the wind outside, there was something about the village that felt . . . pleasant. Like an embrace at the end of a long winter—one Emma thought she could learn to love. A place to put her feet up after a lifetime of service and two months on the run.

She found herself a seat near the exit, facing the bar so she could keep an eye on the sorcerer. She wouldn't concern herself with him much, but she had been trained not to take any chances.

"Anything I can grab for you, hun?" A young lady with a glow in her eyes and a smile that could sweeten tea approached the table. Golden curls hugged her bubbly face, which only amplified her persona. Emma wondered for a moment if this was an act to entice more tips or if it was her natural demeanor.

Gods, when did I get so cynical?

"Just an ale," Emma replied. "But I do have a question for you, if you don't mind."

The server raised an eyebrow skeptically. "O . . . kay, I guess."

Emma laughed. If this was an act, the girl was damn good about it. But given the crowd a pub in a port-side village like Cuanmore might see, she supposed the girl was expecting a proposition, even at this early hour.

"Nothing insidious, I promise." Emma raised her hands in concession. "But I suppose I should first ask what your name is?"

That didn't seem to ease the server's concerns. She paused a few moments before responding, "Liesel."

"Nice to meet you, Liesel. I'm Emma. I've been traveling through the kingdom, looking for a place to settle, and this seems like a quaint village. It's quite nice here."

That was almost true. Though 'traveling' might not exactly have been the way most would have described her hiding from her fellow Hunters. Former fellow Hunters, that is. One could hardly possess magic and claim to be a part of those who would hunt her down and haul her to London for execution.

"I've lived here my whole life," Liesel responded. The suspicion hadn't completely faded from her voice. "Ships come and go monthly now, so there's never a dull moment.

You're here at the best time of year. The days are getting longer and warmer. Our winters can get long and cold."

Liesel took a moment to survey Emma's outfit. She had, of course, discarded her Hunter's uniform. But old habits died hard. She still sported a dark green hood that she wore down now, allowing her red hair to flow over her shoulders, but her fitted tunic and trousers stood out among the loose-fitting, brown apparel worn by most people in the room—not to mention the various belts and straps that held her collection of blades close to hand. Emma's knee-high leather boots were certainly not fit for the fields either.

Even though Cuanmore wasn't a busy port, Liesel was likely accustomed to travelers from all walks of life, and Emma's garb didn't fit the description of a prospective new resident.

"We *are* far away from most of the kingdom. Surely a place like London or Dublin would be a better place for an adventurous woman such as yourself."

Emma nodded, making a show of truly considering Liesel's response. She had to admit, the long winters weren't ideal. But they would be a minor inconvenience for anonymity. "I grow tired of crowds," Emma stated simply.

"I think it'd be exciting." Liesel beamed, her smile wistful as her shoulders relaxed, her suspicion melting away. "So many people, and nobody knows who you are, or what your business is."

That was true enough, as long as nobody was looking for you. "There is some appeal," Emma replied. "But a city has more eyes watching. And besides, I've had enough adventures."

Liesel's eyes lit up, and Emma got the sense that if she didn't change the subject fast, the barmaid would ask for details she didn't want to discuss. Instead, she nodded to the sorcerer in the corner. "What's his story?"

That did it. Liesel's face darkened, and she shook her head subtly as though afraid the man with his back turned to them might see her. "He calls himself "the professor" and often comes in with unusual trinkets and objects. He keeps to himself, mostly."

"You seem frightened," Emma observed. "Has he threatened you?"

Liesel shook her head. "No, he actually seems nice enough. He's just peculiar. He lives by himself, near the lighthouse. It's rumored that he's . . . ." She glanced at the nearby tables, then, not wanting to be overheard, she mouthed the word—*Magic*.

Although that would confirm Emma's suspicions, it wasn't unusual for hermits and outcasts to be accused of witchcraft when they were only eccentric. Still, there was something about this man that rubbed Emma as being . . . otherworldly. Something she couldn't quite put her finger on. But she wasn't going to badger Liesel about it further. Besides, she wasn't chasing after magic users any longer. The professor wasn't her problem.

"One more question, then I promise I'll let you continue your rounds. Is there any work available here? Perhaps behind the bar?"

Liesel took a moment, digesting the question before a smile graced her lips. "There might be an opening for a server later this month, but the main barkeep is the owner, Mr. O'Malley. Evenings are covered by his nephew, William. He's the one at the bar, now."

"It's just the two of them?" Emma asked. "Seems like a lot of work for two people."

"Only them who work the bar, at least. They have others helping with other tasks, of course. But the bar's been in the O'Malley name for generations. Mr. O'Malley has loved being behind the bar ever since he was a boy."

Emma tried not to let her heart sink. From what she could tell, there were two taverns in this village. The Cursed Dragon and one down the road called O'Sullivan's. If the only two bartenders were the owner and his nephew, there was little chance she would have an opportunity here. The situation at O'Sullivan's could be similar.

Emma bit her lip. It had been a long shot, anyway.

"Will that be everything?" Liesel looked both relieved that the question had been as tame as Emma promised and anxious to get back to the rest of her patrons.

"Just that ale, please." Emma handed Liesel a few handsome coins. "Thank you for your time."

Liesel's face lit up again as she saw the amount Emma had given her and scurried off, nearly forgetting to stop at the next table where two middle-aged men were desperately trying to flag her down.

The Cursed Dragon was reasonably busy for it being early in the evening. Nobody was acting rowdy or contentious, and there was an air of contentment enveloping the pub.

Spring's on the way, Emma thought. Just as Liesel had said, this was likely the beginning of the best time of year to be in Cuanmore. The long chilly nights were behind them, and soon the springtime celebrations would welcome longer days and warmer weather.

It didn't take long for Liesel to bring her the ale she'd ordered then dart off as if no amount of coin were worth the risk of Emma continuing her line of questions.

"Quite the charming place they've got here."

The familiar voice nearly caused her to spit out her drink.

On the high back bench of the table behind her rested a muscled arm, connected to a red-hooded Hunter's uniform, and the same smug face she'd been trying to outrun.

A Normal Life

Chapter Three

There were two impulses Emma had to resist.

The first, and easier to control, was her jaw falling to the table.

The second was instinctive and much more difficult to resist—to reach for her blade and lift it to the throat of the man who now stood beside her.

To her credit, instead of doing either, she gripped her copper beer stein tighter. Her knuckles turned white as she struggled to maintain a straight face.

"Hello, Liam." Emma added a slight crook to her own smile and a sickly sweetness to her voice. "To what do I owe the pleasure?"

Despite all the years she'd spent growing up with, training with, and hunting with the man who stood before her, he was still notoriously hard to read. Presently, she couldn't tell whether he was concerned or smug.

Perhaps he was both.

That damned smirk he hid behind made it impossible to tell.

There were twelve steps to the nearest exit. Emma knew this because, like any Hunter, she always knew the quickest path to escape. It wasn't something she had to consciously calculate; it was just something she knew.

Unfortunately, and most uncharacteristically, she had allowed herself to grow complacent in the quaintness of The Cursed Dragon. The disappointment of her dwindling chances of working the bar and the mystique of the professor in the corner had distracted her. Now one of the few mortal men who stood a chance of stopping her escape stood between her table and the way out.

Out of the corner of her eye, she noticed more Hunter guards, Liam's men, filling booths nearby. It was clear Liam had ordered them to stay close but not engage. Not until he'd talked to her, at least.

She chided herself for being so careless while Liam bore a smug look that she recognized. It was the same one he'd often worn while they sparred during training—he believed he'd bested her.

"You didn't really think," he muttered, his tone just as cocky as his face, "that after all these years you'd be able to hide somewhere I wouldn't find you?"

Emma swallowed. Liam was nothing if not a stickler for the rules. Abandoning her post as a Hunter would face a stiff enough penalty on its own. Never mind the secret she held.

"Come here to arrest me, then?" She took a sip of beer and lifted an arm onto the back of her chair, feigning nonchalance. "I hope you realize I won't go in without a fight."

"Fight?" Liam slid onto the bench and raised a hand to Liesel, indicating he'd like a round. "Come on, Emma. Don't make this harder than it needs to be. I know you see the guard. The rest of our squad is waiting outside with a carriage to take you back to London."

Emma snorted. "Carriage? You mean a cage wagon."

"Only if you do something stupid. But it doesn't have to be that way. You abandoned your post; you haven't killed anyone. You're the best Hunter they've got, they're not going to lock you away for taking off. You think you're the first one to crack under the pressure of fighting unspeakable horrors day after day? We'll chalk it up to a mental breakdown, and you'll either be put on leave or assigned to an administrative position, even if it's temporary. We don't need to arrest you unless you refuse."

Emma took a relaxing breath. Liam hadn't figured out what had happened. Not yet, anyway. But she wasn't sure how long she'd be able to keep what she could do a secret. Maybe indefinitely, maybe not at all. But even if she wanted to return, it wasn't like they'd let her back on the field—not for ages. And being stuck behind a desk all day sounded like its own special type of torture.

"Why did you do it, Em? Why didn't you just talk to me?" Liam's face had softened, but his dark brown eyes pierced through her, searching, as if he could glean an answer from her expression. "We could have worked something out. We could have faked an illness so you could have a week, a month, hell, even a few months off without all of this."

Emma wondered if she'd ever seen these two sides of her friend so at odds with one another. In one breath, he was the Hunter, so bound by rules and protocols that he'd do the right thing, even if it was against his own interests; in the next he was her friend, the boy she'd grown up alongside who'd become the man who would lay down his own life for hers.

He would do that, wouldn't he? Would he still if he knew the truth?

How many times had she told him she didn't need him to fight her battles for her?

"Why do you think?" Emma asked. "You know me better than anyone."

Liam blew a puff of air out of his nostrils.

Liesel arrived with his ale, set it on the table, and left

again. Liam barely seemed to notice the server's presence and didn't waste any time before pulling the mug of ale to his lips. He wiped the foamy liquid from his upper lip with the back of his wrist before answering. "Honestly, Em? I don't know what to think. We've hunted together for five years. Trained for it since we were kids. All I know is that this isn't like you. You don't bloody run. You dig in your heels and fight. If I had to guess, I'd say you got scared by something. But by what? I've been trying to figure that out since you left."

"Then you know you should have let me disappear."

"You think nobody's going to find you? Eventually, they'd have someone track you down. And you know you'd rather have me find you than one of the others. I'll advocate for you at least."

Emma swallowed a mouthful of ale before replying. "Not for this you won't."

Liam reached across the table and grabbed Emma's arm. The gesture was sudden but not without compassion. "There's nobody more important to me than you, Em. I would have tracked you into the fairy realm if I had to. I don't understand why you won't talk to me. Please. Tell me what's going on."

What she wouldn't give to believe that Liam could understand. He was her best friend, yet he would never accept this. How could he? They'd been raised to hate the very thing she'd become.

Cursed.

"I just needed to get away. To start over. This was my opportunity to do something more. Something *I* wanted to do."

"Like what?" Liam laughed and raised his drink toward the room. "Travel to the ends of the kingdom to drink stale ale?" He slung the remainder of it back and raised a hand to Liesel for another.

Emma cringed. "Not exactly . . . though that does seem to be all I've accomplished."

"There are better ways to go about retiring." The softness in his voice was disappearing. "Ones that don't involve desertion."

"There weren't." Emma let her gaze survey the guards at the nearby tables. She was already trying to devise a plan in the back of her mind. But if there were more guards stationed outside, she didn't know if she had much of a shot. Not yet. "I did what I had to do. Though, it seems I wasn't as good at covering my tracks as I had believed."

"Well, if it makes you feel better, you provided a hell of a chase. If I didn't know you as well as I do, it would've taken another month—at least."

"Great," Emma said, sarcasm coating the word as it left her mouth.

Liesel set down a second drink as the fiddler finished his song and the tavern erupted into applause.

"I love these small-town pubs," Liam said as he clapped along. "It hits differently from the cities. Everyone's more sincere."

Emma struggled to reconcile the man before her. Those two versions of him pulling at her—the man of duty and the man of compassion.

Once he found out who she truly was, that would all change. The man she'd grown to care for would evaporate.

"You always loved the music," she said, hanging on to that spark for a bit longer.

Liam took another sip of ale. Emma could feel it. Feel the ale in the same way she could feel the wine back in Grenaa. It sang to her, calling for her to make the change. She closed her eyes momentarily. It was only a moment, though it felt like an eternity. This time, the call was different though. It wasn't just that it wanted to be a better version of itself. It was as if it actually *wanted* to loosen Liam's inhibitions. It wanted to bring out the side of him that was more fun-loving.

In another moment, it was done. Emma exhaled briefly, trying to comprehend what the magic had compelled her to do. Something in his drink *had* changed.

"And you always loved traveling," Liam carried on, oblivious that anything had occurred beneath his nose and hand.

Emma cleared her throat, shaking off the remnants of magic that clung to her. "It's really the only part of the job I enjoy." She shifted in her seat.

"Come now." Liam's voice had softened again. This was just another chat with her friend at the bar. "We're doing God's work. Ridding the kingdom of those who would turn it over to darkness."

"And what would we think of it if we weren't recruited as kids?"

Liam raised an eyebrow. "We were given a chance most orphans only dream of. A place in the king's guard, food in our bellies, and a purpose."

"Didn't you ever wish for something . . . different? A normal life? One aside from monster hunting and witch wrangling?"

"How could I want anything more than this?" Liam took a deep drink of ale and set the mug back on the table, wiping his mouth on the edge of his sleeve. "We're protecting the kingdom."

Emma shook her head. "I feel like I've been living someone else's life."

Liam locked his dark eyes on Emma's, reaching across the table and taking her hand. Through his touch, she could feel the magic that she'd imbued in his drink coursing through him as the alcohol entered his bloodstream.

Whatever it was doing, it had managed to circumvent his medallion by entering his body. The magic affected him from the inside out.

"If it hadn't been for the Hunters that pulled us off the street that day as kids, we would be sitting in a jail cell right now. Or dead." Liam gripped her hands with calloused fingers. "You wish for another version of your life? We were spared from a cruel reality."

Emma bit her lip as she considered Liam's words. He wasn't wrong, but should she be forced to spend an entire life in chains because a stroke of luck saved her from another?

"Though, maybe I see why you decided to come here," Liam continued without waiting for her response, his voice raising over the whine of the strings. "The simplicity of it all. London can be so pretentious."

"What London taverns have you been to lately? What about the Stag's Haul, or the Shoemaker's Inn?"

"Bah!" Liam swatted toward Emma as though shooing a fly. "You know what I mean."

Emma barely heard him, though. Her attention had been pulled from their conversation toward the patrons around them, who clapped as the fiddler's tune increased its cadence. The melody vibrated through the pub with an electrified energy, and every single person, except for Emma, began slapping their hands together to the beat.

A big, dumb grin had found its way to Liam's face. He enjoyed music, but she'd never seen him like this. He was almost . . . lost in its hypnotic rhythm.

Then she saw it. Sitting on top of the table next to his drink was Liam's medallion. He must have taken it off while her attention had been drawn to what was happening around them.

In all the years Emma had known him, Liam had not once removed the talisman from around his neck.

Before she could say anything about it, Liam reached across the table once again and grabbed Emma's hand, pulling her to her feet.

"Let's dance!" he exclaimed.

She allowed herself to be dragged along but maintained her awareness of the surroundings. Something peculiar was happening—she'd never seen Liam's inhibitions slide away from him so earnestly.

If it weren't for the rest of the pub getting caught up in the same melody, she'd have believed it was her magic that had caused Liam to respond in this way, but she was completely sure she hadn't enchanted the entire pub's drinks.

Had she?

To be fair, she hadn't yet worked out all the intricacies of her newly developed power, but as she was swirled and dipped by Liam along the dance floor, she did her best to concentrate on the rest of the ale in the room—at least as much as she could without tripping over her own feet.

From what she could tell, each and every glass contained nothing but ordinary, if mediocre, ale. Only Liam's beer seemed to have shifted.

But was it the ale that had caused him to remove the medallion?

Emma let herself follow Liam's lead for the moment. She might be able to take advantage of the fact that he was momentarily distracted.

But something told her she needed to discover what exactly was causing the entire pub to dance to the fiddler's song like fools.

And why it wasn't affecting her in the same way.

Dance With Magic

Chapter Four

The entire tavern was on their feet, moving to the fiddle player's tune. Those patrons who had managed to set down their ale were clapping ferociously; some were singing along.

The tune was familiar, but the lyrics didn't match the version she knew. She allowed Liam to spin her through the first and second verses as she ran through different scenarios of what could be happening. There was no doubt someone had enchanted the patrons of The Cursed Dragon, including Liam.

Something else didn't sit right with her. Why hadn't she been affected?

She was willing to believe that her actions were the reason Liam had removed his medallion, but there was no way the rest of this had been her doing. To be sure, for a second time, she did her best to study the drinks in the hands of each of the dancing patrons. She could sense them all. Each of them was the same. Simply ale. Nothing special to set them apart from any other.

She'd almost believe the behavior of the rest of the patrons was their own, except for the buzz of energy in the air that she couldn't reconcile it as being anything but magic.

Emma tried to shake the thought that the sudden euphoria was something she'd caused. It was unlike anything she'd done so far. She certainly hadn't intended to cast anything.

Maybe the pull of power grew until one day you were turning your neighbors into forest creatures.

She shook the thought off. No, this energy didn't speak to her the same way the beverages did. This enchantment wasn't her doing. It couldn't have been.

Then the answer struck her.

The man in the corner.

Liesel, who had also joined in on the dancing, pulling up her skirts so she could kick her heels in traditional Hibernian fashion, had called him the professor. A funny title for a man who was living at the edge of the kingdom by a lighthouse.

Emma tried to find the unwieldy mop of brown and gray hair or a hint of his mismatched clothing among the crowd but came up short.

Had he been behind this? If there was one thing she had been good at during her time under the king's service, it was sniffing out magic users.

Emma sighed as she spun around once again. She had so desperately wanted to leave that life behind.

Then Emma caught the eye of a young woman. Despite being of average height, this woman would have stood out in any crowd. Both her flowing brown hair and dazzling green eyes sparkled in the golden light of the tavern's lanterns. A solid green dress hung off her shoulders, held up by a brown strap, perhaps made of leather. Her skin was smooth, almost glowing, with freckles around her eyes that hinted at her being a local.

Except this woman hadn't been swept up in the fervor that overtook the rest of the pub. She offered Emma a knowing smile and casually strolled out of The Cursed Dragon's main exit.

Emma's grip tightened on Liam's hands. She did not want to follow this woman; she had no desire to chase after witches any longer.

But what choice did she have? Emma was the only one in the place with her wits about her—for some reason, she alone had been singled out. And she certainly had no desire to continue on the dance floor for all eternity.

She'd heard of this type of enchantment before. In another part of the kingdom, an entire village had danced themselves to death. Some poor merchant had come across what was left of them as he was making his springtime rounds. Emma and Liam had been called to investigate. It was the result of witchcraft, but no suspect had ever been found, and it had been assumed the culprit had moved on to terrorize another village.

Was that witch now here?

Were all witches doomed to cause this type of behavior? That was what she'd been taught to believe her entire life. That's why the Hunters rounded them up and hauled them to London.

The Curse would spread.

Would she eventually lose control as well?

Perhaps she wanted to speak to this woman after all.

She spun Liam toward another laughing, breathless woman, whom he unquestioningly continued his dance with. She tried not to allow the ease of his distraction to bother her, and she bowed out of the room without saying a word.

The night air slapped her skin as she stepped outside, its cold bite a reminder that winter's grip held on longer this far north. Emma shivered as she pulled her hood over her head and her cloak tighter around her. Apart from Liam having discovered her with ease, the chill served as an untimely reason why Cuanmore wasn't the best place for her to settle.

But where else could she go?

Outside, the melody of the fiddler spilled into the streets. The music interspersed with the rhythmic crashing of waves upon the rocky shoreline. Each hammer of their relentless force proclaimed that this was indeed the edge of her world. She could board a pirate vessel, she supposed, perhaps find work on a ship. Traveling had been her favorite part of being a Hunter as she'd said to Liam. In service to the king, she had seen nearly all of Lancastria. Perhaps life aboard a ship wouldn't be so bad. She could explore unknown parts of the world and maybe create drinks with foreign ingredients.

Emma paused. There was a certain appeal to that. Perhaps Liam and the other Hunters wouldn't bother following her out to sea.

But she was getting ahead of herself. First, she had to find the woman responsible for the dancing enchantment. While she needed to leave Liam behind, she didn't want him dancing to his grave.

Then suddenly the woman stood before her, appearing out of the night itself.

"You can see me?" The woman's voice was lighter than Emma had expected. Not high-pitched, per se, but airy, almost as if the wind might have picked it up and carried it off.

Emma swallowed and tried to ignore the fact that a few moments ago, the woman was nowhere to be seen. "Why wouldn't I be able to see you, witch?"

The woman lifted a dainty hand to her face. "Witch? Realms, I'm no witch!"

Emma raised an eyebrow. Of course, no woman would confess to being a witch outright. It would be as good as a death sentence. "So . . . everyone in the pub is dancing their hearts out, and you had nothing to do with that?"

"I didn't say that." The woman gave Emma a playful smile.

Emma stepped back, her hand hovering above her favorite dagger resting in her belt. The electric current within the pub had intensified since this woman had appeared. "But it's the work of magic?" Emma asked, though she didn't need the confirmation. It was strange that a woman would confess the use of magic while denying being a witch.

"I needed to speak with you. I was about to join you at your table, but then your witch hunter boyfriend arrived."

Emma had to refrain from laughing out loud. "Liam and I are colleagues." She caught herself. They weren't anymore, were they? "Friends . . . really."

This response seemed to puzzle the woman as she cocked her head to the side. "No matter," she said. "This was not for his ears."

"Now wait a minute," Emma said. "You claim you are using music to enchant those in the pub but that you are not a witch."

The woman let out a laugh that sounded more like a giggle.

Emma pressed on. "Was it the man in the corner booth? The professor? Was he responsible for this? Are you working together?" It wasn't all that strange for magic users to find each other and work together to enchant a town. Multiple Cursed working in concert were among the more challenging situations they could encounter. Particularly in the smaller villages where the enchantments could run quite deep.

The woman looked at her with a sweet smile on her face. Emma gripped the hilt of her dagger tighter.

"Why aren't you answering me? Who are you? Why are you doing this? And why haven't I been affected like the rest of them?"

"We will get to all of that," the woman said evenly. "First, you can call me Vespa. I could sense your magic when you arrived in Cuanmore and have been watching you. I didn't believe your magic could help us at first, but after sensing what you did to your friend's ale, I think you might be the person we're looking for after all."

Vespa's response made Emma's head swirl with so many more questions she didn't know where to begin.

"You could see that *I* used magic?"

Vespa's brow furrowed in confusion. "Yes, of course, I . . ." She glanced over her shoulder as if looking to see if someone were standing behind her. "Oh, my. I apologize for that." Vespa shimmied her back muscles like she had a chill.

Emma had to blink several times to ensure what she was seeing was real. Ethereal wings, like those of a translucent butterfly, reflected the moonlight. They spread outward as Vespa gently fluttered them, making them shimmer and dance in a surreal manner that spoke of other realms.

"You're a fairy." Emma heard the words leave her mouth before she even realized she was saying them. Fairy creatures weren't unknown to her, of course. They were blamed for countless supernatural occurrences. But for all the magical creatures she'd encountered in her life, never had she seen a fairy.

Not that she knew of, anyway. Before Vespa had revealed her wings, Emma could have walked right past her on the street and never have known the difference.

Vespa smiled proudly. "Of course I am!"

"I have never encountered a fairy before."

"I'm not surprised. We don't normally make ourselves known to humans. Well, we're not supposed to, anyway."

There was more to the statement, but Emma was too caught off guard to press further. Though she'd spent her entire life tracking down witches and other supernatural creatures, she didn't know why it was so surprising that she'd eventually encounter a fairy.

"Now, with that out of the way," Vespa continued, "I came here to make you an offer."

Emma paused. "Just because I haven't met a fairy before," she said slowly, "doesn't mean I haven't heard of the offers you make to mortals."

Vespa's shoulders sagged and her wings went limp. "We're not all like that."

Emma's fingers never left hilt of her dagger. She was skeptical that it would do any good against a fae creature, but she had no other means of defending herself. "What kind of offer?" Emma spoke the words carefully.

There were too many tales of mortals making agreements they hadn't meant to because they hadn't controlled their tongues. It wasn't lost on her that if she had met Vespa even a month ago, she'd be trying to cuff the creature in iron shackles rather than asking for details about a favor.

"You saw the old man in the pub, right?"

"The professor," Emma confirmed, her reply still hesitant. "Yes, the server said he was peculiar. Probably a sorcerer."

Vespa's smile returned. "I guess he is in a manner of speaking. But Professor Aldrich is only strange in the same way that I am."

"He's a fairy? Do your kind reside so frequently under our noses?"

"Well, we do. But that's not what I meant. Aldrich is just a man. His name is Henry, but I call him by his surname. Both of us find ourselves outside of our element, and we could use your help."

"Help in what way?"

"It's probably best if I let him explain his situation to you himself. But the type of magic you possess might be exactly what we need." Vespa lifted a thoughtful finger to her thin pale lip. "And we might be exactly what *you* need too."

Emma's brow hadn't relaxed through the entire exchange. What value could she possibly offer to some eccentric sorcerer? What could he do for her?

"And what, exactly, do you think I need?"

"You seek rest," Vespa said gently. "You want to help people, but you're tired of fighting. We can help you with those things, take you to a world where people aren't afraid of magic. Where you can make drinks and live your life in peace with understanding friends by your side."

Emma held her stance. There was no shortage of stories regarding fairies and how they couldn't be trusted. She did her best to stand firm, though the words did sound tempting.

"I appreciate whatever fairy trickery you're about." Once again, she rested her hand on her dagger's hilt fully, more out of comfort than feeling threatened. "I'm new to possessing magic, so I get that you might see me as gullible, but I have dealt with magic my entire life. I don't have time for games, and I wish to be left alone."

Vespa blinked several times. "You see your magic as a curse."

The boldness of Vespa's statement caught Emma off guard. She wasn't used to anyone being able to read her so openly, and it was a sharp reminder that she'd already let her guard down too many times for one night.

"I've spent my entire life trying to rid the kingdom of witches, of magic and ethereal creatures. Of course, that's how I see it."

"So, you'll spend your days hidden away?" Vespa's wings stood perfectly still despite the wind picking up. "Wandering the Earth alone?"

"Something like that."

"How's that working out for you?" Vespa nodded toward the bar. She took a few steps forward until she was inches from Emma's face. Emma wanted nothing more than to take two steps back to distance herself. But she stubbornly held her ground.

"It was working great until my well-meaning but oh-so-foolish friend tracked me down."

Vespa tilted her head at the response but carried on as though Emma had said nothing, her wings fluttering once again in the moonlight. "You don't have to help us if you don't want to. I can send you back in there with Liam. He'll be none the wiser that they were under my enchantment. But sooner or later he'll discover the real reason you ran away, and how do you think he'll respond? If you come with us, you may be taking a chance, but life involves risk. Often you have to step outside of your comfort zone to get the life you desire."

Emma bit her lip.

It wouldn't matter that she was Liam's best friend. He'd believe that somehow the devil himself had corrupted her. It would break his heart, but he wouldn't hesitate to cuff her in iron and bring her before the King's Court. If he even let her get that far.

If he didn't find out she was Cursed before they arrived in London, he'd still bring her in for abandoning her post, and the King's Questioners were sure to wrestle it out of her.

She said none of this, though. Vespa already seemed to know far more about her situation than she had any right to.

Fiddle music pulsed from the tavern, muffled by its walls, but carrying out into the otherwise still evening.

And what if she were right? What if, now that she was Cursed, her only refuge would be with other magical creatures?

She shivered at the thought, but it wasn't like she had many options.

"If I come with you, do you promise you'll release your enchantment of Liam and the others?"

"I will. Even if you don't come."

Emma didn't believe her. There was no way this magical being would keep her word if Emma didn't comply.

"And no fairy trickery!" Emma had to refrain from spitting the words. "I come to the professor's cabin, and you release them from your hold. Is that clear?"

Vespa nodded, though there was a glint of something worrying in her eye. "You have my word. Once you meet Professor Aldrich, the enchantment will be lifted."

It was something, at least. Emma allowed her hand to drift from the dagger at her side. Instead, she pulled her cloak tighter around herself to keep out the chill of the evening. "All right, then. This professor, what does he need?" she asked, still unconvinced she had anything that would be worth this sort of trouble. "Someone to fix him a drink?"

Vespa's smile widened, and her wings brightened subtly. "That probably wouldn't hurt."

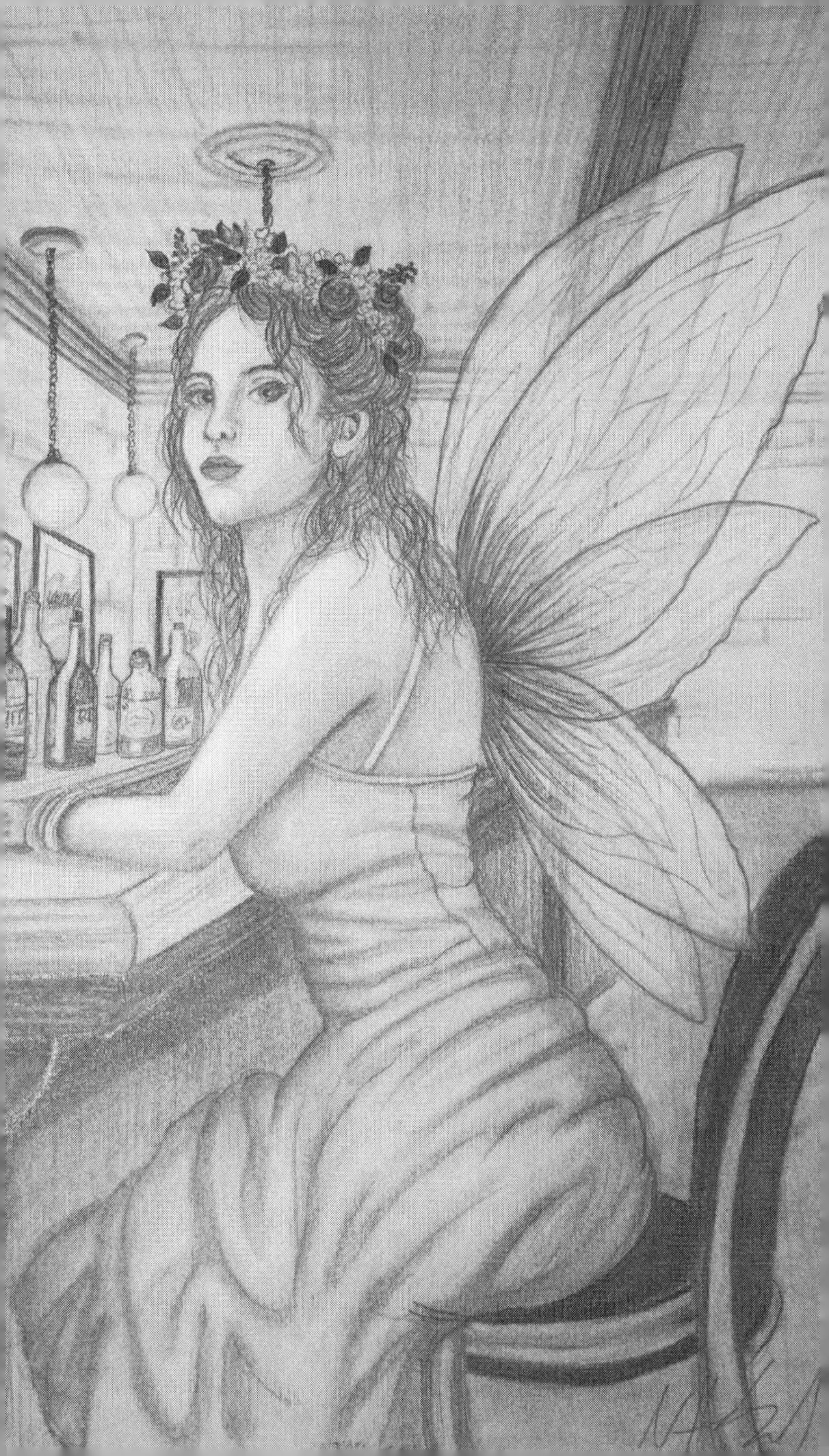

Professor Aldrich

Chapter Five

It hadn't taken them long to arrive at the small cottage situated outside Cuanmore, down a short winding path, and along the rocky shoreline. The home that sat next to a lighthouse had appeared through the mist as they approached, and it was only then that Emma realized Vespa could have been leading her to walk off the edge of the cliff side and she would have never known the difference.

There were countless tales of fairies doing so.

Dwarfed by the lighthouse that towered over it, the exterior of the stone structure was unassuming, almost blending into the edge of the cliff that overlooked the sea below.

It wasn't anything she saw that caused Emma's heart to pound.

"Witchcraft." Emma exhaled as the small wooden door creaked open, allowing the warm glow to escape from within.

Professor Aldrich's house was unlike any Emma had ever seen. The main doorway led into a living area that seemed to be impossibly large for how small the building appeared from the outside. At the room's edge, along a side wall, stood a rugged stone fireplace. It might have been the room's most normal feature, but it was the first to draw Emma's eye. The flame that burned within its hearth gave the room a cozy glow, filling it with a rich scent of wood smoke. The adjacent wall was constructed out of one gigantic bookcase nearly twice as tall as she was. It was filled with more books than Emma had seen outside of London's palace or university, and she wondered how one man in the middle of nowhere acquired such a treasure trove. A ladder rested on a track that allowed it to move from one end of the shelf to the other and provided access to the taller shelves that stretched fifteen feet from the floor.

More shelves stretched across the walls along the rest of the room, each filled with strange mechanical devices Emma didn't recognize, and she couldn't begin to comprehend what their functions might have been. Some churned with interlocking gears, pulling against each other like the inside of a clock. A miniature steam locomotive, something she'd only seen at futurist festivals in the heart of London, circled above them on a small track suspended from the highest point of the wall.

Tunnels bore through the walls into which the train disappeared and reappeared as, Emma assumed, it traveled to and from other parts of the home.

Lights on the devices blinked both in unison and seemingly random patterns. Somehow, this Professor Aldrich had strung electricity through several devices that didn't seem to be connected through any sort of wiring system.

"What sort of sorcery is this?" Emma continued to voice her marvel out loud.

"Sometimes things only seem to be magic when we don't understand what they are," said Vespa. Her smile was more sinister against the shadows of flickering light from the fireplace.

"Do you always talk in riddles, fairy? Is this your doing?" She cursed at her own stupidity—following Vespa had indeed been a mistake. She had abandoned Liam while witlessly following a fairy into the heart of a sorcerer's domain.

If this was a trap, she had fallen into it headfirst.

Vespa appeared undisturbed by Emma's accusations. "These are Aldrich's inventions. He's a scientist."

Scientist. She knew little of the profession. The king, of course, had scientists in his employ. There were a smattering of astronomers and medical professionals throughout London. They were responsible for the kingdom's steam locomotives and dirigibles, but she had never seen anything as elaborate as this workshop. She certainly didn't expect to find it in a home by a lighthouse at the edge of nowhere.

"I don't buy it. I have seen much sorcery in my day. If the professor is not behind the enchantment at the pub, then surely you are. What are you truly up to? Do these inflict your wiles upon the townsfolk?"

Vespa's hand went to her mouth as she let out a faint gasp. "Why would you assume I'd want to inflict any sort of malice?"

"I've heard the stories. Isn't that what fairies do? Inflict hardships on humans? Perhaps you require gifts from the people of Cuanmore, and they haven't delivered. In what way have they offended you?"

Vespa crossed her arms and leaned back. "And all magic users are the hands of the devil! Don't witches steal children and draw the blood of virgins in order to preserve their youth? Is that what people should think of you?"

Those *were* the stories told of witches. Some were likely true, others were rumors the Hunters allowed to spread, perhaps even fueled. As long as people feared magic, they wouldn't hesitate to report it.

"I'm not a witch."

"You can call yourself whatever you like," Vespa said. "But

others would disagree. Isn't that why you've been running from your friend, Liam?"

Emma stood quiet, unsure how to respond. Vespa was right, of course.

"You'll find that many of your preconceived notions are built on prejudice and lies," Vespa continued. "Once you let yourself get to know the people behind the stories, they might surprise you."

Emma wasn't exactly sure she'd go that far. "Explain all of this, then." She waved a hand around the room. "What other purpose would there be to build devices such as these, other than to bring fire down upon the mortal realm?"

"You think humans are so incapable of doing that on their own?" Vespa didn't raise her voice, but it had lost its airy tone, becoming firm with agitation. "All humans do is seek ways to destroy themselves!"

"The items are mine." A man's voice echoed into the room. "Leave poor Vespa alone."

Professor Henry Aldrich, whom Emma had only seen the back of at The Cursed Dragon, stepped into the light. His salt-and-pepper hair was cut and styled peculiarly. It was pulled up on top, sort of like he existed in an organized windstorm. His mustache had been pulled out at the ends, styled, and twisted up, while his beard has been trimmed back to be neat and tidy, shaping his face into a distinguished 'V.'

His jacket had been patched, but it was a close representation of some of the ship commanders Emma had come across in the kingdom's naval yards. She took a second look at some of the devices that circled the room. Some of them did resemble ships, and others might have been dirigibles. There were also goggles that she recognized from some of the modern airfields that were just starting to be developed as part of the king's military. As far as she knew, though, these were prototypes that weren't in active service.

"Are you a pilot?" As she said the words, Emma realized how odd of a first question it was, but there had been so many oddities happening around her that night that it no longer mattered. "Or a ship's captain?"

"Of sorts." If Aldrich thought the question odd, he didn't let it show and began to remove a pair of thick gloves, one finger at a time, as though he'd just finished some sort of heavy labor in another part of the dwelling.

Once his hand was free, he stretched it out. "I'm Professor Aldrich," he said. "But you knew that already, didn't you, Emma?"

Emma gripped the man's hand firmly. If he thought she was just some silly girl he could pull the wool over, he'd be sincerely mistaken. But she did have to admit the man had surprised her in more ways than one. "I see you are already familiar with who I am as well?"

"Vespa has been keeping track of you ever since you arrived in Hibernia and it was clear you were headed our way."

"You've been spying on me?" Emma spun to face Vespa.

"I had to be sure." Vespa's cheeks reddened. "I could sense you had an ability. Like I told you at the pub, I thought it might be what we needed."

Emma held back a growl. It more than grated on her nerves that both Liam and this fairy creature had managed to track her down. Because of her own carelessness, all illusions of disappearing and living a quiet life as a bartender were fading like a mist rolling out to sea.

"Unless you were hoping to throw an epic kitchen party, I'm afraid there's nothing I can do to help you." Emma crossed her arms. "This . . . magic . . . that I seem to be in possession of, can't do much of anything but fix a drink."

"I had my doubts, at first." Aldrich fidgeted with his mustache. "Vespa believes you're able to help us in other ways, though. Of course, a kitchen party does sound like a novel idea, but it would only be the three of us. So perhaps not the best use of your talents."

"I've been telling you to take time to befriend others in the village." Though the words were said lightly, it still sounded like a scolding. "They wouldn't spread as many rumors about you if you did."

"Bah!" Aldrich waved a hand. "I've never planned on staying here long enough. I still don't. But I never planned on being stuck here, either. Hopefully, that's where this young witch hunter comes in."

"Stuck?" Emma couldn't help but ask. "How does one end up stuck in Cuanmore? Why not travel to Dublin? Or London? Surely you could find somewhere more fitting to do your . . . research. What is it exactly you do here?"

"Cuanmore? What?" said Aldrich, ignoring most of Emma's questions. "No, no, you misunderstand. Come, follow me. Let's put your abilities to the test."

Without waiting for a response, the professor turned and scurried deeper into his house. Vespa, without a word, went after him, leaving Emma with nothing to do but follow.

To Craft A Cocktail

Chapter Six

Aldrich grabbed a bottle and set it on the bar along with a clay pitcher.

The fact that Aldrich had a full bar inside this house amazed Emma. Whether the room had been like this when he moved in or he had installed it himself, she didn't know. It was impressive either way.

Dim electric lighting glowed off dozens of bottles racked on a shelf on the back wall. A mirror, etched with a pattern of circles and lines, reflected the lineup, making it appear as though there were double the bottles. Two small tables had been set up in the room, tall enough to stand at, each surrounded by three wooden barstools.

It wasn't a particularly large room, but Emma hadn't ever been in a home that held its own personal bar and room for entertaining, never mind one with electricity. As it stood, there wouldn't have been room for more furniture, but it wasn't so full that it was cramped, either. The room had been designed to entertain, but since the man confessed that he had made little time for friends, Emma wondered how often it had been used.

Vespa stood behind one of the tables, ignoring the stools. Her wings glowed a faint green. Emma moved to take a seat next to her, but Vespa shook her head as she gestured to

Aldrich who was puttering around the bar. "This is all about you."

Emma snorted. "You're really having me pour you a drink? Are you kidnapping me so I can be your own personal bartender?"

"We're not kidnapping anyone," Aldrich said, before pausing and looking up at a corner of the room. "No, not kidnapping. Not now at least."

Emma concentrated on the weight of the dagger on her hip. She didn't think she'd have to use it to get out of the professor's house, even if the situation turned ugly. Though, the more she thought about it, the more she realized it probably wouldn't take much for Vespa to hold Emma against her will. She had no defense against fairy magic.

Aldrich, though perhaps eccentric, didn't seem like much of a threat. Although she had been around long enough to know that when magic was concerned, looks could be deceiving.

Vespa tsked. "No, *not* kidnapping anyone. Emma has already been a prisoner for her entire life."

"What do you know of my life?" Emma tugged at her collar. The room was growing warm.

"Enough." Vespa smiled cryptically. "I also know that you wanted the chance to make a drink. That's what you told your friend at the bar."

Liam. Suddenly, she realized her friend was likely still dancing away with the village folk.

"You promised you would release him once we arrived here. Have you kept your promise? Or are you planning on dancing them over the edge of the cliffs?"

Vespa's face reddened. "I would never! How could you ever think I'd do such a thing?"

"I know what fairies are capable of."

Vespa crossed her arms with a huff. "Human stories paint fairies as villains. Just as fairies view humans as destructive. We share this world yet there's so much mistrust."

Emma gritted her teeth. "Answer the question."

Vespa sighed. "Your friend is fine. Though, I would imagine, confused as to where you disappeared to."

Emma let herself relax. There was always the chance Vespa was lying, but Emma didn't believe she was.

"You said you wanted to be a bartender," Vespa carried on, not waiting for Emma's response. "Take this cider and warm it with your magic."

"Warm the cider? With my . . ." Of all the things Emma had expected to come out of the fae's mouth, that hadn't been something she'd considered.

"Come now," Aldrich said. "Don't be shy. This is merely an . . . experiment. A test which will allow us to see what you can do."

Emma rested her forearms on the bar and leaned forward. "You seriously want me to warm this? What makes you believe I'm even capable of doing that?"

"This is a chance for you to prove to yourself what you've known all along. To prove to yourself that this is what you were made for." Vespa tossed Emma a cup, which she caught in midair.

Vespa grinned. "You've certainly got reflexes. Though that's not exactly useful to our needs."

Emma cleared her throat and set the mug down on the bar gently. "And what is it you *do* need, exactly?"

Vespa leaned forward, her eyes unnaturally wide. Though Emma wasn't sure she could classify anything about a fairy as being *natural*. "I sensed you came to town for a reason."

"Because I'm Cursed."

"Magic is not a curse. It's a gift."

Emma couldn't help but unleash a laugh. "Please. There's no gift in turning every tongue in the village purple or ruining the crop of your entire county."

"Of course you focus on the bad things magic has done," Vespa said. "People only call for you when they have a problem. Nobody is complaining if a village plague is cured or if the harvest is three times as bountiful as the year before. It's only when things go wrong that mortals look for someone to blame."

Emma scratched the hair at the base of her scalp. She supposed what Vespa was saying made sense, even if it wasn't entirely accurate. There was the odd occasion when the news of a string of good fortune reached the ears of the Hunters. Jealousy was a powerful motivator.

"Just because there are good scenarios along with the bad," Emma continued, "doesn't mean it isn't a curse."

"Your magic *is* a gift. It could help bring the professor home."

"Vespa,"—Emma set down the drink and raised her hands —"I don't know what you think I'm able to do. I've been able to turn stale ale into something drinkable and restore wine that's turned to vinegar. Enchanting Liam's ale might have gotten him intoxicated enough to take off his medallion. Maybe I can help the professor forget where he lives, but otherwise, unless he's looking for a shortcut to obtain the worst hangover ever, I don't see how my abilities will help him."

That earned a chuckle from Aldrich. "Perhaps what I need is help curing a hangover." Then to himself he added, "Yes, the most disastrous hangover in any version of history."

Aldrich laughed, but Emma wasn't sure she understood the joke. She certainly wasn't convinced she *could* cure a hangover. More and more she regretted following the fairy to this place.

Emma could sense the drink right away. It was a bit sweeter than wine, and unlike most of the alcohol she'd encountered on her journey, this was in almost pristine condition. There wouldn't be much she could do to improve it.

The professor took the bottle from the bartop and poured a small portion of the golden liquid into a clay mug. The drink sang to her. It differed somewhat from what she'd had in taverns before. For starters, it was made from fermented apples.

Emma shook her head, trying to ignore the drink's call. "Professor. Do you believe any of this? You claim to be a man of science, yet you'd entertain that me pouring drinks could be beneficial to you?"

What sort of scientist would trust a fairy to bring a strange woman into his house and begin serving drinks?

And what kind of Hunter was she that she was willing to go along with it?

Though she supposed, for the moment, it beat riding in a cage wagon back to London—she hoped it was better than that, at least.

Aldrich ran his thumb and forefinger over the tip of his mustache in contemplation. He mused for a moment before replying. "There's a lot that exists in this world that I would never have believed possible. Vespa is a prime example of that. If she thinks you could get the accelerator working, I won't argue. It sure as hell can't hurt."

The what now? Emma didn't voice the thought, unsure if she even heard the professor correctly.

Vespa happily moved to take a seat at one of the tables.

"Now what?" Emma asked. The golden elixir still sat on the bar. It hadn't gone completely quiet, but its song had quietened after the professor had finished pouring his own drink.

"I want you to pour a cup then use your magic to warm it," said Vespa.

Right, warm it. The fairy had completely lost her mind. Everything she'd done with a drink to that point seemed to be an extension of what the drink wanted to do. Inflicting her own will onto the drink . . . "I . . . I don't know how to do that."

"I believe you do." Vespa nodded encouragingly. "Just try it."

Aldrich had leaned against a door frame with one arm crossed over his chest, supporting the opposite hand that was holding his drink, studying her intently.

There was a part of Emma that couldn't shake the feeling that the entire thing was a ruse, and that somehow all of this had been some elaborate attempt to lure her into some fairy trap.

Here she was, in the presence of a fairy and a . . . scientist. She had blades in her belt, in her boots, and throwing blades tucked inside her cloak. The fairy sat at a table, expectantly smiling at her like she had a grade-school crush. At any other juncture of her life, she'd be working to bring Vespa back to Liam so they could haul her back to London. Instead, she was being asked to pour the same fairy creature a drink.

The thought gave her pause. Wasn't this what she had wanted? A chance to become a bartender? To leave her past behind and do something she wanted to do?

Being in a stranger's house with a fae and a probably enchanted man was certainly a loose interpretation of that vision.

That was the crux of this whole scenario. This was not something that happened to ordinary people. This *had* to be a setup. Fairies, after all, enjoyed playing games with humans.

Could she make this all go away? Refuse to make the drink and take Vespa back to Liam? They could bring the fairy back to London. She'd likely be expunged of all charges against her if she brought in such a magical creature. Then she could return to her old life.

Even as she held the decanter in hand, her eyes flitting between Vespa and Aldrich, she considered the prospect. Of course, there was one thing that made the entire plan a mere fantasy. One that became clearer as she unstuck the top of the container and the liquid within called out to her.

She was still Cursed.

The apple smell of the cider wafted from the decanter. A clean, crisp aroma that made Emma's mouth water.

Emma lifted the decanter and let the golden liquid flow into the cups that Aldrich had set out.

It took only a moment for the cider to settle in the smaller containers. As soon as it did, the song quieted to a content hum, and Emma stared at the trio laid out before her. Nothing was happening.

"Now what?"

"Don't overthink it," Vespa said. "Take what you feel from the cider and make it warmer."

"This is so ridiculous," Emma said. But without declaring the entire thing a farce and marching out of the house, she had no choice but to see the silly experiment through.

Plus, not that she'd admit it, she was curious to see what the game amounted to.

Emma could feel the cider just as she could sense it in the cup Aldrich held. Just like Liam's beer back at The Cursed Dragon, the wine in the pub in Kalmar, and each of the barrels of ale at pub after pub on her way through Lancastria.

But this, and what was expected of her, was different than each of those times.

She let her mind weigh on the beverage and tried to focus on its temperature. It was slightly cooler than the surrounding air, which was surprising given that it had been stored beneath the counter, as far as she could tell. She allowed her mind to probe the cider for several minutes. It was so ridiculous, and she had no way to confirm whether the sensations she was experiencing were all in her mind or if she was actually sensing the cider.

Then it hit her all at once, and Emma realized that merely warming the drink simply would not do.

She had been wrong. She didn't need to force her will upon the drink—it would tell her what it needed to complete the task.

It needed more—she could feel it in her bones.

A smile crossed her face. She *had* wanted to become a bartender, and as such, this would become her domain. Forget what Liam thought. She'd be the best bartender the kingdom had ever seen.

She began opening cupboard doors, rummaging through them in search of what she needed.

"Err . . . excuse me," Aldrich piped up. "Can I ask what you're snooping around my cupboards for?"

"Ingredients," Emma said, only barely aware of the question.

"Ingredients?" he repeated slowly. "For what, exactly?"

"I'm not entirely sure yet."

Emma paused. The answer surprised even her. But the magic coursed through her now, and all she could do was allow it to do what was needed.

This was what she was born to do. She could feel it in every inch of her bones.

There was something else that wanted to be part of this concoction. Something else calling to her . . . but what? She studied the bottles lined up behind a glass cabinet door. There was a wide range of alcohol for a private residence. From the languages scrawled on the bottles, some had traveled a great distance. She pulled out a bottle of Hibernian whiskey that she recognized, and a wave of relief flowed from the bottle and into her.

A sense of peace overcame her. This had been the right choice. She found a cooking pot and poured the cups of cider as well as what remained in the decanter into it. She added about half as much whiskey also.

"My whiskey!" Aldrich took two steps toward her before Vespa stopped him with a gentle placement of her wing. Aldrich grumbled as he gave Vespa a perturbed look, but he stayed put.

"This will be worth it." Emma barely looked up.

Will it? She wondered. She'd never made a drink before, not like this. But it was as if her actions were no longer of her own accord. She was sure she could stop, but she didn't want to. The drink had compelled her to carry on this task to its completion.

Emma poured the cider into the pot, but it wasn't quite time to add the whiskey just yet.

Aldrich pulled up a seat next to Vespa, either coming to terms with Emma rooting through his bar or attempting to keep himself still.

"Now for a bit of sweetness." It didn't take much effort for Emma to find the jar labeled 'honey' sitting on the counter. She grabbed a spoon from a drawer under the counter and measured out a few scoops.

"Err . . . I don't know how old that is," Aldrich said. "It might not be good anymore."

"Honey doesn't spoil," Emma said, momentarily ripped from her work because the comment struck her as odd. "I thought you were a scientist."

Aldrich shrugged. "My studies are more on the quantum level."

Emma wasn't sure what that meant, but she'd need to ask about it later. Right now, the calling of the two alcohols in the pot was whipping her into a fervor.

It needed something else . . .

"Do you have any spices?" she asked. It might have been a long shot in this corner of the kingdom. It was a long way for spices to travel, and she didn't expect to find more than some basic salt, but she had to try.

"In the kitchen, but . . ." Aldrich didn't finish answering before Emma took off.

The kitchen was next to the bar, so it wasn't difficult to find. The space was filled with even more contraptions that Emma didn't recognize, but she ignored them all. Right now, her mind had a singular focus.

She rummaged around until she found what she needed. His spice rack was surprisingly well stocked for a bachelor living in a secluded village. Emma grabbed a couple items—cloves and cinnamon sticks.

Next, she needed an orange and a lemon. Something told her citrus fruits were also hard to come by in Hibernia, but she'd lucked out with spices, so it almost didn't surprise her when she spotted a fruit bowl on the counter with two oranges resting on top of the pile and a lemon sitting off to the side.

She returned to the bar with her spoils. Aldrich stared at her in earnest, and Emma couldn't tell whether he was upset with her or simply dumbfounded at what she was doing. At the moment, it didn't matter.

Emma peeled one orange and added the peel and the spices to the pot. She stepped back and paused, resting her gaze on the pot of liquid she'd concocted.

It was an odd thing to have to do, like watching a pot of water on the stove, willing it to boil.

But then a torrent of magic filled her—all at once. Vespa's gleeful expression hadn't changed, and Aldrich sat up with an intent focus. Nothing visible happened, but it was clear Vespa sensed something.

"Not too much now." Vespa's voice was almost a whisper, but it was as clear in Emma's head as if she had shouted.

No, not too much.

Emma could feel the cider hit a comfortable drinking temperature—like that of hot tea. She didn't stop though. This needed to boil.

The energy flowed through her, just as it had in Kalmar. It wasn't that she consciously channeled the energy out of her and into the drink, but more like the drink was *pulling* magic from *her*, thirsty for whatever she could provide.

"Remarkable!" Aldrich exclaimed as he stood from his seat. He lifted his glasses as though unsure he could believe what he was seeing. Emma couldn't blame him. Here, sitting on his counter, with no flame to be seen, was a boiling pot of spices and apple cider.

Nearly fifteen minutes passed before the hold on her was complete, and almost as quickly as it had begun, the magic stopped.

Now time for the whiskey. She poured in a cup, then added a little more for good measure.

The drink was really coming together now, but it needed one last step. She cut the lemon and squeezed it over the drink, allowing the juice to drip into the pot, then gave it a good stir.

The drink sang sweetly to her. It was everything it was meant to be. She could feel contentment radiating from the beverage.

How is this even possible? she mused.

"Here, Professor, why don't you try it and let us know how it is?" Emma took one of the cups already set out and filled it with the steaming beverage as the fragrance of cinnamon and cloves filled the room with its luxurious odor.

Vespa remained at the table but nodded in approval.

Aldrich lifted the cup to his mouth, pushing the hairs of his mustache out of the way as he took a sip.

His eyes closed as he lowered the cup and swallowed. "Why . . . this is marvelous!" He opened his eyes and met Emma's gaze. "I have not had anything like this in quite some time. What is it called?"

She hadn't thought of naming a beverage before, but she assumed the blending of new ingredients should be called something.

"What about, Spiced Apple Hibernian Bliss?" A bit of an explanatory name, but it felt right.

Aldrich nodded. "A fitting name indeed. It appears you do have a talent for this."

Emma's heart raced as she considered the possibilities of what being able to craft a drink like this meant. Perhaps she could really become a bartender. Not only could she salvage and serve ale and wine that would have otherwise spoiled, but this . . . this was drink making on a whole new level.

At the same time, her stomach dropped, and she had to steady herself to quell a sudden bout of nausea.

She *could* become the bartender she'd always hoped to be. But at what cost?

I might have just struck a deal with the devil.

"This is most excellent," Vespa said as she sipped a cup that Aldrich had brought to her, blissfully unaware of the battle waging inside of Emma. "Better than I had hoped!"

Aldrich nodded in agreement. "She can do this, but will this translate into what we need?"

Vespa set her drink down. "There's one last test to see what you're capable of. Hurry, we must see if you can affect the portal!"

"Portal?" Emma asked. "What the blazes are you talking about?"

"You'll see!" the fairy called back over her shoulder as she glided across and out of the room.

Aldrich finished taking another sip, his eyes closing as he savored the drink. "Before we do that, I must ask that you write down this recipe!"

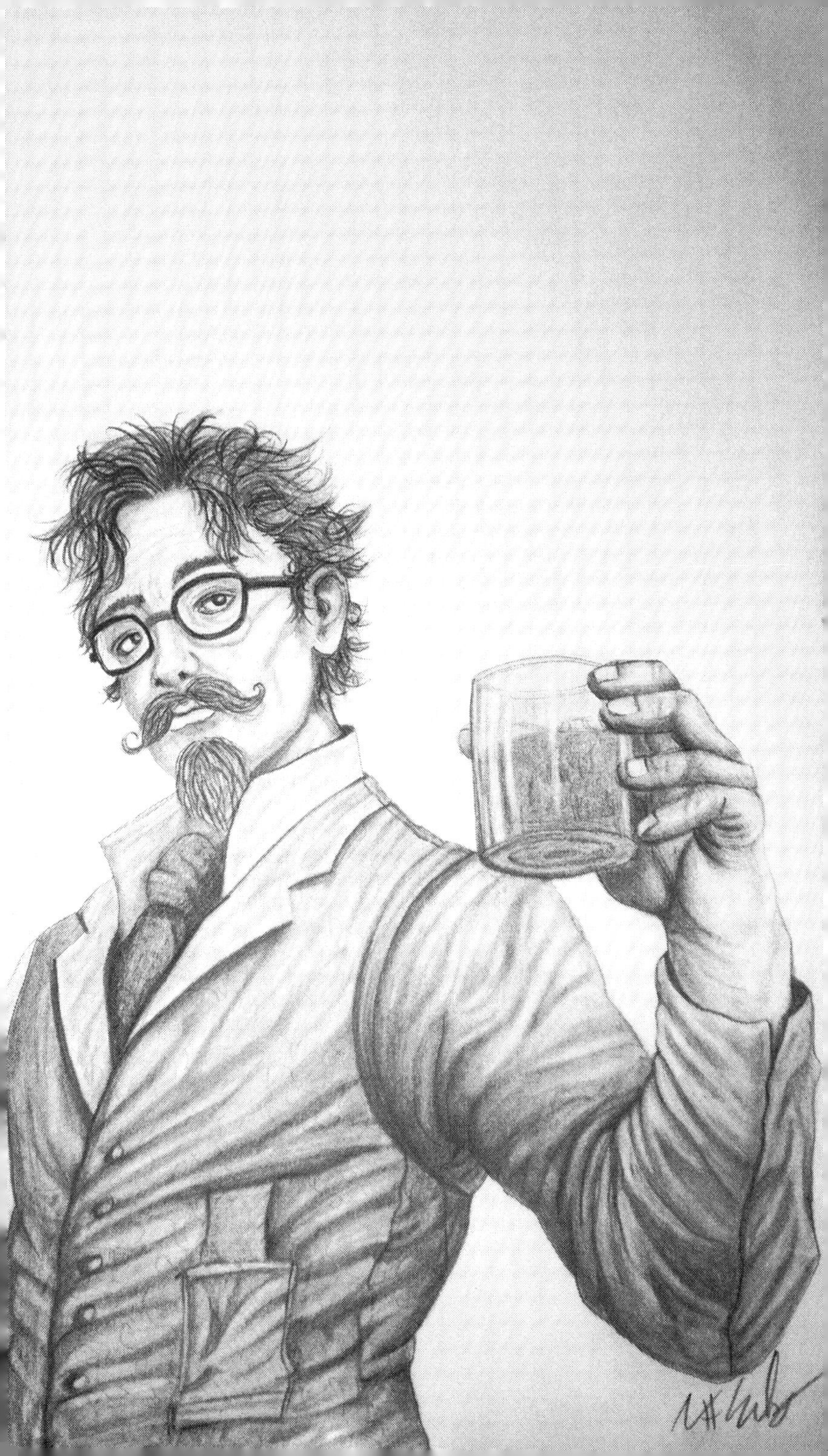

Spiced Hibernian Bliss

Drink Recipe

(No Magic Required)

Serving Size: 6

Ingredients:
- 9 oz Irish whiskey
- 6 oz apple brandy
- 2.25 cup apple cider
- 6 apple slices
- 6 cinnamon sticks
- 2 teaspoons of whole cloves
- 3 tablespoons of lemon juice
- 1 orange peel

Directions:

1. In a small saucepan, combine the apple cider, cinnamon sticks, cloves, and an orange peel. Bring the mixture to a boil, then remove from heat and cover, allowing it to steep for 15 minutes.

2. Strain out the spices and orange peel from the mixture, then stir in the Irish whiskey and freshly squeezed lemon juice.

3. Divide the aromatic blend among six mugs.

4. Garnish each mug with a slice of apple and an additional cinnamon stick for that perfect touch.

5. Serve hot for greatest enjoyment!

The Device
Chapter Seven

That any house in the rocky and wet terrain of Hibernia could have a functioning basement came as a surprise to Emma, but the trio descended hastily down a stairwell. A long way down.

The staircase spun in a spiral, stone walls on either side of the narrow descent, like something Emma would have expected to see in a castle dungeon. Sconces on the walls were lit, not with flames, but electricity. How anyone had managed to build a system of electricity so far from a major center and so far underground, she couldn't have guessed.

Everything that Emma had ever known told her this could only be the work of magic.

"You're sure you're not a sorcerer?" she asked. "These lights! They must be the work of magic."

There was no point for him to deny it now. It was clear she possessed magic as well, so it wasn't as if she could hand him over to Liam. She was all in at this point. Still, she expected Aldrich to protest.

Instead, he said, "Magic is only something that science hasn't explained yet. There are a vast number of marvels in my world that would appear to be magic to you."

"Your world? What do you mean?"

Aldrich sighed but didn't answer. He merely raced ahead, down the stairs faster, as though trying to escape the question.

Emma decided to let it go. He likely meant wherever he was from—perhaps there was a land she was unaware of that lay outside the kingdom. One with technological marvels such as those scattered across his home—but it was unlikely.

Instead, she focused on the stairs in front of her that descended stories underground.

Stone lined the narrow walls and paved the staircase itself. It did indeed remind her of some of the castle dungeons beneath the king's abbey in London. Minus the electricity, of course. Though the lack of smoke made the descent easier on the lungs.

She wrenched her feet to a standstill, stopping on a random stair when she glimpsed the bottom. The pair was leading her down a very long, very narrow flight of stairs, into what definitely resembled a dungeon.

Emma wondered how long she'd be willing to ignore her senses. How long would she allow the threat of discovery to override her instincts? "Where exactly are we going?" she asked.

"My lab," Aldrich replied.

"Your . . . lab?"

"Yes. My laboratory. That's where I keep my quantum accelerator."

"Oh, so we're just making up words now?" Emma wanted to laugh, but neither of the others appeared amused. She ran her hand over the hilt of her dagger once again.

"You can quit rubbing your blade," Vespa said from farther down the staircase. Emma didn't think the fairy had even turned around. "You won't need it."

There was no way Vespa could have seen Emma's action, which didn't help to ease her anxiety. "I'm being led down a narrow stairwell into an abyss by a fairy and a lunatic. Forgive me if I seem a little on edge."

Vespa didn't say anything, but Emma was sure she could see the corners of Aldrich's lips curl into a smile.

Emma had subconsciously counted the stairs as they descended. Seventy-two by the time they'd reached the bottom, she realized.

Through a small doorway, a room opened before them. It wasn't large, running about eight meters wide and probably twenty long. The gray brick of the stairwell shifted sharply into a smooth, black stone wall. More electric sconces lined the walls, four on each side, and two at the end glowed, dimly illuminating the room's contents.

Which was . . . nothing.

Almost nothing. The room was completely empty, save for a mid-sized table, which stood at its center. On its surface rested a bag about the size of a man's head.

Emma's senses tingled. There was something in the bag. Something that felt sort of like alcohol, but . . . different. For starters, it was far more powerful than the pot of cider and whiskey she'd crafted upstairs. "What is this? Why did you bring me to this place?"

Aldrich stepped to the center of the room and carefully unzipped the bag. "It's why Vespa brought you to me. As soon as she knew you resonated with the frequency of drinks, she thought you might be able to help me with this as well."

"This is how Professor Aldrich will return home," Vespa said.

Aldrich reached into the bag and pulled out a cube. The box was black and sleek, with a glass surface so dark it reflected the room around it like a mirror. However, it almost disappeared where it sat, almost like light bent around it instead of hitting its surface.

Whatever this box contained, Emma could tell it was

powerful. Its invisible tendrils were reaching out toward her, trying to wrap her in its snare.

"Now this is sorcery," Emma thought out loud.

Aldrich's focus was on the device. He nodded subtly.

"There's no sorcery here—only a fool scientist who leaped before he looked and got stuck in a world that hasn't developed a power source strong enough to get him home."

His tone was soft. Longing even. His eyes lingered over the device with a sadness that Emma had seen in the family members of those who'd succumbed to the Curse.

Something about this device had once held something dear to the professor. Something that had been taken away from him. Something that he had been powerless to retain.

Home.

Emma followed his gaze, confused. "What do you mean *home*? In this box?"

Aldrich's eyes stayed on the cube, picking it up as gently as one might a child. "It's more like through it—this is the device that brought me here years ago."

Emma took another look at the dark box on the table. It wasn't anything she was familiar with. "What's it supposed to do?"

Aldrich closed his eyes. "I would swear that it's supposed to haunt me for the rest of my days." He turned from it, shaking his head, and focused his deep brown eyes on Emma. "For the last six years, I've wandered this world. Trying to discover something that might help me. But it's like being stuck in the damned Victorian age. You've hardly begun to power things with steam. I've managed to generate barely enough energy on my own to power a lightbulb, never mind a quantum accelerator."

Professor Aldrich may as well have been speaking another tongue for the amount that Emma understood. But the device he was holding—there was something about it she did understand. It spoke to her, just as the cider had.

"It's Cursed." Emma thought out loud, then to herself: *Just like me.*

Even with that thought, she couldn't help but try to allow it to interact with her magic in the same way the cider had.

Immediately, a wall went up within Emma's mind. Her magic still brewed, but there was a barrier between her and the device, like it rested behind a film.

It wasn't an impervious wall. She could probably push through it if she allowed herself. But once that barrier was penetrated, there'd be no turning back.

"It's not cursed." Aldrich rolled his eyes as he set the device on the table. "I built the damned thing. It's highly advanced tech. There's nothing supernatural about it."

Emma didn't know what to think about that. Based on the pull it had on her own magic, if she were at any other point in her career, she would have marked this talisman as the devil's own device. A demon box.

Whatever it did, it was indeed otherworldly. Even though Aldrich didn't *seem* to possess any magic of his own, she wasn't yet ready to let go of the notion that he might indeed be a sorcerer. It was all too likely that this box held the key to his power.

"But it needs my magic to . . . to what? Turn it on?"

"I know it's a long shot." The professor pursed his lips and let out another sigh. "But truth be told, I'm out of options. If Vespa wasn't so convinced this would work, I wouldn't bother, but . . . well, she hasn't steered me wrong yet. And what the hell, if fairies can exist in this world, then certainly someone can have a magic that will power my device."

"How?" Even as she asked, the magic pressed against her mind's invisible barrier. She knew she just had to allow it access. But what she didn't understand was how this related to her other abilities. "My ability has only affected alcoholic drinks."

Light, she prayed that was all she was able to affect.

"Vespa believes that your magic will work. That, for whatever reason, the energy resonance of my quantum crystals is on the same magical wavelength as alcohol."

Emma raised an eyebrow.

Aldrich held up his hands in defense. "I'm as skeptical as you. Magical frequencies aren't exactly something that I'd ever considered to be . . . real. But, well, frankly, I'm out of options. This is a last-ditch effort. If it doesn't work . . ." His shoulders slumped. "Well, I suppose I need to accept the fact that I'm stuck in this place. Perhaps I can do some good here—utilize the knowledge I have to improve it."

"Don't give up before she's even tried!" Vespa lamented.

"Even if she *can* activate it," Aldrich said, his voice still sullen. "The return mechanism was damaged along with the power conduit. There's no telling where we'll end up."

"That doesn't mean there's no hope," Vespa urged. "That doesn't mean we don't try." She turned to Emma. "You can feel it, can't you?"

Emma could, but her internal warnings screamed, waging war with the magic that was itching to be released.

It's a trap. What if this device allows demons to exit the pit of hell? What if this is the key to their prison?

"Why me?" Emma asked. "You're a fairy; why can't you use your magic?"

"Fairy magic doesn't seem to influence these . . . crystals. Aldrich calls it a frequency. I can feel the resonance they project, even though I'm unable to touch it. It seems to be the same as yours."

So, this is a doorway, and I hold the key. But a doorway to where? The professor suggested it was a way to reach his world, but Emma couldn't shake images of a dark fairy realm from her mind's eye.

What if this device unleashed a war that pitted humans against fairies? What if Vespa unleashed a darkness upon the land? Was she willing to be a part of that reality? It was too real of a possibility, and she feared she was being coerced into becoming the catalyst to bring such a hellscape to life. From every story she'd heard, and every magical creature she'd fought, Emma knew it would be exactly like a fae creature to trick a victim who'd only just discovered their power.

She never thought she'd be the one to be fooled so easily.

Whatever this power was that she possessed, she could only imagine she was about to see Vespa instigate a war between human and fae. In the moment, she felt powerless to stop it.

Despite the ever-increasing volume of warnings sounding from within her mind, she couldn't stop herself. The box called to her. She *had* to know what the device did. It was hardly a conscious effort at all, but she allowed her magic to puncture through the veil and unleash in a firestorm.

Flame raged through her with such veracity she worried she'd become a fireball herself. The device held a life of its own. It had lain dormant for years, and now it was hungry for power.

A torrent of magic erupted from within her—one she couldn't stop, even if she had wanted to. The device demanded every bit of Emma that she could possibly give, and she was powerless to refuse.

The devil's device sprung to life. Lights flickered on the edge of her periphery, and a crackling energy filled the room. The hair on her body stood on end. It was like lightning had charged the surrounding air.

The device lit up, the black glass flooded with an intense light that pooled at its front then vomited out a stream of light and energy. The stream pierced through the room in a thick beam, before spreading into a vertical pool, meters away. Somehow, the light transformed into a mist and coalesced into a dark, disk-like shape, the size of a melon, floating against the wall.

Aldrich's mouth had fallen open. His eyes were as wide as saucers as they reflected the swirling vortex that had formed in his basement.

Whatever this is, perhaps Aldrich is just as much a pawn as I am, Emma thought.

Vespa had her hands clasped to her chest. If it weren't for the roar of the machine, Emma was sure she'd be able to hear the fairy squealing in twisted delight.

What poured out of the machine next was a combination of light and darkness. The lab's lights flickered and an eerie glow shrouded the room. The disk grew large enough for a person to step through. Its size appeared to rip a hole in the wall itself, except there was no dust and no debris. Instead, the energy spun, like a whirlpool in a river.

As the machine's hum waned, the beam disappeared, but the disk it had created remained.

"You've done it!" the professor gasped.

Emma tried to wrap her mind around the Cursed gateway before her and failed. This couldn't be happening.

"What is it that I've done?" she asked. "You claim that your world is on the other side of that?"

"Hmm, it's possible . . ."

"Possible? What do you mean?"

The sinking feeling in Emma's gut was worsening by the minute.

Aldrich held a hand to his head, while lifting the other,

gesturing for her to hold her line of questions. "This device creates gateways between multiple versions of our world. There are an infinite number of realities that this could lead to. If the device were working correctly, yes, my world would be the default destination. But with so much time since I've arrived and your magic an unknown variable in the equation, I have no way to know for sure."

Emma froze in horror. What lay in front of her couldn't have been anything but a gateway to the fairy realm.

Or worse . . .

And the power to open it came from within me.
Not just drinks . . .
Cursed . . .

Emma sank to her knees.

"This shouldn't be possible." Aldrich's voice was hardly more than a whisper.

"That's what you said when you first met me." Vespa grinned.

"Yes . . . yes, I suppose I did." He adjusted his glasses and turned his attention toward Emma. "Vespa had said this was a possibility, but I never truly thought . . . May I ask, how are you doing this?"

"Yes. How *are* you doing this?" The gruff voice was less than enthused.

Liam filled the door frame, his broad shoulders blocking out most of the light of the stairwell. He stood, nearly a silhouette, with his short sword held at the ready, blocking their only escape.

Cursed

Chapter Eight

How was she doing this?

More than that, what were her options now that Liam had not only tracked her from The Cursed Dragon, but he had *witnessed* her creating this . . . gateway.

Liam's eyes darted from the portal to Emma; his short sword remained trained on her. Somehow, despite her best efforts of covering their tracks toward the lighthouse, Liam had found her.

Damn, that man was a skilled tracker.

Who knew how long he had been standing there—Emma had been too focused on the cube—but it was clear he had seen enough. She wasn't getting out of this one alive.

The swirling disk had settled. No longer was the room filled with the whirlwind of its wrath. Instead, it hovered peacefully against the wall. A warm light glowed from its center, like a mist slowly lifting from the early morning sea.

Aldrich had said he needed a power source to get him home. Was that what this disk was?

What did home mean for Aldrich?

What did it mean for her?

Ten steps separated her and Liam. He'd been her home once. The one thing she could count on no matter where she traveled—he was always there. But now . . .

Beyond him were seventy-two stairs and no doubt a cage wagon bound for London. Even if she went with him, his part in her life was over. Her mouth went dry as she considered her new reality. Regardless of whether she complied with Liam or not, her future would not be with him.

And what would her life be without him? Even if she could get past him and race him up the stairs, then what? Disappear into the darkness? Where could she go where he wouldn't find her? He'd already proven how fruitless those efforts would be.

Her unlikely accomplices stood by silently. The devil's box talisman would be all the proof the King's Court would need to convict the professor. If he weren't executed, he'd certainly be imprisoned, and that device would be confiscated and likely dismantled and destroyed.

Then there was the fairy. If Emma were to flee now, Vespa would be left to the Hunters, and Emma had been among them long enough to know the cruelty they'd enact on a fairy creature would be far worse than the fate that awaited her.

She was suddenly aware that both Aldrich and Liam were still waiting for her to answer.

"I . . . I don't know." Emma looked at her hands. Whatever this gateway was, wherever it led, she had been the one who created it.

Liam wasn't waiting further. In true form, he slid across the room and grabbed the professor. The clay mug Aldrich held shattered as it hit the floor, warm cider splattered across the gray stone floor. The slight breeze that originated from the portal made waves on the liquid's surface as it spread along cracks until it formed the vague shape of a tree, its branches reaching out in every direction.

Vespa, who had fortunately hidden her wings before Liam arrived, smiled sweetly, as though he had come over for biscuits and tea rather than in a Cursed Hunter's fury. She lifted her pale arms and offered a small but cheeky wave of her fingers. Liam obviously didn't believe her to be the threat and instead focused his attentions on Emma.

Liam replaced his short sword with a dagger in a lightning-fast motion and pointed it toward Emma's neck. She knew that if he threw it, she'd be dead before she comprehended the action.

"Is this some sort of trick?" Liam's voice was firm. "Have these two enchanted you? Used you to create this . . . evil thing?"

Emma couldn't say she hadn't asked herself that very question. But she didn't believe this had anything to do with Vespa. She'd felt the power flowing through her. Somehow, the power to open whatever this thing was had come from her.

But Emma knew that if she were to say that outright, Liam would have every authority to slit her throat where she sat. Despite their history together, Emma wasn't convinced he wouldn't.

Her options now were to tell him the truth and risk being executed by the only friend she'd ever had, or to say nothing and be brought before a tribunal who would likely tie her to a pyre and set her on fire.

Is this how all witches felt when the Hunters arrived on their doorsteps? Confused, defeated, and scared?

Her eyes flitted toward the portal. Liam would never follow her through the gateway. It might offer her the only escape, but two problems stood in the way. The first was that she'd never make it that far. Liam would land his dagger in her chest so fast that the only other realm she'd enter would be the afterlife.

Second, even though she was the one who created it, Emma had no idea where the gateway went. Another world . . . but would it be any friendlier to her than this one? She wasn't about to hop through to find out, at least not on her own.

There was a third option. She could try to take on Liam, but she was currently at a disadvantage. Against anybody else in the kingdom, she'd like her odds. She was nearly unmatched in most forms of hand-to-hand combat. Unmatched to almost anyone but Liam—and with a dagger in hand, he held the advantage.

Not to mention, one of them would end up dead, and no matter who the victor was, that wasn't a path she wanted to travel down.

She took a steadying breath.

Liam stepped back and gestured with his dagger for Emma to stand. Tired of sitting on the cold stone floor, she had no reason to argue. She studied his dark eyes as she did so, searching for her friend, finding only uncertainty and concern. He was studying hers as well.

"How long?" He lowered his voice and relaxed his hold on the knife, though he held it at the ready in case anyone in the room got any ideas. It amazed Emma that through this entire endeavor, he regarded Vespa as the lesser threat among them. She knew if Liam realized the creature was fae and not just another witch, the dagger would have already been cast in her direction.

Emma sputtered as she tried to sort through her own thoughts.

"How long, Emma?" he repeated with more grit in his voice this time.

"Grenaa," she said quietly then cleared her throat and straightened her posture before she unleashed all her thoughts at once. "The wine the barkeep served *had* been spoiled. I willed it back to a drinkable state. I realized I'd used magic, got scared, and ran. I don't know how I acquired the Curse, but I did not want to be executed because of it. I still don't. I thought if I could disappear, I could live a quiet life without hurting anybody."

Emma held her ground, braced to taste the steel of Liam's blade. But his stance remained unchanged. "Where does this go?" he asked, gesturing to the portal still swirling behind them. "Is it meant to unleash Hades upon Lancastria?"

"I don't know where it leads. My magic unlocked the potential of Professor Aldrich's device."

Liam took the cue to shift his attention to the professor, who seemed relatively unfazed about being held in iron cuffs. If anything, by the way his eyes lingered on the floor with a disconcerted frown, he was more displeased about the spilled drink. "It leads to another world." Aldrich answered.

"A dark realm?" Liam growled. "This is mad sorcery, Emma. How the hell did you get mixed up with this? After all we've been through to rid the kingdom of darkness! Are we to expect hordes of creatures to come pouring through at any moment?"

"You Hunters are so dramatic." Aldrich rolled his eyes. "It leads to another Earth. Another version of here. It is neither dark nor light, it just is. And it's a one-way trip. We can enter on this end, but no person or creature will be able to exit it into your world."

"Another . . . Earth?" Liam said. "You make no sense, old man. What you say is nothing but dark sorcery." He turned back to Emma. "Can you close it?"

Emma shook her head—she truly didn't know. But Aldrich jumped in and answered for her. "She won't need to. It will close either after we pass through with the device or when the energy crystal has depleted. Which won't be long now."

It was at about this moment that Emma realized Liam

hadn't cuffed her. It was unlike him to break protocol, which would have seen all three of them restrained. Either part of Liam still trusted her, or he was so thrown off by her involvement he'd forgotten. If she was going to get out of this without being put to the stake, she had to think quickly.

"Liam, this is not something I asked to happen. I have not given myself over to the darkness."

"They call it a curse for a reason, Emma." He shook his head seemingly disappointed. "It doesn't matter if you chose this path. If even you can be overtaken by its grasp, it proves evil's root can spread. Why do you think we've been fighting so hard to remove this blight? If even those who fight against it can be afflicted, we must stop it at all costs."

Liam turned his dagger to Aldrich. "What is the purpose of this device, wizard? You say this leads to a different Earth. Explain yourself."

"It's complicated," Aldrich replied. "And it's a lot for me to unpack with a knife pointed at my throat."

"Try," Liam hissed.

Aldrich deflated and shook his head. "The simple version is that I am a scientist. I am not from this world but from another reality. *Not* a magical realm." He paused for effect. The professor clearly wanted Liam to be certain of that. "However, the foundation of my research was studying the fabric of space and time. I built this device to test my theories. The device allowed me to travel to your world, and well, I hadn't expected the differences in our world histories to be so expansive.

"The power source used to charge the device's quantum crystals was damaged during my journey here. I had no way to activate a gateway to return. To be fair, I made a lot of errors of judgment in my excitement to test the device out. Suffice to say, this world—your world—is lacking in the technological capabilities to replicate the power source I needed to return to my universe. However, your universe does seem to possess energy signals that mine does not. For whatever reason, the resonance of my quantum crystals seems to be on the same wavelength as what your friend here possesses."

Emma and Liam exchanged confused glances, blinking at each other as they attempted to comprehend the explanation. Vespa stood with her hands clasped, appearing delighted at the professor's words.

Liam turned to Emma. "What the hell is he talking about?"

Emma shrugged. "Not a clue."

"Lacking in technological developments?" Liam snorted. "You need to get out of the small town and into the wider streets of the kingdom's cities! We live in a golden age. We have electricity powering lights and locomotives that can get us from London to Edinburgh in two days."

The corner of Aldrich's lip turned up slightly. "Boy, in my world, you can fly from London to Edinburgh in an hour. And in two days, you could travel around the globe twice over."

Liam's hand twitched, and Emma feared he was about to slit the professor's throat right there.

Aldrich continued. "This device requires more power than all your steam-powered engines combined. Quite substantially so."

"What sort of evil place do you come from?" Liam asked. "A land full of magic?"

Aldrich's stare didn't leave Liam as he answered. "To you, it would likely appear that way. But there's no magic in my world."

Emma's gazed moved to the portal once again. It seemed so unlikely that someone could step into that strange mass and walk out the other side in a completely different realm. One that didn't possess magic.

"Do they hunt witches in your world?" Emma asked.

Liam cleared his throat, making it clear he was annoyed that Emma took over his line of questioning. But he didn't object and seemed equally intrigued at the question.

"Not anymore," Aldrich said, his words measured. "In our past, we did. Then we realized magic, what you call magic, doesn't exist. At least not in our world. Here, it appears, there are forces at work other than what we would consider natural."

A world without magic. Emma wondered what that would be like. Where would life have led her if she hadn't been orphaned and brought under the king's service? If she hadn't been raised to hunt magical creatures and people. Would she still have worked for the king? Or would she have been left destitute on the streets of London? Maybe she'd have been picked up by some farmer to work as a farm hand.

The possibilities of who she could have been were endless.

The puddle of cider on the floor caught her attention. Its tendrils had now spread out in all directions with an infinite number of branches, being pushed along by the invisible forces of the portal.

Perhaps she didn't need to be sentenced to a life that was no longer within her control. Perhaps there was a place out there where she *could* be free to do as she wished. Even become a bartender if she chose.

Cuanmore was at the edge of the kingdom, but maybe that wasn't far enough. Maybe her fate hadn't been decided.

Emma looked thoughtfully at Aldrich. "I'd like to see your world."

Something More

Chapter Nine

Emma's statement hung in the air among the group. The hum of the demon box filled the otherwise quiet room. It had quieted since the portal formed, but it continued to emanate a dull background noise.

Vespa broke the silence by giggling, and Emma turned sharply to the fairy. She didn't know if she should be offended, but the reaction was like a dagger thrust into her ribs.

Is it so ridiculous that I desire to be something else? Something more?

Vespa's eyes were wide, a huge smile painted on her face. It was a look, not of mockery, but of delight.

Emma didn't know which reaction she'd prefer. If this decision delighted a fae creature, perhaps it wasn't the right one after all.

"What are you so happy about?" Some of the intensity had dissipated from Liam's voice, but it still couldn't be considered anything other than a growl.

"Emma was *meant* to come with us," Vespa said. "She's just like me and the professor."

Liam pursed his lips. "Cursed."

Emma flinched. The word struck harder than it should. Especially since she'd had the same thought moments before. It was more painful coming from Liam, though.

"Not cursed," Vespa replied. "Lost."

Lost. That word resonated with Emma. It was exactly how she felt.

"And that makes you smile?" Liam asked.

"Of course! It means our journey has only begun. Our destiny has not yet been set. There's something exciting in knowing that infinite possibilities await us."

Aldrich's mustache twitched.

Liam lowered his weapon for the first time since he arrived. "Em, you can't be serious."

He looked at Emma's two unlikely companions, the furrow in his brow deepening. Emma knew what he was thinking before he even said it. "They've enchanted you. We can go back to London, get this all straightened out. Your reputation, your achievements, the Court will take all of those into consideration. Perhaps we can still get you off with a warning if you agree to time under exorcism."

The thing about being a former Hunter of the Cursed was that Emma knew every strategy that had ever been used to bring a witch, wizard, or sorcerer in without a fight. Bargaining wasn't a tactic Liam often grasped for, but he must have sensed he was running out of options to fulfill his duty peacefully.

"This isn't about them," Emma sighed. "This is about me. I . . . I don't belong here. I've traveled to the edge of the kingdom, and I *still* don't belong. I may be in over my head, but what these two offer me is something I never thought possible, but perhaps something I've always known I needed."

Liam tightened the grip on his dagger, his face bearing gritted frustration.

Emma took a cautious step forward. Perhaps she could speak to her friend rather than a Hunter. She had to get him to let his guard down . . . just a little. Liam didn't move, but his eyes stayed fixed on hers. She risked two more calculated steps before lifting a hand to place on his shoulder.

He tensed but didn't back away.

"Liam, you and I both know, time served under the king's command or not, if you bring me back to London, they'll execute me."

Liam shook his head. He must have known that he'd lost any control of the situation—if he'd ever had any—as tears welled in his eyes. "It's a trick, Em. I won't let them steal you away."

Emma tightened her grip on his arm. "This is no trick. This is who I am. Perhaps who I've always been, and I had just never realized. My entire life I've been a Hunter because that was who I was told I must be. Perhaps now I can learn who I truly am. Away from here. You could haul me to London, but we both know what will happen to me if you do. At least if you let me flee, I'll live."

Liam held his stance in silence. Emma could sense the war that raged inside of him. It mirrored the one that roared inside her own mind.

Tight-lipped, he responded. "Light, the sorcerer must have me under enchantment as well. I may come to regret this." He handed Emma the keys to Aldrich's cuffs.

Emma blinked.

"You're letting me go?" She neglected to hide the disbelief in her voice. Despite her plea, she'd never expected Liam to bend.

Liam closed his eyes and sucked in a deep breath through his nostrils before opening them again. "Years ago, you helped me fight off a nightfang in the village where my younger brother had stayed. Do you remember?"

Emma snorted. "Of course I remember. You lost your

brother that night. Despite running at the monstrous beast like a damned fool."

It was one of their first missions. It was unfortunate that Command had sent them to a town where Liam's only living family member was, but there was no way for them to have known. Nor could they have expected Liam would abandon all his training to protect someone he loved.

"If it hadn't been for you that day . . . I don't think I would have survived either. You put your mouth on my dirty ass leg and sucked the bloody poison out yourself." Liam shook his head. "Nobody has ever cared for me as much as that. That day solidified our friendship. If we weren't both Hunters . . . light, Emma . . ."

Emma's pulse quickened. She couldn't let him finish that thought. Not now. "You're my best friend, Liam." She would not cry in front of him. That wouldn't be his last memory of her. She clamped down on her resolve. "That will never change. Whether or not I'm Cursed."

"The point is," he said, "I've never felt like I've fully repaid you for saving me. Now, once you step through that portal . . ." He let the thought drift off.

"I wish it didn't need to be like this," he said instead. "I already lost my brother. I hate to think I'm losing you, too."

Emma stood quiet for a long moment before replying. "I'll miss you too, Liam."

A grin grew on his face. Emma knew him well enough to know he was fighting off his own emotion with humor. "And if hordes of demons follow you back, I will slay them all one by one."

Emma allowed herself a smile. "I would expect nothing less."

Aldrich cleared his throat. "I don't mean to rush this

exchange, but the gateway won't remain open for much longer. We have to go."

Liam sheathed his dagger and wrapped his arms around Emma. His familiar smell of sweat, leather, and pine enveloped her. How long had it been since they were kids sneaking around the training grounds? How many times had they had one another's backs?

It was hard to believe that in this sorcerer's basement it was all coming to an end.

"Take care, Emma." Liam grasped her head and pulled it into his firm chest.

"You too." Tears she'd been holding back broke free. These were tears of relief, not sadness. For all the strangeness of this situation, it seemed right. As though it were always meant to be.

Liam turned to Vespa as Emma stepped away, his demeanor turning dark in an instant. "If I ever find out that this was some sort of fairy trick, I will spend the rest of my days hunting down each and every last one of your kind."

Emma blinked. She shouldn't have been surprised, but Liam had been savvier than she'd thought. Had he known Vespa was fae this entire time?

"If this was a trick," Vespa replied smoothly, "you wouldn't have even known I was here."

The edges of the portal warbled. Swiftly, Emma unlocked Aldrich's cuffs, and the professor calmly walked to the center of the room and picked up his device. "We will still need this," he said.

He rejoined Vespa and Emma, peering into the void of the tunnel. "It'd be best if we all cross the threshold together, just to be sure we aren't separated within the fabric of space-time."

"Is that possible?" Vespa asked, and for the first time that evening, worry crossed her face.

"It's unlikely," Aldrich answered, "but I've never done this with more than one person."

Emma looked at the fairy with a quizzical furrow of her brow. "You're coming too?"

Vespa tilted her head, appearing puzzled by the question. "Of course."

"There'll be time to get to know each other and our motivations better once we're through," said Aldrich. "Now, everyone, through the portal. Hurry!"

Emma turned to Liam one last time and found hurt in his eyes. He must have felt betrayed, confused, angry. Perhaps all those things and more. Emma could only guess based on how she felt herself. How could life have taken them on such different paths? She wondered if she'd ever see her friend again, but deep down, she knew this was the last time she'd look upon his stupid face.

"If I discover a way to undo this curse, I will return."

He returned her gaze, tight-lipped and unwilling to let his emotions display on his face. "You can never return," Liam replied. "Nothing good awaits you in this realm."

Remorse flooded her. This had to be a mistake.

What am I doing? I've worked my entire life to rid the world of magic, and now suddenly I'm throwing myself headfirst into its literal maw.

"May you find the answers you seek, Emma," Liam said, allowing a touch of emotion to intrude upon his voice. It wasn't much, but it was enough to tear down the wall Emma had erected, and tears streamed freely down her face.

"Three!"

The time for second chances was over, and Emma was all but pulled along with Vespa and Aldrich as they stepped into the unknown.

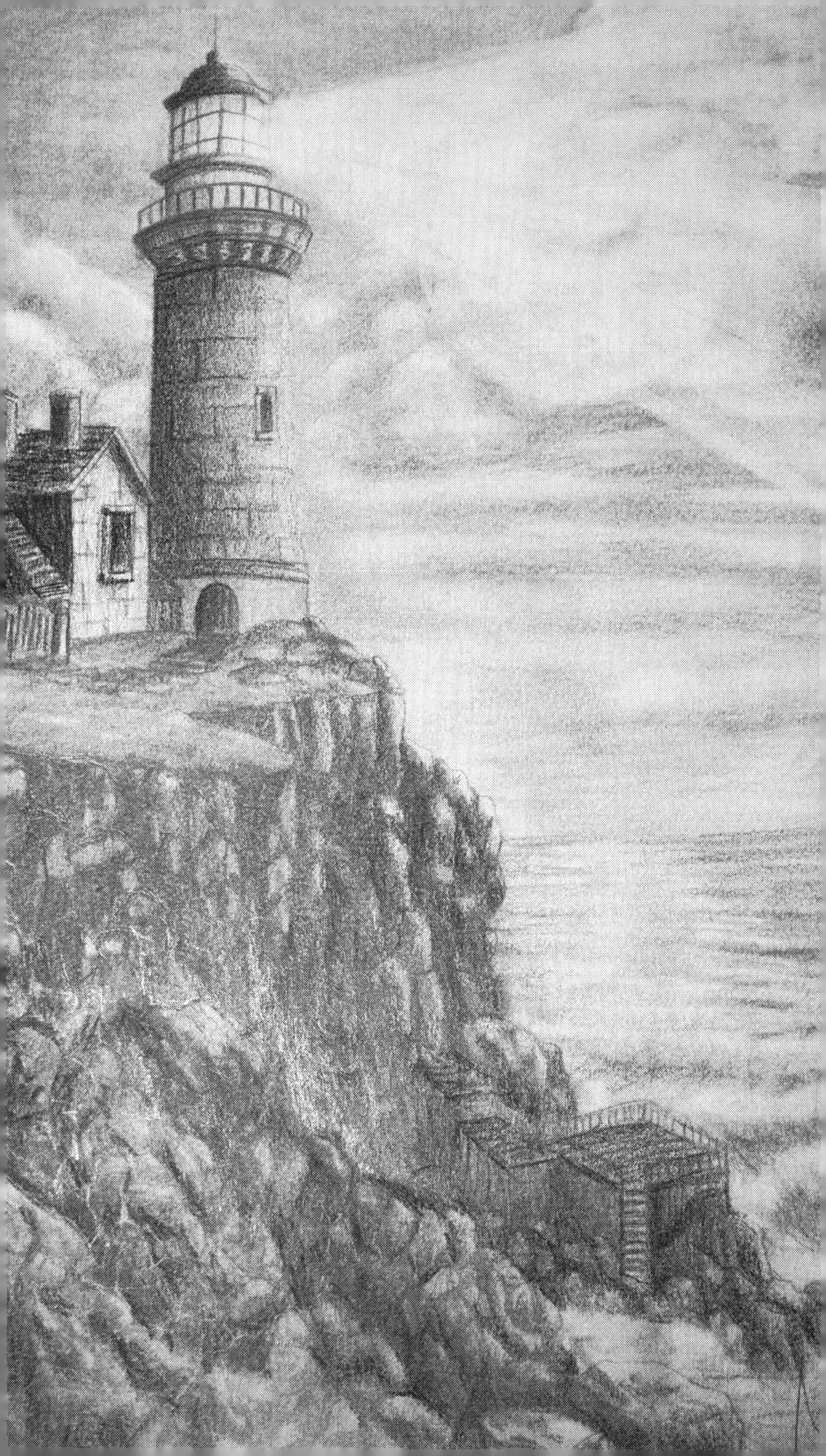

World Two

A New World

Chapter Ten

Aldrich's home vanished as they stepped from the portal and onto a grassy knoll. The lighthouse still stood strong and unwavering, but its light had been extinguished. As if nobody cared about ships that might crash into the rocky terrain.

"This is another world?" Emma asked. "Other than the house being gone, it looks the same to me."

"Things here may appear similar to your world," Aldrich said "It's much too complicated to get into now. Different choices have been made here, and they'll have resulted in different outcomes."

Emma wanted to press the professor for more answers. She'd just left behind her only friend and her own world. She thought it was only fair that she receive some sort of explanation as to what she'd gotten herself into. But the early spring chill from the ocean bit at her face, and she decided any conversation they might have would be best had indoors.

But Aldrich pushed ahead toward the village, making it clear he wasn't discussing the matter further.

The rest of the walk was carried out in silence. The distance back to town was the exact same distance as it had been on the trip to Aldrich's. But it was like traveling through a shell of her own world. If it weren't for the crashing of waves on the rocks in the distance, there would have been no noise whatsoever. At first, she believed they'd spent longer at the house than she'd originally thought, perhaps into the early hours of the morning. But even then, the town was far too quiet. Emma had traversed through plenty of villages in the middle of the night—that was when most dark creatures came out to play. Even at a late hour, there would be the sounds of babies crying, dogs barking, and squabbles between partners over one of them returning home from the pub later than promised.

There was none of that now.

Vespa was the one to break the silence. "Something is not right here."

The fairy didn't elaborate further, and Aldrich didn't seem bothered enough to pry, so Emma let the statement sit and kept her eye out for some dark creature that may have run amok. Whatever choices Aldrich was referring to, they had apparently led this world to silence.

It hadn't taken long for them to arrive at the pub that appeared, at least on the surface, to be The Cursed Dragon.

If Emma didn't know better, she could have said she was looking at the very same pub she'd been in only hours before. The tavern sat on the same corner lot, had the same brick exterior and the same stables out back. The same sign, bearing the name The Cursed Dragon, accompanied by a painted image of a dragon circling a beer stein, hung above the door. Even the dirt street leading toward it felt the same beneath her feet.

But there were subtle differences here that made her skin crawl. Things were almost the same, but just different enough that she wondered if she'd stepped into a dream.

The paint on the buildings and fences was faded, obviously it had been neglected for years. Pots which once held greenery and flowers were now filled only with dirt. Though the windows had previously been filled with darkened glass, they were now boarded over.

And everything was too quiet.

The Cursed Dragon stood silent. The stables were empty. No laughter emanated from its walls; no music billowed into the streets. There was no sign of merriment from inebriated patrons who had stayed too long or imbibed too much.

Only silence.

If it weren't for a faint glow between the slits of the doors and boards shuttered to the windows, Emma would have believed the place had been abandoned or had closed in the brief hour they'd been away. Dips in the light suggested movement from someone inside.

"It's like they don't want customers," she said as she stared at the heavy wooden door.

Was it thicker than it had been before? She hadn't paid close attention, but for a small pub in such a remote village, this door had been built extra sturdy. There was no doubt it had been installed to keep people—or trolls—from breaking in. It was crafted with thick oak and overlaid with intricate ironwork, both around the frame and overtop of the wood itself.

Aldrich gave the door several firm tugs with no luck. "Very peculiar."

The Cursed Dragon doubled as an inn, and there would be no reason for the door to be sealed shut. It wouldn't close for the night, as patrons would need some way to get to their rooms.

That was in my world, she reminded herself. Though she didn't quite grasp what that meant yet, she had figured out enough to know she had not rented a room at *this* version of the tavern.

Aldrich shuffled his feet a bit, as though preparing himself for a race, before banging the edge of his fist on the door three times. The sound echoed through the village streets, breaking the overbearing silence of the night.

Moments stretched on as the echo fanned into darkness and faded once again to quiet. Emma strained to hear any semblance of noise coming from within the tavern. Just as she was about to suggest they try some place else, the door creaked open a notch, allowing a slim bar of warm lantern light to stream across the street.

A set of beady eyes poked out and studied Aldrich for a good several seconds before turning to examine Emma and Vespa. The man's face hid in shadow, but there was no mistaking the nephew of The Cursed Dragon's owner, William O'Malley.

"What's the matter with you?" William hissed. "Are you trying to get us all killed?"

"Er . . ." Aldrich stuttered. "My apologies, good sir. We're travelers from the east, and it took us longer to arrive than we had expected. We're looking for a room for the night. We can share if necessary."

Emma balked slightly at the presumption that she'd be willing to share a room with a middle-aged man and a fairy creature, but she supposed she'd survived worse—if not stranger—arrangements.

"We don't let travelers in at this time of night." William's voice was rough like gravel and didn't match the starry-eyed youth Emma had seen working the bar earlier. This William looked older, more run down and eyed each of them with the suspicion of someone used to things not being quite what they seemed. "You should have planned better, and you shouldn't be outside."

"Yes, well,"—Aldrich straightened his vest—"we would be most appreciative if you could help us rectify that."

The man shook his head vehemently in a short but determined fashion. "I'm sorry, there's no refuge here. If you are who you say, O'Sullivan leaves his tavern unlocked for those who find themselves stuck in the street after sundown. Just be careful and keep quiet. May God keep you safe."

Before Aldrich could plea further, the door closed without another word.

"That was only mildly unsettling," said Emma.

Aldrich scanned their surroundings, his gaze lingering on the dark, cloudy sky. His mustache twitched, and he heaved an uneasy sigh. "You could say that. There's no telling what he might have been afraid of. We should probably do as he says."

Familiar with a version of the city's layout, Aldrich swiftly led them down a short stretch of zig-zagging road to O'Sullivan's pub. At first glance, the pub appeared to be abandoned, but no more so than any other building on the street.

Aldrich tugged the handle of the door, and as William had claimed, it was unlocked.

The pub was empty, but clearly not abandoned. Like the owner had closed up for the night but simply forgot to lock the door. Chairs were neatly tucked in beside their tables, the bar was clean and free of dust, and even the floors had been recently scrubbed.

As far as Emma could tell, O'Sullivan's was a typical Hibernian pub . . . with a few peculiarities. As Emma studied its decor, it became apparent that its owners were extremely wary toward magic users. That wasn't something uncommon in these small villages—one never knew when a doppelgänger or banshee might attempt to impersonate one of the patrons, and that was never good for business—however, this was bordering on paranoia. Horseshoes circled the door frame and were hung above every table. Jars of iron nails lined the bar and small bundles of St. John's Wort dangled from the rafters wherever there was room.

At the back of the bar was a storage room door, which would have gone unnoticed, except it had been barred shut with two solid steel beams.

"Is this normally what happens when you go through that gateway?" Emma asked.

"Normal is a tad hard to define, I'm afraid. I had only been through it a handful of times before I got stuck on your world. What normally would happen after visiting one world is that I'd return to my own. Either it's been too long, and the device couldn't lock onto my world's coordinates, or it didn't respond as it normally would have due to your unique ability. That said, every world presents its own unique history. Every combination of choices results in something new. Other than some peculiarities, this world seems relatively similar to yours."

Emma thought this was as good a time as any to broach the question. "That man at The Cursed Dragon; I recognized him. He's the nephew of the owner."

"Hmm." Aldrich seemed uninterested. He grabbed a stool by the bar and pulled himself onto it, all the while distracted by the details of the establishment they'd entered.

"How is that possible?" she pressed. "How can a person inhabit more than one realm?"

Aldrich's attention became more focused. "Remember earlier when I mentioned that the events of your world made it different from mine?"

Emma nodded. "Yes, but you didn't elaborate."

"What if, for every decision you made, every possible outcome happened?"

Emma tilted her head. "What do you mean?"

Aldrich removed his glasses and inspected them in the lantern's light. He took a moment to blow on the lenses before continuing. "Take, for example, when we were back at the lab.

You had a decision to make about whether to go with your friend."

"Right, to stay with Liam and be taken to London for trial, or to travel with you to . . ." Emma looked around her and gestured a hand to their current accommodation. "Wherever this place is."

"And you chose to come with us."

"Well, it was this or facing execution."

"But you *could* have stayed with Liam," he said.

"I suppose . . . but I don't understand . . ."

"In that moment, another world formed, a version of the world where you stayed behind and are chatting with Liam right now instead of me."

Emma grasped what he was saying, but it sounded more complicated than what she wanted to deal with. "I think I need a drink."

Black Velvet

Chapter Eleven

There was something unsettling about O'Sullivan's pub that Emma couldn't quite put into words. It wasn't all the trinkets or charms spread around the place—she'd encountered her fair share of superstitions in villages throughout the kingdom. Nor was it the reaction of William at The Cursed Dragon, though she couldn't deny it was unusual. No, this was an unease that ran deeper than that, but she couldn't pinpoint its source.

"I don't like this place, Henry." Vespa's voice trembled with trepidation. "William was terrified. I can't tell of what, but something doesn't feel right here."

Aldrich nodded but appeared unconcerned. "Just because the locals are superstitious doesn't mean there's anything to fear. As far as it not feeling right, it's possible your magic operates on a different frequency than magic does here, if there is magic here at all."

"You're certainly handling the prospect that there could be magic here rather well," Vespa said. "I remember how hard it was to convince you that it existed on my world."

"Yes, well," Aldrich adjusted his vest, "if you've taught me anything, it was to not make assumptions about anything. Not even the possibilities of magic. All I can do is observe and record what is."

Emma didn't know what to think. All the talk of worlds with magic and worlds with *different* magic than her own was making her head spin.

Aldrich continued. "We'll rest here tonight and reassess how things look in the morning. Perhaps we'll be able to find someone who can give us more answers in the light of day."

Vespa didn't appear convinced, and Emma couldn't blame her. She really could use that drink to help calm her nerves.

Emma let her eyes wander over the bar. Behind jars of nails and vases of dried St. John's Wort, the shelves were fully stocked. She let her senses reach out to each container. Without approaching them, she could tell what their contents were, and some even inspired drink recipe ideas. She tried to ignore those for the moment.

It struck her as odd that the owner of O'Sullivan's would leave their liquor unlocked overnight. Superstition or not, if this were London, the staff would return the next morning to find their shelves emptied.

Emma stepped behind the bar, where a sparkling wine bottle sat in a bucket of cold water. An *open* bottle. She could tell just by sensing the liquid that it had only recently been opened, and it was still full.

"Well, there's no point in letting this go to waste." She lifted the bottle, causing water to pour off the glass and back down below. Emma grabbed a towel to catch the water dripping down its side.

"Emma! What are you doing?" Vespa hissed. "Don't touch anything!"

"Don't worry." Emma waved a hand. "I'm not going to steal anything. I'll leave sufficient coin. Besides, it's already open! It will be flat by morning if we don't. Plus, they left the inn unlocked. Who's to say it wasn't left out here for people like us who need a place and a drink? But I think it needs something else . . ."

"Emma, you should probably listen to Vespa," said Aldrich. "This might look like your world, but the rules might be very different here. You don't even know if they use the same currency."

"Why wouldn't they use the currency of the kingdom?" Emma barely looked up from what she was doing as she grabbed three pint glasses from behind the bar. She had an idea.

Emma lifted a glass to the beer tap on the counter and slowly pulled back the handle, filling it to the halfway mark with a dark, rich stout. Then she repeated the process for each glass, watching the rich chocolatey drink flow and foam. The stout, though a couple of days old, was still good. She didn't even think she needed to manipulate it. The sparkling wine would create the balance she needed.

"Someone opened this bottle of wine, set it in chilled water, then left." Emma took the wine and poured it over the velvety stout in the first glass. The two liquids intermingled and swirled together, creating a rich symphony of bubbles, dark stout, and clear wine.

"How do you know the wine's not tainted?" The professor was squinting to see in the pub's dimness and adjusted his glasses as he spoke.

A smile crossed Emma's face. She didn't need to, but she let her mind probe the wine she'd just poured. It spoke to her loud and clear, almost as if someone were reading her the tasting notes. Cool, crisp, with light acidity and yeasty remnants. The bottle might have been one of the finest examples of sparkling wine she'd ever seen.

"With this new ability I have, I'm able to tell the makeup of the wine before I even try it. I just know things about it.

How it tastes, what it should mix with, I can even change properties about it if I want—like how I heated the cider at your home. I can manipulate it to highlight some of the existing flavors and complement the drink." She slid one of the glasses across the bar toward Aldrich. "Like this drink, for example. The sparkling wine has a nuttiness that I brought out by mixing it with the stout."

"New?" The professor's face scrunched. He picked up the glass and brought it to his lips, but paused there, considering.

"Didn't Vespa tell you? I've only discovered that I have this magic recently."

"She hadn't." Aldrich's lips fidgeted, and he took a sip of his drink. His eyes lit up as the drink hit his tongue, and Emma thought that was as good of an excuse as any to try the drink herself.

She allowed the drink's bubbles to swirl around her palate. Just as she said, the stout was rich, and its flavor brought out the nuttiness of the sparkling wine. It had a thick mouthfeel that coated her throat. Notes of chocolate, molasses, and even a hint of peanut butter danced along her taste buds.

Emma inhaled deeply as she enjoyed the drink she'd crafted. She could definitely get used to crafting cocktails like this.

Vespa still held her glass, studying it curiously. Understanding crossed her face as she let out a gasp. "Don't touch the wine!" she cried as she took a few steps toward Aldrich.

The professor stopped with the glass at his lips for a second sip and lingered. "Why not?"

"Because it's ours." From the darkness of the other side of the pub, a deep voice, as silky smooth as the stout, danced across the empty tables.

Vespa disappeared.

Emma had to catch herself from dropping her glass.

Professor Aldrich stood and backed up against the bar. His steps were calm, but his posture was uneasy.

Three figures stepped out from the shadows. Two appeared to be male and one female. Dark iridescent wings unfolded from behind each of them.

"Fae," Aldrich whispered.

Black Velvet

Drink Recipe

Ingredients:
- 4 ounces chilled Champagne or sparkling wine
- 4 ounces chilled stout

Directions:

1. Gather the ingredients and ensure they are well chilled.
2. Pour the Champagne into a wine flute, filling the glass about halfway to create a sparkling base.
3. Slowly top the Champagne with the chilled stout, allowing it to blend.
4. Serve and enjoy!

Tips:

- For a fancy touch, use a wine flute for serving, although a beer mug or pint glass works just as well.
- Ensure both ingredients are well chilled for the best taste experience.
- Experiment with different sparkling wines like prosecco or cava for a unique twist.
- Adjust the ratio of Champagne to stout based on

personal preference; a 1:1 mix is traditional, but a 2:1 pour can also be delightful.

Important Note: It should go without saying that it is ill-advised to use any wine that has been left out as a gift for the fae. Do so at your own risk.

Three Fairies

Chapter Twelve

These fairies didn't look at all like Vespa.

Each was still beautiful—there was no doubt about that—but it was the type of beauty that came with being a badass rather than a dainty flower ready to blow away with a harsh breath. However, what truly set them apart was the way they carried themselves. They hovered just above the floor, floating with shoulders taut, ready to pounce. Their wings, instead of being translucent and reflecting the light of the room, seemed to absorb the flame and leave shadows in their wakes.

"He knows we're fae." The closest fairy jeered at Aldrich, responding to his comment. Horns, similar to those of a goat, protruded from the top of her head. "Very insightful."

A shiver ran down Emma's spine. It was the menacing glares that left no doubt of their malevolence.

"We are fae, indeed." The fairy moved toward Aldrich, her face curled in a sneer. "Yet, he is not so clever that he would leave our gifts be."

"Most disrespectful," another stated. His voice was comparable to nails scratching on metal. Emma could feel the reverberations in her teeth. "Perhaps we should burn their village to the ground and make them watch—as punishment."

"Vespa's betrayed us," Emma whispered just loud enough for Aldrich to hear.

Aldrich had backed up so that he was against the bar. "No." He shook his head. "She wouldn't do that."

Emma's worst fear had become reality. The fairy had tricked them both. "Clearly, this is her realm!" Emma did her best to keep her voice down, but it was no use.

"Enough talk!" the third fairy hissed. "You know the rules. Humans stay hidden until morning light."

Emma took a deep breath and stepped forward cautiously. "We are not from here. We didn't know."

The lead fairy glided across the room until she was right at the bar. Flecks of yellow and green danced in her eyes as they reflected the torchlight. The fairy smiled, revealing teeth as sharp as a wolf's.

Emma was sure they'd be used to take a bite out of her throat. She backed away instinctively and reached for her dagger. At least she tried to. But she found herself immobilized.

This was her worst fear come to life. A dark fairy realm. "Who are you?" She nearly spat the words.

Even as she wrestled against her invisible bonds, she couldn't help but think Vespa had led them to this world intentionally. A trap to gain . . . something from them. But what? Aldrich didn't seem to think Vespa was capable of such a thing, but Emma was at a loss as to how else her fears had become reality.

"Refer to me as Aja," the lead fairy snarled.

Against all hope, Emma tried to invoke her magic, but it slipped through her grasp like she were trying to grab the wind. It was just as well as she had no idea what use it would have been, anyway.

The fairy's left eyebrow arched. "You have magic?" She sounded surprised, and the edge in her voice momentarily faded.

Emma cursed her stupidity. Of course, if Vespa had been capable of detecting her magic, these three could as well.

The other two exchanged glances as though searching for an answer to an unasked question. "Maybe it's a trick," the second fairy said. "Humans are deceptive."

"They are," Aja agreed. "But they aren't usually clever."

Aja's gaze fell upon the three glasses on the counter, her small nostrils flaring as she studied the drinks Emma had just poured. "But this human *does* have magic." Before Emma could even begin to follow the fairy's movements. Aja landed directly in front of her. "Was your intent to poison us? To create an elixir that would be our ruin?"

Warmth filled Emma, and she could feel the answer forming on her lips before she could even think of refusing to answer. "No," she heard herself say. "We've had a long day. I was making us drinks to take the edge off. This bottle was open. I thought it would go bad."

"Where could you possibly be from that you are unaware of this exchange? Is there a land you've rid of fae?"

"We *are* from Cuanmore," Emma said. "Just a Cuanmore in another realm where we have never heard of such a deal." Emma winced at her words. She didn't want to divulge the information, but she couldn't help herself. Whatever magic the fae held on her forced her to speak truthfully.

Aja paused, considering. "How is that possible?"

Emma bit her lip in an attempt to control her answer, but it was in vain. She nodded to the professor, feeling the muscles in her neck straining against the compulsion, and spoke through the lump in her throat. "He's developed a machine that can traverse between different realities. I don't understand its workings, but my magic has the power to activate it."

The fairy glanced at Aldrich, lifting a perfectly manicured finger to her thin lip. "I'll get to him yet. But first, I want to know of this magic you possess. What is it that you did to these drinks?"

Emma couldn't help but smile. "To these drinks? I enhanced their flavors. My magic worked between the wine and the stout to bring out the nuttiness of the wine and mellow the sharpness of the stout."

Aja frowned. "An interesting task for a human. Yet, I can sense you likely cannot do much else with the little magic you have."

"That is true," Emma said. "Except the crystals in Aldrich's device operate on a similar wavelength. I can affect those as well."

Blast this enchantment! Why couldn't she control her traitorous tongue?

"Interesting . . ."

"Perhaps we can use this," the male fairy said. His voice grated on Emma's nerves, but she had heard far worse from the grimmawraiths deep in the Black Forest—growls that could kill a weaker person just through their vibrations.

This fairy's skin was a light shade of blue. His pointed ears clung close to his hair, which flowed down his back in silver waves. Emma decided she'd call him Blue in her mind.

"Drink weakens the will of humans. This might be the perfect medium for us to use." He turned his attention to Emma. "Could you infuse a magic that would enhance this effect, that would enable humans to become more susceptible to our magic?"

Emma's mind went to Liam and how the magic she infused in his ale loosened his inhibitions enough that he removed his medallion. A power such as that, in the hands of these dark fae, would be more than she was willing to bear responsibility for. More than any other question so far, she did not want to answer this one. She bit her tongue to still it for the moment.

"Why would you need such a spell?" Emma asked, surprising herself that she was able to deflect the answer to a question. "You can clearly control us well enough."

"Fool human!" Blue snapped. "If that were the case, would we have lost the war! We can hold you for questions, one at a time. Anything more extensive is beyond our control."

Vespa had held an entire pub enchanted for at least the hour while she'd led Emma to Aldrich's home. Did that mean Vespa was *more* powerful than these three?

But something else the blue fairy said had caught her attention as well.

War? Emma tried to voice the question but couldn't get the word out. Whatever conflict he was speaking of, it was apparently not a topic they'd allow her to address.

Blue didn't seem to notice her struggle. "Could you, say, enchant all of the town's ale, so that if we served it to the people, it would weaken their will enough that they would remain enchanted?"

No, no, no. Emma struggled against answering, but in the end, it was no use. She couldn't fight the thought of Liam's uncharacteristic smile, of the way he'd pulled her up to dance. She'd already done the very thing Blue was asking of her.

"It would tire me. But yes, I believe that's possible." Emma's heart sank as the confession flowed from her mouth. Emma would rather be burned on a pyre at the hands of Liam and the Hunters than succumb to whatever twisted plot these three envisioned.

The three fairies, however, all danced with glee in a strange imitation of how Vespa had reacted when Emma agreed to join her and the professor.

The air closed in around Emma's throat, and she wasn't sure if it was the fairy magic or the gut-wrenching realization that her own magic could be used against the poor people of this Cuanmore. This wasn't her war, and she wanted no part of it.

She wished she hadn't left her world. If there was, as Aldrich claimed, another version of herself in the back of Liam's cage wagon, making her way to London to stand trial, Emma was envious of her fate.

Aja turned her attention toward Aldrich, and she studied him with intensity. Some of Emma's tension deflated as a sliver of the compulsive magic released its hold on her chest.

She instinctually tried to move, tried to will her way out of her invisible restraints, but it was no use; their magic held her immobile.

Aja seemed content to ignore Emma now, confident that the fairy magic was keeping her in place. Blue and his companion had stepped back into the shadows deeper in the room.

Perhaps it wasn't Aja but one of them who was holding her. Emma couldn't tell, but if their powers were limited as Blue had suggested, it would be in their best interest to allow one of the others, or perhaps both, to hold the captives so Aja could carry on with the questioning. Blue and the third fairy both had their arms crossed as they leaned back, as if into the very air itself. Their shadowy wings moved almost imperceptibly, keeping them upright, despite their feet not touching the floor.

"You're a sorcerer?" Aja stepped toward Aldrich, but instead of towering over him, as she had Emma, she left a two-meter gap between them. Her ears twitched as she studied him. "How? I sense no magic in you. How did you accomplish this task?"

"Science." Aldrich's voice was hollow and empty—

Emma could only assume he had been placed under the same spell she'd been with no choice but to respond to Aja's query.

Emma held her breath as she waited for Aldrich to launch into excruciating detail about the machine and the quantum whatevers that he had babbled on about to her and Liam, but his answer ended there.

"Science?" the fairy asked skeptically. "And who is this *Science*? What great force do they possess that you are able to harness a jump between realms in this manner?"

The response confused Emma. Certainly, science was not a foreign concept in this world.

"Science possesses all power in every universe. It controls everything that is, was, or will ever be."

Blue and his companion gasped, but Aja didn't seem convinced. Her face contorted.

"Enough of this." Aja waved her hand. "I grow tired of this nonsense. We will have answers from you. But right now, this witch is of more immediate value."

Aja pointed to the Black Velvet drinks Emma had poured. "Witch, enchant one of these drinks so that it would make a person more susceptible to our magic. So that any spell we place on its consumer would last for a significant amount of time. You can give one to your sorcerer friend here as a trial run."

Emma paused as she contemplated the command. She could tell magic was rising within her, but the fairy had been vague in her description. How long was a "significant" amount of time? Emma smiled inwardly. She could use this to her advantage.

One could do something significant in a minute, after all . . .

She considered again. No, that wouldn't give her enough

time. After a minute, the fairy might catch on to the loophole she'd found and demand something more concrete.

Perhaps she didn't have a choice. Outside of her control, the warmth of the magic spread through her core, then radiated down her arms and toward her fingers. She could feel the Black Velvet cocktail calling out to her, demanding to be enchanted. Why the beverage had changed its tune from earlier, she had no idea. But if she'd learned anything in her time as a Hunter, it was that magic was an unpredictable thing, and magical creatures could often hold sway over their surroundings in a way that defied logic.

Then the call ceased. The magical hold dissipated, and the three fairies froze where they floated.

War

Chapter Thirteen

A wall appeared, separating humans and fairies.

No, it wasn't quite a wall, more like a barrier. A translucent mass that hadn't been there a minute ago filled half of O'Sullivan's pub. It encapsulated the three fairies, the nested tables and chairs, and everything else in that half of the room. It was a bluish-green substance, like thick water. The fairies were entrapped, snared within the viscous gel.

With the fairies' hold on her gone, Emma exhaled a sigh of relief as she could move once again. Aldrich stretched and rubbed his arms to work the blood back into them.

For a second, she didn't care why the fairies were frozen—she just needed an exit. But the main door was located through the newly appeared substance. There was a door behind them, beside the bar. But Emma had been in enough bars to know it likely led to storage, not to mention it was barred shut with iron. There was a staircase leading upstairs to what was sure to be guest rooms. The windows of the tavern space had been boarded shut and it was likely those upstairs would be as well.

"We don't have much time." Vespa appeared out of nowhere between Emma and Aldrich.

Aldrich jumped, and out of pure instinct, Emma drew the dagger from her belt.

"Explain yourself, fairy," Emma growled. "What is happening? Why have you brought us here?"

"*You* were the one to bring us here, Emma," Vespa said in her usual soft tone, brushing off her arms as though dirty and scanning the trapped fairies. She all but ignored Emma's blade. "But we must leave. Now."

Vespa focused her attention back on Aldrich. "Professor, where is the device?"

Aldrich was still rubbing his shoulders. He shook his head. "It needs to cool down, at least for a couple of hours. If we use it sooner, we run the risk of damaging it permanently. Without being able to make any repairs or replace the crystals, I don't want to run that risk. We might not be able to leave whatever world we find ourselves in next."

Vespa eyed the gelatinous half of the room warily. "I won't be able to hold that barrier for long. Once it fails, we might be in a whole host of trouble."

"Might be?" Emma hadn't lowered the blade yet. "They were about to force me to make a drink that would enchant the entire village! Where did you disappear to?"

"I sensed them coming. If I had been here when they arrived, I wouldn't have been able to help you. They could have immobilized me as well."

"I don't know about that," Emma said. "From what they wanted me to do, I think you're much more powerful than they are."

Vespa nodded. "I tried to gain answers from other magical creatures I sensed nearby. Many didn't want to talk to me, and I didn't want to leave you alone for too long. But what I was able to gather is that somehow the veil between the fairy realm and the mortal world here has solidified. Nothing can cross. Any fae who were on this side when the rift occurred were stuck here. Any who were in the fairy realm were unable to leave. Those who remained have been weakened without being able to draw power from the magic realm. I imagine my powers will also diminish if we remain here for too long."

"Their leader mentioned a war." Emma examined Aja, frozen in goo, as she spoke. "Was that what caused the rift?"

"It might have been the other way around." Vespa's wings sagged only slightly, and her face darkened. "Those who were stuck here understandably grew enraged and started taking out their aggression on humans. Anyone who had magic started fighting back. There were great losses on both sides. Human witches and sorcerers were all but eradicated in the fight. In the end, the mortals and fae who remained came to this arrangement. Humans would leave out gifts for the fairies in apology for their part in sealing the fae off from their realm. The fae, in return, would only wander the villages at night, and keep out of areas that were locked up tight with humans inside."

Now that they posed no threat, Emma was able to study the three suspended in animation a little closer. At first, she noticed their wide eyes, their open mouths, obviously in surprise at the sudden spell cast upon them. But upon closer inspection, other things became apparent. There were bags under their eyes, and their skin had gone slack. Their frames were a little leaner than they should have been, as though they hadn't been getting the right amount of nutrition. Where Vespa appeared soft, they were hollow and jagged.

Those who remained have been weakened.

Something had chased these fairies from their homes, and they had been stuck here in a realm that was unwelcoming to them. They had been guarding the small reparations they had received.

Emma realized what they had done. Into their safe space, walked a human. One who was breaking their treaty and had the power to give them something more—a way out of this hell they'd found themselves in.

"Can you allow them to speak?" Emma asked.

Vespa appeared alarmed at the question, and Aldrich eyed her curiously. "You . . . want to talk to them?" Vespa asked. "They were trying to force you to use your magic against the townsfolk."

"They were." Emma nodded. "But if what you say is true, perhaps they were trying to defend what little they have. I don't want them to use their magic, not yet. But please, let them speak."

Vespa shuffled anxiously. "If this goes badly, I may not be able to stop them again. I might be stronger than any one of them, but combined, they could overpower me."

Vespa made a sweeping motion with her hands, and the gelatinous wall lowered from the ceiling like a bathtub draining. The movement stopped just below each of their heads. All of them shook their heads furiously, as though trying to remove bits of gel from behind their pointed ears.

"What is the meaning of this!" Aja boomed. Then her eyes rested on Vespa. "You!"

"Aja," Vespa said calmly. She turned to face the others.

"You know them?" Emma looked at Vespa in horror. Fear bubbled within her as she gripped her dagger tighter. The only thing stopping her from launching it was the fact that Vespa had been the one to freeze them in the first place.

"I know who they are." Vespa gestured to Blue. "This is Drafdor. The other is Faolin,"

"How do you know us?" Drafdor replied. "We've never met."

"You perhaps never met the Vespa from this world," Vespa said, "but in my world, we used to be best friends." Vespa had clearly adapted to the multi-worlds theory quicker than Emma had.

Drafdor's face twisted with offense. "I would never be friends with the Forsaken one."

Vespa didn't flinch; instead, her voice hardened. "You were once." Her face momentarily tilted down before lifting her eyes to meet Drafdor's. "But you abandoned me in my world as well."

Drafdor's voice was little more than a sneer. "If you betrayed your kind there as you did here, then I don't doubt it."

"You're supposed to be dead." Aja glared icily at Vespa, seemingly pondering what the fairy had said. "These humans also claim to be from another world. You are helping them, too?"

Vespa visibly deflated. Her wings dimmed as her head lowered.

Aja took that as enough of an answer. "Even if what you say is true, you're no different from the Forsaken in this realm." The fairy spat, and drips of saliva landed on the gelatin's surface, causing Emma to wrinkle her nose.

"All I want to do is help people." Vespa lifted her head, meeting Aja's gaze with her own. "Humans and fairies—they share the same space. Why is working to help each other so wrong?"

"Because you're fae!" Aja barked. "We don't help humans. They destroy the very world that provides for them. We stay out of their way."

Vespa scoffed. "We don't stay out of their way—we trick them. We play games with them. Make deals with them they don't understand. Replace their children with changelings. And for what? For a few trinkets? To be entertained? To pretend they don't also inhabit this world? There's no denying humans are destructive creatures, but there's good in them as well. If I can sense their suffering, why shouldn't I help them?"

"Look around you!" Faolin spoke for the first time. His face contorted in anger, but his voice was smooth like glass. There was a deep, haunting melody behind it. Anguish echoing in its sound. "You've tried to access our realm by now, yes? Then you know we've been cut off. Your helping them caused this! Our magic has withered to almost nothing. If not for this agreement, the fae would have been completely extinguished." Faolin was vibrating with rage, barely holding himself together.

"That isn't my fault!" Vespa exclaimed. "How could helping humans have done this?"

"You helped a human sorcerer try to reach our realm!" Aja pressed. "And here you are, claiming to be from yet another one, and you've brought yet another human who can wield magic and a sorcerer who can travel from one world to another. Will you bring down destruction wherever you go?"

"I never meant—"

"It doesn't matter what you meant. What matters is what happened. It doesn't matter that you're from another realm. Vespa has been banished from this one. If this device can take you back to where you came from, leave now. We would kill you where you stand if we had the strength to do so."

Vespa turned whiter than a fresh blanket of snow.

Fire burned within Emma's gut. "She's only trying to help!" Aldrich laid a hand on her shoulder, but Emma continued. "I needed to flee my world. The professor wants to get back to his. Vespa would never wish harm on anyone. You can't blame the result of an entire world's history on one person!"

Color returned to Vespa's face along with a faint smile that didn't reach her eyes.

"Do you have any idea how many fairies were killed because of what she did?" Aja's voice melted from anger into languish. "I have not had contact with my brothers and sisters in decades. The ones who remained perished in the aftermath of the Fae-Human War. We have nothing left but this meager offering the humans pay to keep us at bay."

"Have you tried working something out with the humans? Perhaps you could better coexist in this world."

"Humans only want to kill us," Aja said. "They don't care if we live. They'd prefer if we were eradicated from the face of this world."

"They're scared of you because of what you've done," Emma countered. "What if you made a more permanent solution? One where you both can share this world without fear?"

"You do not understand, human." Aja's eyes lost focus, her thoughts elsewhere. "Please. Just leave this world with the Forsaken. We cannot stand more heartache."

Aldrich's mustache twitched back and forth.

"What can we do?" Emma asked. "We must be able to do something to help this world."

Aldrich sighed, his hand still rested on her shoulder, but the tone of his voice shifted from cautionary to consoling. "We can't undo an entire world's history. On this journey, I've learned to accept the value of small changes. All we can do is strive to make a positive impact on the corner of the world we touch. That's true no matter what world we find ourselves in."

"We should go," Vespa said. "Once my hold lifts, they will bring others to take me."

Emma scanned the faces of the three dark fairies. They weren't as intimidating now, but Emma couldn't overlook the sadness reflected in their hateful stares.

"We will leave," Emma said. "Vespa will come with us. But in exchange, we ask that you at least try to speak with the townsfolk. You hold the power to make this world better for all of you."

"You don't know what you're talking about, witch." Aja snorted. "Even if we wanted to coexist with the humans of this realm, they wouldn't listen."

"It won't be easy," Emma agreed. "But living as you are, off the scraps they provide for you, sneaking around at night as they cower in their homes, that can't be easy either."

Aja grunted. The other two muttered under their breath, but neither said anything further.

A bead of sweat trickled down Vespa's brow.

"We should go, Professor," said Emma. "Regardless of if they acknowledge my request or not, I don't believe these fae will be willing to forgive Vespa so easily."

Aldrich shook his head. "If you force magic into the crystals now, we might not get another shot. They will burn out, and if we don't arrive in a land where we can acquire more, we'll be stuck there."

Emma focused on the professor's bag. Just like the bottles on the shelf, she could feel the crystals. She could tell that, as Aldrich had claimed, they wouldn't survive more than one use. There was not enough energy in them and burning them out would render them useless.

The drinks she had altered had always given her direction. The ale wanted to be good. The wine wanted to not be spoiled. The cider wanted to be heated and made into Hibernian Bliss. These crystals only wanted power.

But *she* was the one who channeled the power into them. Could her magic work the same way here?

She took another look at the world around them. Dark. Run by fairies trapped away from their own realm. Despite their position, these fairies still enacted their will against the humans here. Wasn't that what she had been afraid of when she activated the device the first time?

Of a war between humans and fae.

Everything she'd feared when she opened the portal.

The thought struck her. What if that was exactly what had happened?

"What if my intentions control where we end up?"

Vespa looked up thoughtfully and nodded. "You do set an intention in the drinks you make," Vespa said. "That's how you were able to heat the cider."

"Before the portal opened, I was worried about Vespa leading us into a fairy trap. That's exactly what happened here. This world is the way it is because of Vespa's actions. It is precisely what I was afraid would happen. What if I can use that to our advantage?"

Aldrich's mustache twitched again. He seemed unconvinced. "What are you suggesting?"

"If I can influence the crystals enough to open the portal to your world, Aldrich, would you be able to get new ones there?"

Aldrich lifted a finger to his chin. "I have been away for quite some time, but there should still be a supply at my lab. Are you sure you can do this? You'll only have one shot."

"One shot," Vespa whispered, her voice distant. Then louder she said, "Maybe I should stay here. Aja's right. I cause trouble no matter where I go."

"That's rubbish!" Emma admonished. "If it weren't for you, I'd be on my way to London right now to face execution. We came here together, we leave together."

Vespa nodded, though her heart didn't seem to be in it. Her gaze was distant and unfocused.

Apart from ensuring the fairy joined them, Emma couldn't worry about Vespa just yet. Instead, she let her thoughts drift back to the effect she'd had on Liam's ale. Vespa was right. Emma *had* enacted change on that drink.

Without even realizing it, she had changed the properties so Liam loosened up enough to remove his medallion.

Then there was the cider. Emma had managed to heat it through intention alone. If she could do that, why not this? She didn't understand how the magic worked, but if she could convey intent to the drinks, and the properties of the crystals were as similar as Aldrich claimed, then perhaps this could work as well.

She couldn't help but think her conclusion out loud. "What other options do we have?"

Demon Box

Chapter Fourteen

Once the device was set up, Emma did her best to focus, but the task seemed insurmountable.

First, because there were three dark fae staring at her menacingly. Despite her speech encouraging them to appeal to the local humans, she got the distinct sense that they had not been convinced.

Second, the fairy they had brought with them was pacing beside the bar, worrying about the effect that another version of herself had had on this world.

Third, because she didn't exactly know how to communicate what she wanted to the crystals. It all felt so ridiculous and outside of herself. It wasn't like she understood how this magic worked. Hell, until a month ago she'd have hunted down anyone like her and brought them before the London courts.

And fourth, she knew *nothing* about Aldrich's world. She couldn't feed any specific thoughts about it toward the crystals other than thinking the words "Aldrich's world" repeatedly. But was that something the crystals would understand if she held no concept of it? Nevermind the possibility that the crystals might take their own interpretation of any instructions given and send them somewhere even worse.

While she contemplated these thoughts, the crystals began warming. It was just as they had done back in Aldrich's lab, although this time they struggled to wake up. Like she had felt many a time the morning after a successful hunt. Just as Aldrich had said, they weren't ready to go yet.

The panels on the outside of the box lit dimly, blues and yellows pulsing faintly.

Just five more minutes.

The voice was gruff and grumpy. It sounded like an old man being shaken awake from a restful slumber. But it was definitely a voice, and it caught Emma off guard.

"You've got to be kidding me," she said.

"What's happening?" Aldrich asked.

"You didn't hear that?" she asked. Though she knew they hadn't.

Both Aldrich and Vespa shook their heads. For a moment, Emma wondered if the voice was real. But it was so clear, so strong, that it was impossible to shrug it off as a hallucination.

Unless I'm going mad.

Had the device . . . spoken to her?

Yes, yes, we're all mad. The voice said into her mind once again. *Now please, could you quit being so noisy for just a few more minutes!*

Emma had to work to keep her face from contorting in incredulity. "It's asking for five more minutes."

"Is there a problem?" Aja asked with a smirk.

Emma could have sworn the fairy enjoyed watching them sweat.

"Emma, I don't want to alarm you," Vespa whispered. "But I'm not sure if I'm able to hold the barrier for five more minutes."

Listen, demon box. Emma directed her thoughts toward the device. *I don't know if we have five more minutes.*

There was no response. And it certainly wasn't listening to her calls to turn on.

She was out of options and running out of time.

Five more minutes it is, then, she thought.

Emma took a sweeping look at the half of the tavern filled with goo and considered what their options might be. "Vespa, you've solidified half the tavern. Would it use less magic to shrink the amount of gel down to only contain the three of them?"

Vespa lifted a finger to her chin, considering. She then moved her hand to wipe a bead of sweat from her temple. "Yes, I suppose it would. But I can't promise it will be enough."

The gel around the room shrank, appearing to melt in the heat of Vespa's struggle. Almost instantly, the burden on Vespa appeared to lighten, her breath returned to normal and the tension in her shoulders eased. The fairies' prison now only extended a short radius around the group of them.

"Better?" Emma asked.

Vespa simply nodded. Her eyes didn't leave the fairies encapsulated in her spell.

Five minutes was excruciatingly long, and Emma had no proper way of marking the time. It didn't help that the jeers from the fae nearly caused Emma to request the gel to be encased around their faces again. Aldrich paced along the bar, muttering something to himself that Emma couldn't hear, and Vespa seemed to be locked into a staring contest with Aja. Emma wondered how much of her energy was going into beating herself up for something her alternate self did in this world.

After what she believed had been a sufficient amount of time, she opened herself up to the device once again.

Come on, demon box, we've got to go. Time to wake up.

Ugh. Are you kidding me?

Was the machine giving her sass?

Listen, Emma thought, feeling quite ridiculous, and most happy this conversation was happening in her head and not out loud for the rest of the room to hear. *We're all going to be in a lot of trouble unless you're able to fire up and go.*

Don't get your knickers in a twist. I'm up, I'm up.

This was more than unexpected, but Emma supposed speaking directly with the box was a lot easier than trying to imagine what she wanted and imparting her will upon it.

Have you always been able to talk? Why haven't you said anything before?

I did, the machine grunted. *You just weren't listening.*

Surprised, she quirked an eyebrow at the remark, though in truth, she hadn't been. She hadn't known she needed to "listen" to the device. Yet, despite all the grumbling, the machine hummed, its lighted panels blooming into life.

Emma decided it was best to ignore the snarky comment and give the device her instructions.

We need to go to a world where the professor can fix you. Preferably the world he brought you from. Can you do that? Do you remember that world?

The noises the device made shifted slightly in pitch, and Emma could feel through her magic that the crystals were beginning to warm.

It's . . . difficult. It won't be quite the same, but I can get us close enough to matter . . . I think.

Emma had held conversations with enchanted objects before. There was the enchanted hat in Mesopotamia that wouldn't stop swearing at people and calling them names. There was the enchanted snowman in Lancastria's hinterland which cursed his maker when it realized it would melt when spring came. But this was different. She'd yet to have met an entity that could reach into her mind, and it was extra peculiar that she was the only one who could hear it.

Do you have a name? What can I call you?

There was a brief pause as the machine's lights dimmed then brightened again.

The professor always calls me "Quantum Accelerator." Quite bland, don't you think? It does nothing to accentuate my bursting personality. I like the name you've already given me. It sounds much nicer.

Emma paused, not entirely sure what the device was referring to, then it struck her. "You want me to call you demon box?" she said out loud before she realized she was doing so. "That's . . . I didn't mean . . ."

Yes. Demon Box. I like the sound of that. Please call me that from now on.

Before she could argue, the pull of magic tugged at her insides.

There was less resistance from her magic this time, and the outpouring was less dramatic. In case the device didn't get the message, she clung to the thoughts of Aldrich's home world until the portal was open and glimmering in front of them.

"They are going to get away!" Drafdor shouted above the rush of wind the portal created.

"Better she rains terror on another world than more on ours." Aja's smugness faded to resignation.

Ignoring them, Aldrich picked up Demon Box and tucked it under his arm.

Woo hoo, that tickles!

Emma almost burst out laughing.

Aldrich then linked his free arm with Vespa's and the fairy grabbed on to Emma.

"This will lead us to the professor's world?" Vespa asked.

Emma steadied herself. "There's only one way to find out."

World Three

True Purpose

Chapter Fifteen

Before the gateway even had a chance to close behind them, Emma had to keep her heart from thumping out of her chest. The world where they had landed was nothing short of miraculous.

Buildings loomed over her, reaching taller than she ever could have imagined possible. She strained her neck trying to see the tops of them but got dizzy with the effort.

The sun was just beginning to appear. Shadows of towers striped the road, and Emma imagined their imposing presence would ensure the city rested in perpetual shade. The road they landed on was made of a hard stone that stretched from one edge of the building to the next. It was mostly empty with only a few bodies moving in the distance, heads down in a hurry to get somewhere. Wherever this place was, it was not the same sleepy village of Cuanmore they'd just left.

A world of stone.

But it was more than stone, she realized as she studied their surroundings. There was also glass and metal in abundance here, lights and sounds. It was an overflow of visual stimuli that her brain struggled to keep up with.

Behind them stood a small vestige of the familiar—O'Sullivan's Pub. Despite everything that loomed around it, the tavern appeared nearly the same as the one they'd left. The awnings looked newer, the paint fresher, and the sign . . . different. Painted in such a precise way that Emma struggled to imagine the craftsmanship that must have gone into creating it. But otherwise, it was as though the pub had been transported alongside them.

Emma tried to focus her attention on this recognizable anchor, lest she be swept away in the sea of chaos they'd landed in.

Aldrich stood with the bag containing Demon Box by his side. Emma mused over the newly found consciousness of this machine. Its energy spent, the device had once again gone quiet, and she couldn't help but wonder about the implications of such magic taking on a life of its own. Had it been her enchantment that had brought it to life? Or had Aldrich unwittingly created a life form?

The professor inhaled deeply, his face stretching into a smile, as though reacquainting himself with a familiar friend.

His expression was so enchanted that Emma couldn't help but do the same, trying to capture the essence of what he was smelling. She nearly gagged. The air was filled with a stench reminiscent of London garbage and a sourness that she associated with that of a boiler room.

"What in the blooming hell is this place?" she asked. "What magic has been used to build such colossal structures that dwarf the pyramids?"

She had been on a hit in Cairo only a few months ago with Liam. The southern most edge of the kingdom was home to more than a few witches and even more spirit beings.

A smile touched Aldrich's lips. "This is Cuanmore. The city as I know it. And there is no magic here at all."

Vespa stumbled next to her on the walkway. The sun had found a gap between buildings, and its warm light landed on her wings, causing them to sparkle and cast a rainbow of colors around her. The effect only lasted a moment, however, as the wings faded into nothingness. The fairy's face, normally pale like the rest of her, had turned various shades of green.

"Is everything all right?" Emma asked, rushing to her side. Vespa leaned her feather-light body into her, and Emma couldn't help thinking that the fairy was so light that she might blow away with the faintest breeze.

Aldrich appeared on Vespa's other side, though there was barely enough weight to justify one person holding her up, never mind two. Even so, Vespa sighed, giving both companions a nod and a smile of appreciation. Plus, since the ground appeared to be made of solid stone, a fall would have been more than a little painful, so perhaps the extra caution was warranted.

"I'm okay," Vespa said after a moment. Some of her normal color returned to her face as she composed herself. Emma couldn't tell whether she was feeling better or putting on a brave face. "But if you were trying to kill me, you could have left me in the last world." Despite the quip, Vespa doubled over, clutching her stomach.

Aldrich gestured toward the edge of a wider street running next to them, and the two helped Vespa to a metal bench. Emma sat beside her, allowing Vespa to hold onto her hand as a means of support.

"Wait here." Aldrich dug through his bag. "I'll be back in a moment."

"You're not going to leave us alone here!" Emma demanded. "Who knows what horrors might attack us? I may have hunted a variety of threats, but I'm unfamiliar with the creatures of this place."

Aldrich surveyed the empty street. "If this is indeed my world, there won't be anything like that here. You'll be fine. Just don't wander off." He scurried away, his gait noticeably lighter than it had been in either of the previous worlds.

Emma had been in every major city in the kingdom. No place she'd ever encountered, or even imagined, compared to the overwhelming labyrinth that stretched out around them.

Her senses were normally impeccable. She'd been trained from a young age to find her way through any situation, but she didn't have to venture far to realize this place would have her turned around in a matter of minutes. Everything was gray, stone and uniform. Regardless of Aldrich's warning, she wouldn't have dared to move on her own in fear of getting lost. Instead, she gawked at the megalith structures that towered over them.

How could human hands have built these?

Loud carriages rolled past on the street behind them. A roar filled the sky as some sort of giant mechanized bird flew far above the tops of the buildings. Her fingers danced along the hilt of her blade—a reflex of anxiety. But there was no doubt in her mind that none of the tricks she had up her sleeve would be useful against the cacophony of machines.

"I can't believe there's no magic in this place." Emma's mouth hung so far open it nearly grazed the paved surface below.

Vespa righted herself on the bench. Most of her color had returned, but her wings had been put away. "There is little magic here. More than none but not by much. It caught me off guard when we first arrived."

"That's why you feel unwell?"

Vespa nodded. "It's a bit hard to explain, but magic courses through my being. It's part of who I am. It's like the air is thinner here, and I'm struggling to breathe. I will manage, but it will take some time to get used to."

"What about other fae here? Is there a hidden realm here where your kind might gain their strength?"

Vespa shook her head slowly. "There might be, but I don't

have the energy to try and find out now. Perhaps later when I've had some time to rest. Holding the barrier in the last world already weakened me, and now I'm barely able to access a trickle of magic."

The two sat in silence for several minutes; Vespa leaned onto Emma's shoulder.

"Vespa?" Emma wasn't sure exactly how to put this into words, but it had to be said.

"Yes?"

"I know I didn't exactly trust you at first. But I want to say thank you. For saving us back there. If it weren't for you, we would likely not have made it out of there without being under Aja's enchantment."

"Don't think anything of it," Vespa said. "Helping people, it's what I do. And I couldn't let anything happen to you or Aldrich if I had the ability to do so. You're both important to me."

It had been less than twelve hours since she'd met the fairy, yet it felt like a lifetime had passed. Who would have thought she could ever have become friends with a fairy? Here she was with the light weight of Vespa pressed against her, and Emma had to admit she was grateful to have her in her life.

"Vespa, I have to ask a question. Back in our world, you approached me knowing I was a Hunter. I could have shackled you in iron and brought you to the King's Court. How did you know I would help?"

A smile crept over Vespa's face. "You know how when you approach a drink or the professor's device, it speaks to you? It tells you what it wants so you can craft it into what it's meant to be?"

Emma smirked as she thought of Demon Box. She still wasn't sure what to make of the contraption. She also wasn't sure where Vespa was going with her question, but she nodded anyway. "Yes," she said. "It's like I'm able to provide the exact piece they're missing to complete them."

Vespa nodded. "That's how I am with people. I can sense what they need, even if they don't know themselves. If I'm lucky, I'm able to provide that missing piece. It's like their spirit speaks to me. Especially if that person has any sort of magical ability.

"When I first encountered Aldrich, I knew his need was great. Though I didn't understand it at the time, I could sense his device needed a powerful magic. I tried to manipulate the crystals myself, but fairy magic doesn't seem to be on the same frequency. Nothing I tried worked. When you arrived in Cuanmore, I could sense that the vibrations of your magic matched the crystals'. I also could tell that you both needed the same thing."

Emma cocked her head. "We did? You knew we had to leave our world?"

Vespa's warm smile crossed her face again. "Each other. Aldrich . . . he's been in your world for years, yet he hasn't made an effort to make any friends. A scientist in a realm full of magic. I've befriended him, but he has to understand that humans need relationships in order to thrive."

Emma slid from underneath Vespa, forcing the fairy to sit up on her own. She raised her hands in protest. "Whoa, whoa, whoa. I'm not interested in the professor like that," she said. "Never mind that he's probably twice my age. If you've pulled me into this thinking to set us up, I—"

"You misunderstand," Vespa said. "This isn't about romantic relationships. Although, those are important too. I'm talking about friendship. The professor has no friends, and it's not good for him to be alone the way he is."

Emma lowered her hands and sighed. She knew that

feeling well. Liam had been her only genuine friend, and now even he was no longer in her life.

"You sensed I would need a friend as well," she said.

"I can sense that you both need each other," Vespa continued. "Not romantically. But you both have things in common, even if you don't recognize it. He needed you to activate the device. And you need him to help uncover your true purpose."

"True purpose?" Emma scoffed. "I was perfectly happy with what I was doing before I discovered I'm Cursed."

"You are not cursed," said Vespa. "Just because others don't understand what makes you unique, it doesn't diminish who you are."

Emma snorted. That was hard for her to swallow. Especially since she had spent her entire life seeking magic users and removing them from the rest of society.

Vespa smiled sweetly. "Do you really believe you were happy with what you were doing?"

She hadn't been. But Emma didn't want to admit it, so she pushed down those feelings of restlessness. For most of her life, Emma had been raised and trained to make a difference in the world, to do what she could for the kingdom. Without that . . .

"At least I had a purpose." She didn't fully believe the words, even as she spoke them. She'd been disenchanted with her life as a Hunter. But now, she felt lost. "Now what will my fate be? Nobody has ever saved the world by mixing drinks."

Vespa leaned into Emma's shoulder again. "Not everyone is destined to save the world. Some people find purpose in giving their best every day, and often that's more than enough."

How many hours had she spent being told the exact opposite? That her purpose had been to keep the world safe? "I've worked my entire life to advance the kingdom . . ."

"Advance the kingdom?" Vespa sat up again, her emerald green eyes fixating on Emma. "Look at who you are, Emma. Who you *truly* are. Look at everything you're capable of. Do you truly believe you are a threat because you possess the magic you do? Do you believe you deserved to be hauled back to London with Liam? Knowing what you do now, even if your magic was taken away from you tomorrow, would you really want to go back to that?"

Emma startled at the statement. It was so hard to reconcile everything that had happened with the picture of the world that had been painted for her. She took in her surroundings and felt the weight of it all pressing down. Not just the city—that was overwhelming in its own right. But the immensity of everything she'd experienced in the past few days. It threatened to crush her.

"I don't know what to think." She struggled to put her thoughts into words. Despite what Vespa said, it still felt as if she were Cursed. She didn't know if she'd be able to shake that unease. Emma sucked in a breath.

She was here now . . . whatever strange place this was. That realization alone was enough to stir her thoughts.

"I believed the world had an order to it. I was raised to see things as either good or evil. Black or white. But look at this place! I'm in another world! I've only seen a small slice of it and already I feel as if my understanding of order, structure, and chaos is small and insufficient. I just don't know how to reconcile who I am with who I thought I was. How can I come to terms with what my life has been until now? I did many horrible things for a cause that was unjust."

Vespa turned away. The street was growing busier, but still nobody paid any attention to them.

"Perhaps," said Vespa. "But you were put into circumstances that were beyond your control. Now you've been given the choice to live another life—one that's truly yours to make."

"I left because I had no other choice."

"Your choice was to submit yourself to your old way of thinking or to forge a new path. You chose this. You needed to see there are more possibilities for your life out there."

Emma wasn't sure about that. She was also not sure she was quite ready to discuss the implications of it all yet. "You chose this too," she said. "Why would you do that?"

"I made an oath to the professor. A debt I need to repay." Vespa's eyes followed a few pedestrians walking along the side of the street. The people had their heads down, ignoring each other, but almost all of them held a small white cup in one hand and a small glowing box in the other. Focusing on either one as they went, determined to get to their destination, but seemingly oblivious to their surroundings. "I thought there might be more for me as well. But it seems my destiny has been determined. I'm meant to be an outcast. Now I fear even he will reject me now that I've brought him home."

"What's that supposed to mean?"

"You saw what happened in the last world! Their version of me had been banished for trying to help that sorcerer?"

"Yeah," Emma said. "What about it?"

"It's the path I'm destined to follow. I was banished in our world, too. Only helping Aldrich didn't end up as cataclysmic."

"So you like helping humans. What's the big deal?"

"You don't understand. Fairies view humanity as a blight upon the world. Humans destroy nature while they expand their empires. But, instead of playing games with your kind, I chose to believe in the best in you. That wasn't a popular opinion. Fairies believe it's in our best interests to either avoid or be rid of humans. They thought helping humans would eventually lead to ruin. But my gift is sensing what they need! How could I ignore that?"

"That's crazy!" Emma said. "How can they cast all of humanity in such a negative light?"

Vespa laughed, only this time it wasn't her typical sweet giggle. "Isn't that what you did with witches?" She lifted her hand in mock oath. "The kingdom shall be rid of all who use magic?"

Emma winced, then opened her mouth to respond but couldn't. Instead, she grabbed Vespa's hand and held it, pulling it in close to her chest.

"You never have to apologize for helping others," Emma said. "Sometimes the best intentions don't go as we planned, but that doesn't mean we shouldn't try. It doesn't mean it wasn't worth the effort."

"You saw how that last world ended up because of me!" Vespa was on the verge of tears. "I should have listened to the elders and stayed away from humans altogether."

"First, that Vespa was not you. She chose a path that you are not on. You can't beat yourself up for decisions you didn't make. Second, if you had stayed away from humans, you never would have met me." Emma flashed Vespa her most charismatic smile.

Tears flowed down the fairy's face, but her eyes glimmered with amusement. Vespa bit her lip but its corners curled upward, and she failed to hold back a laugh.

"If you hadn't found me at The Cursed Dragon," Emma continued, "there's no doubt I would be on my way to London right now to stand trial, and Aldrich would be alone in his shack by the lighthouse drinking drams of whiskey, forever stuck in our world. Our choices, whatever they are, will have consequences, both good and bad. We can't change the decisions we've made, but we can learn from them and move forward."

Emma did her best to ignore the acrid air of the city as she inhaled.

And what of my decisions? she thought to herself. *Where have they brought me?*

Before she had to fully let the thought sit with her, Professor Aldrich returned.

"Here," he said, as he shoved a container at Emma and another at Vespa.

Emma studied the object he held for a good long moment, trying to understand what it was he was holding out to her. It was clear like glass, but flexible as Aldrich tensed his fingers around it.

"What is this?" Emma asked.

Aldrich rolled his eyes as he twisted a white lid off the top. "It's a water bottle."

Like a canteen of sorts, Emma understood, but the water inside was clearer than she'd ever seen! "Where did you find water so clean?"

"There is a lot about this world you'll find surprising," Aldrich said. "Clean potable water is only one of the things I took for granted before I was stuck in your world."

"So, is this it then?" Vespa livened up after taking a few sips of water. "Is this your world?"

Aldrich surveyed the street with a pained look. Emma could almost sense the longing coming from him as his misty eyes took in the street around them.

"At first glance, it seems like it might be. But it's going to be hard for me to tell until I can check some of this world's histories. Our first stop should be my flat. We need to rest before we come to any conclusions."

Then Aldrich stopped and took a long, hard look at Emma and Vespa. "Actually," he said, "maybe we need to find you some clothes that are more suitable for this place."

Family We Make

Chapter Sixteen

The sun was high in the afternoon sky by the time Emma woke up. Half-asleep, she absently scratched at her new outfit. There had been unlimited options at the massive indoor marketplace Aldrich had taken them to, but only one caught her eye. She tugged at the hood of the black jumper she'd chosen. There was a comfort to the hood, but the rest of the outfit was unlike her normal attire. For starters, it was soft. It lacked the buttons and belts she'd grown accustomed to. The pants were made of an equally soft and stretchy material. Both lacked adequate places for her to hide her weapons.

But based on the selection that had been available, apparently the women of this world didn't believe in pockets.

She snapped awake, checking the short table beside the couch to ensure her weapons were still where she'd left them. It wasn't like her to fall into such a deep sleep, especially with her weapons out on display. She did a quick count of the knives, daggers, and iron she always kept on her.

Relieved to find everything accounted for, she let the tension fall from her body and sunk back into the comfortable orange sofa she'd used as a bed to sleep most of the day away. After two months of travel and a full night without rest, sleep had been inevitable.

Aldrich had apologized numerous times for the inconvenience of it, but after a lifetime of sleeping in haylofts and backrooms, it was one of the most comfortable surfaces she'd had ever slept on.

After their quest for new clothing, which was a separate adventure all on its own, Aldrich had brought them back to his flat. They all needed rest, and he needed to conduct research to determine if this was his world and how much had changed since he'd left.

The apartment complex was shorter and flatter than many of the buildings around the core of the city, but it still stood eight stories high. The unit itself was much smaller than Aldrich's home by the lighthouse, and most of it appeared to be an open space so that she could see nearly the entirety of the home from where she lay. Two rooms were the exception—a small bedroom and a room that, to Emma's surprise, held an indoor toilet that used water to flush away waste without odor.

Despite its smaller size, the home was no less impressive. A small kitchen was lined with cream-painted cupboards, what Emma could only guess was a cooking stove, and a large white box that looked like it might have been an oddly crafted cupboard. Immediately next to this space was a small room with a table meant for dining, but it had piles of papers and devices strewn across its surface. Aldrich sat at the table, staring into a glowing gray box. Emma could only guess that the man had been sitting there since they'd arrived without a single wink of sleep.

Only a few feet away from the table was the room where Emma lay now. It was filled with shelves that were lined with dozens of books, reminding her of the libraries in the King's Court. Much like the professor's home in her world, among the books and along additional shelves hung from the wall, were gadgets and trinkets. Some held the rust of many years, others held the clean modernity of the rest of Aldrich's world. There were some Emma recognized: binoculars, clocks, and jars filled with various substances. Others had purposes she couldn't begin to guess.

Despite the mass of papers on the dining table suggesting it was the chief place of study in the abode, there was also a desk that sat against the wall, topped with even more books and trinkets. Vespa had settled into an office chair in front of it, fumbling on a glowing gray box of her own.

The fairy appeared so drab and dull in this world—the sparkle of her magic had provided more of a glow to her skin than Emma had realized. And now without it, her color had all but faded.

During their shopping excursion, Vespa had chosen a light summer dress to replace the airy fabrics she'd adorned back home. A floral pattern decorated the fabric, and she'd paired it with a light brown scarf and a wide-brimmed hat to keep the chill of the early spring air at bay. Emma thought the outfit would have been too cold, but Vespa didn't seem to be as affected by the temperature as she was.

"It looks like there once was magic in your world," the fairy said, referencing something she was reading on the screen. "But it disappeared centuries ago. All that's left now are legends and folklore."

"I never expected there to be differences between our worlds at the metaphysical level," Aldrich responded. "It's almost as though there's a sub-dimension within your world that allows for a separate realm. A plane of existence that evolved alongside the physical realm. It's fascinating. Even more so that this world appears to have developed without it."

"If there ever was a fairy realm in your world, it was sealed years ago." Vespa's moist eyes reflected the electric light of the desk lamp. "In two of the worlds we've visited, that realm either does not exist or is out of reach. What if my world was the only one where such a realm exists? I'll be cut off from my magic forever."

"Don't fret about it, Vespa." Aldrich fidgeted with his mustache, considering. "There are an infinite number of worlds out there. You and Emma can travel on to the next. If she can manipulate the destination through sheer will, you are sure to find somewhere that suits your needs. There are likely worlds out there where humans and fairies live in perfect harmony."

Vespa sighed audibly as she turned from the desk to face Aldrich. "Are you in any of those worlds?"

Aldrich stopped fidgeting for a moment and looked up thoughtfully. "Some version of me, perhaps."

Vespa snorted. "I promised I'd stick with you. Not some version of you."

"You've fulfilled what you promised and brought me home." Aldrich's eyes returned to the screen in front of him. "You're not stuck with me anymore."

Vespa was on her feet so quickly that Emma didn't even see her stand. The fairy opened her mouth, then closed it without making a sound, furrowing her brow. She vibrated, grew semi-transparent for a moment, and then completely solid again. Her expression morphed from anger to frustrated before she put her hands to her face and ran into the next room.

Not some version of you.

Aldrich's comment caused Emma's thoughts to drift back to Liam. They'd never been more than friends. Their positions had never allowed it. But there was an ache in her heart that made her realize the man was perhaps something more to her than just a good hunting partner. More than just a friend.

And now she'd likely never see him again.

There might be other versions of Liam beyond the portal,

but they'd never truly *be* Liam, would they? It surprised her how much that realization hurt. She and Liam had always maintained a platonic relationship. No matter how lonely they got during their travels.

They couldn't let feelings for one another impede the job they had set out to do. Besides, it was forbidden for Hunters to fraternize with each other. Sure, there were no rules about blowing off some steam with the locals after a successful hunt, but relationships between the Hunters? That had always been a recipe for disaster.

Yet, she only realized now, she did have *feelings* for the friend she'd left behind—and she couldn't imagine being told there'd be some other version of Liam that could replace him.

"That was rather rude." She grabbed her knife belt from the coffee table and strapped it back on around her waist, doing her best to hide it beneath her new hoodie.

Aldrich squinted and looked up from his device. "Rude? What are you talking about?"

"Vespa! She can't stay here, and you're shrugging it off like it's no big deal."

"She made an oath to repay me. I never asked her for it. She helped me return, and her oath is fulfilled. I'm not asking her to remain here with me."

"You don't see it, do you? This has nothing to do with an oath."

"Of course not. I was happy to help her. I never asked for anything in return. She's free to do whatever she wants."

Emma snorted and shook her head. "What she clearly wants is to be with you. So much so that she'd be willing to suffer here without access to her magic!"

Aldrich blinked as though struggling to focus on Emma. Bags under his eyes confirmed he'd not taken any opportunity during the day to catch up on sleep.

"Fairy rules differ from ours, Emma. They're bound by the words they speak. I would never ask her to stay here with me."

"Then come with *us*," Emma said. "Surely, if there's an infinite number of worlds out there, there's one that would be a good fit for all of us."

"Hmm?" Aldrich studied Emma as though she'd grown wings of her own. "My research is here. I've gathered so much data over the last six years, it would be a shame to waste it."

"Never mind," Emma said. Clearly, the man was too stubborn and self-absorbed to see past his own mustache. Vespa would be heartbroken having to leave him in this place, though.

Perhaps she could approach the topic better if she knew more about their situation.

"What's the deal between you two, anyway?" she asked. "What is this oath you both keep referring to?"

The professor lifted a hand to his hair and ran it through his graying mane. "When I encountered Vespa, she was on the run from her elders. I offered her sanctuary, a place to stay when she had nowhere else to go. It was a series of events I don't care to revisit now, but she claims that my act of kindness saved her life."

"Did you know she was a fairy at the time?" Emma asked.

"What? Heavens no. I hadn't been in your world long. I hadn't even realized magic was a thing. I thought, in a world such as yours, she was being falsely accused of being a witch as many in my world have been throughout the ages. But I would never have imagined there was real magic, real fairies. She promised to help me home in exchange. I don't think she realized what she was committing to. I didn't believe it was possible, but I wanted to help. I wouldn't have ever held her to it, but she insisted. Then the other day, she begins talking about someone with compatible magic. Well, then you showed up. Like I said, I didn't think returning here would ever happen."

"And now that you *are* here, you're done with her? All that time and you're just going to abandon her?"

Aldrich shook his head, his face constricting as he did. "No, that's not it at all. I just don't want her to feel stuck here with me. I never meant for her to have to do that. She should be free to do whatever she chooses."

"Haven't you considered that she *wants* to be with you?"

"Like you said, she can't stay here. But *I* must. My research is here, and I've already left it for too long. I'm sure I've been missed at the university."

"Perhaps some things are more important than research."

Aldrich grew quiet and carried on with whatever he was doing at the table.

Emma considered pushing on the matter but thought it might be best to let it go for the time being. He was so absorbed in his work that he didn't see he was hurting the fairy who'd gifted him years of her own life.

Instead, she asked, "How is it possible that our worlds can be so different from each other? Is this still Hibernia?"

"Actually," Aldrich said, "it is the same land, but here, Hibernia is called the Republic of Ireland. It's not a state of a larger kingdom, it's a country."

"The kingdom . . . fell?" Great towers made of stone and glass she could believe, but the end of the kingdom? Lancastria had no formidable enemies, and there had been relative peace among the territories for centuries.

"The kingdom as you know it never existed here," Aldrich replied. "It was difficult for me to determine what the cause of the shift was, but from what I can tell, about seven hundred years ago, our two worlds split during an event we called the Hundred Years' War. During that period, in our timeline,

England lost much of its territory in Europe. In yours, it seems the British strengthened their claim and expanded to control most of Western Europe. Along the way, it became Lancastria. As you might imagine, there have been seven hundred years' worth of differences in our histories as a result. Throw the existence of magic into the mix, and our two worlds look almost nothing alike."

That timeline added up to what Emma knew of the kingdom's history, though she wasn't overly familiar with the specifics of it.

"Regardless," Aldrich continued, "being stuck in your world for an extended period gave me great insight into what multi-dimensional travel could look like. If I can fix the device and restore its backup power source, I won't run into this issue again. Now that the two of you have rested, we can head to my lab."

Emma shook her head, her thoughts drifting back to Vespa. She was having a hard time believing the professor would abandon someone he'd spent so much time with. On the only family he'd had for the past six years.

But she wasn't ready to give up on Aldrich just yet.

Maggie

Chapter Seventeen

The university campus was as sprawling as its own city. Though not the skyscrapers of downtown, these buildings were just as impressive, standing several stories tall and encased in white. Everything was crisp and clean. Green trees marked the paths around campus, unbothered that spring had only just arrived. Grass was trimmed and vibrant, and gardens that rivaled those at the palace punctuated the campus with bursts of color that were aesthetically pleasing yet unnatural. Even here, all streets and pathways were paved with the same hard and uniform stone. Everything in this world was strangely curated to appear neat and tidy.

The insides of the buildings were somehow both more and less impressive. If there ever was a place that was less cozy, Emma wasn't sure if she could imagine it. Stark white hallways created with stone and glass left her feeling cold and empty. There was no character to the place. Like the grandest palaces and churches in her world had been left completely unfinished, with no decor and no sense of artistry.

They navigated the stark corridors until they reached Aldrich's lab, which was as sterile as the rest of the building. The walls were white, and the floors were a sort of faux marble tile that had been polished until it reflected like a mirror.

There were several counters covered with notebooks and

equipment. Like the rest of this strange world, the amount of new and intriguing things was overwhelming.

A variety of metal machines were scattered throughout the lab, and images hung on the walls, breaking the monotony of white with text and graphics displaying varying degrees of realism, from cats to blobs of color that Emma couldn't begin to sort out. It was as though someone realized these cavernous rooms needed art to invoke some sense of life into the place but created the most straight-edged and lifeless paintings they could imagine.

"Did you draw them?" she asked, wondering at both the means and medium of the pieces. "I've never seen paintings like these before."

"What?" The professor once again moved toward a glowing box that sat on a desk—this world appeared to be filled with them—and looked up absently at the wall. "Oh . . . no, those aren't paintings, not in the sense you're used to. Most of them reflect scientific principles. That large one is a representation of the Standard Model of Particle Physics. The one beside it is a representation of Einstein's Field Equations."

The professor might as well have been speaking Trollish.

Aldrich must have caught her blank expression. "It's a lot to explain, especially coming from a world where there is but a base understanding of physics. Hell, I still haven't worked out why the laws of physics seem to behave differently in your world. Listen, I need to sort out the state of my inventory so I can get some more crystals for you and hopefully restore the backup power source. I also think I've also worked out a way to save locations so I can come find you and Vespa. I know you have a million questions, and that's understandable I suppose, but if you can hold on to them for now, perhaps I can work to explain some basic principles to you later."

Emma nodded and continued to look around.

Vespa had resigned herself to sitting on a metal stool that sat against one of the counters.

More than an hour passed. Emma continued to question Vespa about fairies, and Vespa happily responded. The lightness in her voice returned slowly. The professor ticked away on his device, occasionally standing and investigating a back room of the lab that Emma assumed was storage.

After a while, Emma couldn't contain her curiosity. "You've been gone all this time. How is it that nobody has collected your things? That your 'lab' is still here?"

"I have tenure," he said as if that explained anything. A reticent expression crossed his face. "At least they didn't think I was dead."

"What of bandits and thieves?" Emma asked. "It makes sense that a palace such as this would be secure from outside threats. But I've seen no evidence of guards. They must be well trained to remain out of sight."

Aldrich let out a short laugh. "I wouldn't quite call this a palace. The university employs some security guards, but they're probably nothing like you imagine."

"But despite your long absence, none of your items have been stolen."

"No," he cleared his throat. "It's like I never left. Nothing has been touched." The professor's shoulders slumped.

Vespa must have picked up on it as well. "Is that a problem?" She stood and took two steps toward him, concern painted across her face. She stopped a few feet from the professor, though and closed her eyes with a steadying breath.

Aldrich sighed. "No, I suppose not, it's just . . ." He waved a hand toward his device. "There's no mention of my absence, nothing to indicate anyone even noticed I was away. Not even an email asking where I've been."

"I'm sure that's not the case," Vespa said.

"Henry?"

The three turned in unison toward the voice. A short, curly-haired woman stood in the lab's doorway. She surveyed Emma and Vespa curiously.

"Maggie O'Connor." Aldrich's eyes lit up as he stood. "You are a sight for sore eyes. How the devil are ya?" He approached Maggie and wrapped his arms around her in a warm embrace.

Vespa continued to keep her distance, though, seemingly content to observe the newcomer—for now, at least. The sharp look in her eye had Emma worried that Vespa might do something foolish.

"It has been quite some time, hasn't it?" Maggie said gently. The woman had a calming presence. She appeared younger than Emma guessed she was, based on her demeanor and timbre of voice. Her face bore only a few wrinkles, more like laugh lines from years of smiling. She held the professor's arm for a few seconds longer than the embrace, and her mahogany eyes stared up at him, her mouth moving slightly before she found the words. "I haven't heard from you in ages! I was starting to wonder if I offended you. We haven't talked since . . . well, it's been a while."

There was a flash of realization in Aldrich's eyes, and he stammered out something that sounded to Emma like an apology, but she couldn't quite parse out what for.

"Oh, don't get all flustered now, Henry. It was years ago." Maggie let out a warm laugh. Whoever this woman was had a serenity about her that Emma found enchanting. Like an aunt she'd never had. "It's all water under the bridge. I've moved on, and I'm happily married now. I thought you knew and maybe that was why you've been avoiding me."

"Avoiding you? No, I wouldn't . . ." Aldrich lifted his

hands in protest. "I'm so sorry Maggie. I would have contacted you, but I've been away."

Maggie gave a sullen nod. "You could have sent me an email at least. I was worried."

"It's a lot to explain . . . but I didn't have access to any means of communicating with you."

"Now that's intriguing." Maggie's warm smile returned. "You must have been off on some grand adventure. Like the ones we used to talk about." Maggie's eyebrows lowered for a moment as she surveyed both Vespa and Emma. "Perhaps you fancied one of these lovely young ladies instead?"

Emma was horrified at the insinuation, but Vespa didn't seem to notice and continued to study Maggie suspiciously.

Thankfully, Aldrich stepped in. "Oh, heavens no. Nothing like that, Maggie."

Vespa's lip quivered slightly as she closed her eyes briefly. She inhaled deeply through her nostrils, composed herself, and held firm.

Maggie continued, oblivious to Vespa's discomfort. "Did the university finally convince you to take that sabbatical?"

A smile crossed Aldrich's lips. "More like field research. At any rate, I am surprised nobody contacted you to question my whereabouts."

"Contact me? Why would they do that? Henry, I haven't seen you in six years! I didn't know what to think after you disappeared on me, but I assumed you had your reasons."

"Yes, well . . ." Aldrich's shoulders slumped. "I'm glad things have worked out for you. May I ask, though, what brings you here, then?"

Maggie blushed and stammered a little. "Um . . . I am in the city for a few days. I don't get here too often anymore, so when I do, I try to swing by the university. You know, catch up with some of the old gang. Every time I do, I pass by your lab to see if you're here. I just want to know how you're keeping . . ." she tucked a strand of light brown hair behind her ear. "I guess part of me was curious. The first few times I was disappointed you weren't in. Then I became worried. I feared your lab would be cleared out, or I'd hear some news that you'd . . . Well, you're here now, and I'm glad to see you're alive and well."

"Maggie . . ." Aldrich shuffled his feet. "If it's not too weird, I'd love it if we could catch up some time. I'd like to hear more about your time away."

"Well, I'm only in town until tomorrow. How about tonight?"

"I'm just finishing up a few things here, but if you'd like to join us for drinks this evening. My friends here are new to town. It would be great for them to hear some of our stories about the good old days. I also think you'd be most intrigued to hear what I've been up to the last six years."

Maggie's face lit up at the prospect. "I think that sounds lovely."

The lab door closed as Maggie left the room. Emma and Vespa exchanged uncertain glances as Aldrich kept his gaze on the door for several silent moments.

"Married," he whispered.

"You loved her," Vespa said, laying a hand on his shoulder. Emma expected there to be judgment in the fairy's voice, but there was only concern. "I can sense you're in pain."

"I mean no disrespect when I say, damn your abilities." Aldrich rubbed the edge of his mustache between his thumb and forefinger, which evolved into his palm rubbing up his cheek and over his eyes. He let out a sigh. "We shared a couple of nights before I left. I have a hard enough time connecting to people as it is, but something between us clicked. She understood me on a level that nobody has in . . . well, maybe ever. I don't think it was long enough to call it love. But I've spent a lot of time in the past few years imagining what could have been. I think part of me hoped that, even after all this time, we could have ended up being something more."

Emma shuffled her feet, unsure what to say. "Professor, I'm sorry. That couldn't have been easy."

"Bah!" Aldrich waved a hand. "This is precisely why I study what I do, isn't it? To understand the possibilities our decisions hold. In another reality, perhaps we're together. In this one, it just wasn't meant to be."

He turned back to his lab. The spring in his step had vanished.

"Let me grab a fresh batch of crystals," he said. "Then we can head to the pub. After the events of the last two days, I think I do need a drink."

Chicken Wings

Chapter Eighteen

It was difficult for Emma to articulate, even to herself, how odd it was to be inside of The Cursed Dragon once again. There was a distinct sensation of déjà vu as the interior was so similar to how it had been the night before in her own world. Yet it felt as alien as being on a completely different planet.

Well, technically I suppose I am.

Some things about the pub were identical in both versions. The wide-planked floors, the exposed rafters, and the structure of the building itself. The layout of the interior was the same. In fact, despite being made of a different type of wood than on her home world, the table where she sat with Aldrich and Vespa was in the very same spot as where she and Liam had discussed her future only the night before.

Bloody hell, was it only last night?

The same twelve steps separated her from the exit. The same forty steps between her and the back door. It was uncanny.

What made it that much more peculiar, however, was that the number of differences far outweighed the similarities. Like much of the city in this world, the amount of stimuli in the room was overwhelming, and Emma didn't know where to look first. The music was far louder than anything she'd ever heard, and instead of a local fiddler, the noise was emanating from nowhere and everywhere all at once.

Glowing screens, similar to those on Aldrich's devices, displayed moving pictures of some sporting event. Emma believed it to be a variation of a game she called "Catch the Cat," but Aldrich informed her the sport was called "rugby" here, and somehow in this world, they had devised a way to capture an event and send the images to a far-off destination. The game on the screen was taking place in another part of the kingdom!

"I thought you said there was no magic here!" Emma said, startled when Aldrich explained the devices to her. "I've seen this before, but never so clear. This is nothing more than a witch's scry."

"In simple terms, it's light and wires," Aldrich said. "There's no magic involved."

Vespa shook her head, eyes fixed on the same devices. "I still can't sense more than a trickle of magic. It isn't what powers these viewing portals."

Emma studied the screens, mesmerized by their output. "Lights and wires? And that allows us to see this game, which is being played as we speak, somewhere else in your world? You can't convince me that there is no sorcery involved in this!"

"No magic." Aldrich raised his palms toward her. "As I said before we left your world, there is much that science has discovered here that would appear as magic to you."

Emma couldn't help but marvel.

"Just wait until you try the food." Aldrich's mouth curled in a smile. The man was *enjoying* watching her try to comprehend everything his world offered. "You'll figure this all out with time."

"That's not fair," she said, crossing her arms.

"How so?" The smile faded from Aldrich's face.

"I have no reference for anything in this world. How does one get so accustomed to all of this?" She waved a hand at the room. "I've spent my life tracking magical people and creatures, and still I struggle to process everything that exists here."

"You will grow used to it." Aldrich shrugged. "And after a time, what you once saw as magical will appear ordinary."

Emma didn't know how she could ever picture anything in this world as ordinary.

A server arrived at their table. "How can I help?"

Emma had to do a double take.

The woman's blonde hair was shorter, but the freckled face was the same. This was the server she'd encountered the day before.

"Liesel?" Emma couldn't help but ask.

The woman's eyes widened in surprise. "Yes? Have we met?"

She didn't think she'd ever get used to seeing multiple people with the same face.

The woman stared at her, awaiting a response.

Aldrich leaned against the palm of his hand, his eyes bulging out of his skull, desperate to communicate to her to choose her words wisely. Vespa's gaze diverted between the two others at the table, ensuring Aldrich understood the peril Emma was about to place herself in.

The message wasn't lost on her. She couldn't very well suggest that she'd encountered the woman in another realm. Emma wasn't familiar with the laws of this world, but she was quite sure that would universally mark her as either a witch or crazy, and she didn't wish to come across as either.

"I . . . I have been in here before."

"Oh!" Liesel exclaimed. "I'm so sorry. I serve so many

people, I can't keep everyone's face straight. What was your name again?"

"Emma."

"Well, Emma, I hope I did a good job." The woman had the same nervous laugh as her counterpart the day before.

"Yes, you were absolutely lovely."

"I'm happy to hear it! Can I get you started with drinks?"

"A round of pints," Aldrich said. "Red ale if you've got it."

"Of course. Is that everything?"

"A large plate of wings for the table, please."

"Coming right up!"

It seemed to take no time at all before Liesel returned with three glass mugs and set them on the table. Another server followed closely behind and set a large plate of food on the table. It bore a pile of small chunks of meat, but they looked unusual, with a coating of some sort she didn't recognize. More than that, the serving was massive.

"Is that all for us?" Emma asked. "That's a helping of meat fit for the king's court!"

Liesel gave Emma a sidelong look. "He asked for the large plate. Is this too much?"

Emma's stomach growled. She wouldn't argue, but she had never seen so much meat delivered for three people in a common pub before.

"This is perfect," Aldrich said with a smile. "Thank you."

Liesel returned the smile, winked at Emma, then returned to her duties.

Emma felt a little embarrassed about her response, but it quickly melted as she took a bite of one of the meat sticks placed in front of her.

"These are incredible!" she said as she quickly stuffed another into her mouth. "What did you say these were called?"

"Chicken wings." Aldrich chuckled. He seemed amused, but Emma couldn't imagine why.

They were so small, and different from the wings she'd been used to. She lifted one and inspected it. The meat inside was tender. Most of the chicken she'd had in pubs was tough and stringy. The outside was crisp, the foreign coating giving it a rough texture and pleasingly fragrant smell.

As she took her first bite, a medley of flavors exploded in her mouth—spicy, tangy, and savory notes danced on her palate. Emma's eyes widened with delight. She couldn't explain it, but the crispy skin provided the meat with a satisfying crunch. Along with that, the juiciness of the meat combined with the bold flavors left her pleasantly surprised and eager for another bite.

"The chickens in your world must be tiny!" she muttered through a half-full mouth. "And how did they get them to taste so good?"

"They're half of a wing," Aldrich said, bemused. "And the flavors are likely the result of a lot of salt and sugar."

Emma held one up and inspected it again. "Whatever it is, it's delicious." She ate greedily. It was only then that she realized she'd hadn't eaten since the day before.

"Take your time," Aldrich said, picking up a wing of his own. "You can grow sick eating too much like that."

Emma paused. The professor was right. She was acting like a waif who hadn't known food for months.

"Vespa, you have to try these! They are like nothing in our world."

The fairy shifted uncomfortably. "Er . . . Fairies don't eat meat. Truthfully, we don't need to eat at all, but meat is particularly unsettling."

Immediately, Emma set her current wing down. She turned to the professor on the verge of anger. "I'm so sorry!"

Emma exclaimed. "I didn't mean to offend you. Aldrich! How could you order this, knowing how she feels?"

Aldrich eyes were also wide in surprise, but Vespa spoke up before he had a chance to respond. "It's all right." She rested her chin on her hands, leaning against the table. "I've never told the professor. I didn't want to inconvenience him. Humans have different nutritional needs, and I wanted to be respectful of that. Fairies can eat, but we get our sustenance from the magic around us."

"Vespa!" Aldrich's pupils dilated as he froze. The color in his face shifted subtly, but it was enough that Emma caught it. "If it upsets you, I would have been more respectful! You should have told me!"

"I have grown used to it," Vespa said. "Truly, I do not want to be an inconvenience."

Emma pushed away her plate. "Well, I won't have any of that. I'm not going to eat meat in front of you if it's even a little offensive."

"That's very kind of you, Emma." Vespa said. "But you don't have to."

Emma locked her gaze on Vespa's. "Tell me truthfully. Would you prefer if we did not eat meat?"

Vespa sighed, and Emma could see the battle being fought within her. She didn't want to tell the truth, not if it meant she'd inconvenience her friends.

"Truthfully . . ." Vespa said, "yes, I would be more comfortable without meat being consumed. Living things, even animals, are part of the environment where we typically draw our magic from. It's part of the reason fairies tend to avoid humans."

"Vespa, I had no idea . . ." Aldrich's mouth moved in disbelief. Emma imagined he was picturing the countless times he'd offended the fairy.

"You couldn't have known," she said. "Please, don't make a big deal of this. I . . . I've only strived to help. I don't wish to make you feel bad."

The table grew silent, chicken wings left untouched.

"Wait," said Emma. "If you're sustained through magic, how will you be able to survive here?"

"I'll be okay for a time. But yes, eventually I'll need to access to magic in order to survive."

Aldrich's brow furrowed. "Vespa! You have to share these things with us. How are we to know if you don't?"

"You knew I am weakened here and need to leave. I didn't want you to worry you unnecessarily. I didn't want to be a bother."

Emma grabbed Vespa's hand and held it firm. "You are *not* a bother, Vespa. You needing magic to survive is a big deal. You're so concerned about helping everyone else, but you need to let others help you as well."

Vespa pressed her lips together and gave a shallow nod. "That is something I've never been good at. I've been told that I'm a nuisance my entire life."

"Your wellbeing is important to us," said Emma. "Being able to sustain yourself, your customs, and beliefs, these are not things that you need to hide. We want you to be able to be yourself! We'll find a way to get you off this world," Emma said. "To somewhere with all the magic you need."

Vespa squeezed Emma's hand, as she inhaled deeply.

"It will be difficult for me," Vespa said. "But I'll try to share my needs more."

Emma couldn't help but smile. "Thank you for being willing to do that. I know it's probably not easy, but we want to help."

"Thank you," Vespa said. "But I don't want to dwell on it. It makes me uncomfortable."

Emma nodded. "Understood."

She released Vespa's hand and grabbed the ale that Liesel had set down. Her fingers wrapped around the cool, condensation-kissed glass. The amber liquid shimmered inside, but still it was missing something. Like it was hollow.

The rim touched her lips, and she took a tentative sip. A cascade of sensations followed—a malty embrace and a subtle undercurrent of caramel sweetness.

Like the chicken wings, this ale was far more flavorful than anything she'd experienced before. She reached out with her magic—or at least, she tried. She wanted to speak with this creation, to get a better understanding of the hearty layers she was detecting. There was a vague impression she could gather from the drink, but there was no sense of character. None of the depth she'd grown to appreciate over the last month.

"Beer no good?" Aldrich asked, taking a swig for himself and his eyes rolled back. "It's quite different from what you're used to, probably, but there's nothing like a pint from The Cursed Dragon . . . At least this Cursed Dragon."

"No, it's not that." Emma set her glass down and stared at it, willing it to provide her with *some* of the detail she craved. "It tastes remarkable. But . . ." She was beginning to understand how Vespa must be feeling. "I can feel the ale is there. I can sense the malt, barley, and hops, and that they are all of far superior quality to what we have in my home world . . . but it doesn't speak to me the way it should."

Emma thought it must have sounded funny to miss something she'd only possessed for a short while. Something she had actively fought against.

"Maybe order something else," Aldrich suggested. "There are plenty of drinks in this world that are more exciting than your typical pint."

"Not a fan of the beer?" Maggie appeared beside the table.

She took a small bag off her shoulder and placed it beside her as she sat next to Aldrich. "You should try the hazy pale ale. It's my favorite."

"The what?"

"You'll find the styles here are a little different from what you're used to." Aldrich chuckled.

"Styles?" she asked. "You mean, ale or stout?"

"That's precisely it," Aldrich said. "And there are probably dozens of styles to choose from."

Emma's eyes widened, but she kept her tone flat, not sure if the professor was playing a joke on her. "Dozens?"

"Not one for the craft beer scene?" Maggie asked. "Your accent sounds like it's from England—you must know Ireland has more than stout."

Emma wasn't sure what to make of the information at all. Were there really *dozens* of different ways to brew beer? She had traveled throughout the kingdom, and sure, beer in Kalmar tasted different than beer in Hibernia, and different still in Lisboa, but . . . she supposed she'd never thought of it before.

Suddenly she wanted to try *all* the distinctive styles. Before she could say so, Aldrich carried on. "I think a cocktail might be more to her liking."

"Lovely idea!" Maggie waved to Liesel to get her attention again. "I think I'll order one myself."

Vespa shifted uncomfortably. Emma couldn't help but notice the unsettling glare the fairy was casting in the woman's direction. But she was much more interested in what a cocktail was.

Emma was about to ask, but Liesel was there almost instantly.

"Two smoked old fashioneds, please," said Maggie. "One for me and one for my new friend here."

"Smoked old fashioned?" Emma repeated. "What's that?"

Liesel smiled knowingly. "It's a pub favorite. Come on, you can watch the bartender prepare it."

Emma looked at Maggie, unsure of how to proceed or what societal norms would dictate. She truly felt like a fish out of water.

Another world, indeed.

"Go on," Maggie urged. "I'm going to stay here and catch up with Henry."

Emma forced a smile, nodded, and stood. She'd spent her entire life learning how to blend in during awkward situations. This unfamiliar environment was throwing her off. Though, she had to admit, she'd never imagined or prepared for anything quite as surreal as where she found herself now.

"I'll join you." Vespa rose to her side. "I think these two have a lot of catching up to do." She looked back at Aldrich with a knowing glance before following Liesel and Emma toward the bar.

A Different Witch

Chapter Nineteen

"How are you doing?" Emma whispered to Vespa once they were out of earshot from the table. They hadn't had a moment alone since they arrived at Aldrich's flat, and she had to take the opportunity to chat with her away from the professor.

"What do you mean?" Vespa replied innocently. "I'm lovely, thank you."

"You know exactly what I mean," Emma hissed. "I see the daggers you've been staring at Maggie. You're jealous that she's had a relationship with the professor, and he basically dismissed you out right."

Vespa's smile faded but only slightly. She took a deep breath. "It was a long shot to wish for anything to happen between us. I'm a fairy, and he's a human. I should have known he'd never see me in that way. We're too different."

"Nonsense," Emma said. "I see the way you look at him. And I know he cares about you a great deal, too. He's oblivious, but all he needs is to see past his research and realize how much you care for him. Give it some time. I don't think all hope is lost for the two of you yet."

Vespa's smile returned, but it was dull compared to her usual brightness. "Perhaps you're right. But just in case, I don't want to get my hopes too high. The professor is a man of many mysteries, and I don't know how much more of myself I'll be able to give him if he doesn't feel the same way about me."

The trip to the bar was a short one. Emma half expected to see William O'Malley standing behind the counter, but instead it was a dark-haired woman with an olive complexion and piercing dark eyes.

"This is our mixologist, Mia," Liesel said as they approached. "Mia, these two would like two smoked old fashioneds, but they wanted to watch you make them."

Mia's smile reached her sparkling eyes. "Ah, I see. Trying to steal the master's secrets?"

Emma's guard instantly flared. Trade guild secrets were known to be well protected. She had no intent on getting into a fight here.

Vespa, however, held no such reservations. "Emma wants to become a bartender!"

Emma nearly choked.

"She was joking," Vespa whispered to her so that Mia couldn't hear. "You can relax."

"Is that so?" Mia said as she pulled together a few items behind the bar. "Well, this shouldn't be anything you can't handle."

"Err . . . I'm a little out of my element here, I'm afraid."

Mia nodded as she wiped a splash of water off the bar with a towel. "Say no more. We all need to start somewhere. The old fashioned is your classic cocktail. The smoking part is what people usually want to see. But I'll walk you through each step."

Emma sighed with relief. "That would be most appreciated. I'll try to be an apt student."

"It's nothing too complicated." Mia flashed a pearly-white smile, and a sparkle of excitement flashed in her eyes. "The backbone of the old fashioned is your bourbon."

"Bourbon?" Emma asked.

Mia raised an eyebrow. "You might want to take notes if you really want to become a bartender. You're going to need a knowledge of your basic spirits."

Emma's cheeks flushed. "It's a recent interest," she said. "I know I have a lot to learn."

"It's all right." Mia smiled again. "Like I said, we've all got to start somewhere. You can learn a lot by searching online."

Emma nodded, though she wasn't sure where "online" was. "I'll be sure to do that," she said.

"Anyway, bourbon is a type of whiskey, but it's made primarily with corn, and comes from America." Mia picked up a clear, square-shaped bottle, the liquid inside glowed in the pub's artificial light—its orange-copper color practically shimmered.

"It's got a sweetness to it that other whiskeys don't typically have," Mia continued. "That sweetness, along with deep, oaky notes, is what makes it important for the old fashioned—it already has a bit of that smoky undertone. When we add smoke, it enhances the flavors already there. You don't need anything top shelf, you're better drinking that neat, or on the rocks." Mia placed the bottle on the bar next to two glasses that she'd already set out.

She held up another glass bottle, this one filled with a cloudy white liquid and no label on it. "Do you know what simple syrup is?" she asked hesitantly.

Emma shook her head. The time to save face had passed; she may as well learn what she could.

"So," Mia said while popping the lid off the bottle. "Simple syrup is really just a mixture of sugar and water. You can buy it, but it's really easy to make. Just add a cup of sugar to a cup of water and mix them together."

Emma worked hard not to let her jaw fall. *A cup of sugar?* She looked at Vespa incredulously.

"I know that sounds like it will be extra sweet, but don't worry, we're not adding much. That amount of syrup will last you awhile. It's used to balance out the strength of the bourbon. You can also use a sugar cube, but this way sugar won't get stuck at the bottom of your glass, plus we use the simple syrup in other drinks behind the bar, so it just makes it easier to have a batch ready."

Emma couldn't help but ask, "How easy is it to find sugar?" She almost added "in this world" but caught herself.

For the first time, Mia's smile lessened but only for a moment before she let out a short, sharp laugh. "You're funny."

Emma was bewildered by the reaction. Sugar wasn't rare, per se, but it was a luxury. Something that was used sparingly. For it to be added to a drink, and in such quantities was madness.

Clearly there was no such scarcity in this world, so she tried not to let her bewilderment show—she put a smile on her face and nodded along.

"I'm going to make both of your drinks at the same time. So, I'm going to take four ounces of the bourbon, an ounce of the simple syrup, and add it to a shaker with some ice."

"Ice?" Emma asked and then quickly wished she hadn't. She struggled to imagine where ice might have come from—there was a nip in the air, but it was hardly cold enough for ice. Mia's smile was slowly fading with each question Emma asked. Clearly, sugar and ice were things people of this world wouldn't normally question.

Luckily, Mia misinterpreted her vague question as the need for ice in the drink, and not a question of how one finds ice in the springtime.

"You wouldn't need ice, I suppose," Mia said. "But the classic old fashioned is chilled, and I think it does make it more palatable. I've mixed the bourbon and simple syrup with ice to cool it quickly, but we'll strain that off and add a single ice sphere in each glass. Using an ice ball instead of an ice cube ensures it doesn't melt too quickly. Plus, it looks cool." Mia pulled out a tray from a cabinet below the bar and, sure enough, opened it up to reveal multiple balls of ice. Emma had to bite her tongue from asking how the ice remained solid in such a chamber. She was tired of Mia's peculiar stares. She'd have to ask Aldrich her questions about the workings of his world later.

"Next, we'll add a dash of bitters," Mia said, taking a smaller bottle and tapping a few drops into the shaker. "Think of these like the spices of the drink world. They're concentrated, so you don't need much but they'll add a lot of complexity to the drink."

Snapping the lid onto the shaker, Mia gripped it with both hands and raised it in front of her. "Then you give it a shake!" She violently shook the canister, which made a great rattling noise. After she did that for a minute, she poured the cocktail into two glasses and set a small wooden disk on top of each.

"This is where the magic happens. You can use any type of wood, but cherry wood infuses a delicate flavor."

Emma's ears piqued at the word *magic*.

Mia took what looked like a small metal gun out from behind the bar and lifted it toward the first wooden disk. "It doesn't need much, but once the wood catches, I'll cover it and let the drinks smoke for a good minute."

She pressed the trigger on the weapon and a flame erupted from the barrel with a hiss.

Emma gasped. "Witch!" she cried out before she could catch herself. Old habits died hard.

Mia let out a laugh, as did a handful of patrons around them within earshot.

"I suppose I am, in a sense." Mia continued to chuckle as she set the flame to the wood.

Despite the levity Mia showed, Emma's nerves had been shot. She tried to still her thoughts, but they spiraled out of control. *How can this woman produce fire from nothing without the use of magic?*

As much as the professor had tried to insist there was no magic in this world, at every corner there were things she could not explain by any other means.

Vespa laid a gentle hand on her shoulder. "Are you doing okay?"

Emma jumped out of the daze she hadn't realized she'd been in. It took all her cognitive focus not to pull her dagger out from her belt on pure reflex. The sudden appearance of fire was not the oddest thing that had happened that day by a long shot, but Emma still found herself rattled. Adrenaline coursed through her veins, and she had to fight a decade's worth of instinct not to fling her knife at poor Mia.

Of course, Vespa likely could sense the duress she was under and felt the need to help.

"Is everything all right?" Mia asked, as she set the flame to the wood again for the second drink. "This is usually the part people are the most interested in." Despite the storm that raged within Emma, Mia had been so concentrated on what she was doing that she'd not even noticed. Or at least, if she had, she'd hidden it well.

Emma paused and let her gaze fall on what Mia had done. Indeed, a storm of smoke brewed within the glass, and the effect was mesmerizing. But one doesn't spend a lifetime hunting witches and not react when a person produces a flame out of thin air.

"I've had a long day," Emma said. "I need to sit down." She paused before adding, "But I'd like a copy of that recipe before I leave."

Smoked Old Fashioned

Drink Recipe

Ingredients:

- 2 ounces bourbon
- 1/2-ounce simple syrup
- 2 dashes aromatic bitters
- 2 maraschino cherries, plus a bit of syrup
- Smoke (using a smoke lid or similar device) - optional, see note for smokeless version.
- Orange peel for garnish

Directions:

1. In a cocktail shaker filled with ice, combine the bourbon, simple syrup, and bitters.
2. Shake vigorously for about 20 seconds to chill the mixture.
3. Strain the cocktail into a whiskey glass over fresh ice.
4. Add 2 maraschino cherries and a bit of the syrup to the glass.
5. If smoking cocktail:
6. Place the smoke lid over the glass.
7. Follow the instructions provided with the smoke lid to add smoke to the drink. Typically, you'll ignite wood chips or a smoke pellet inside the

smoke lid, creating flavorful smoke that infuses into the cocktail.
8. Allow the smoke to infuse for a few seconds to a minute, depending on your preference for smokiness.
9. Garnish the drink with a twist of orange peel on the rim or floating in the drink.
10. Sip and savor!

Note: If you prefer, you can enjoy this cocktail without the smoke by simply skipping steps 5-8. It will still be delicious and flavorful without the added smokiness.

Simple Syrup Recipe:

To make flavored simple syrup, combine equal parts water and white sugar in a saucepan over low heat. Stir until the sugar dissolves. If desired, add your choice of fruits, herbs, and spices to infuse flavor. Let it simmer for a few minutes, then let it cool to room temperature and strain before using in cocktails.

Store excess in a jar or other airtight container and chill until next use.

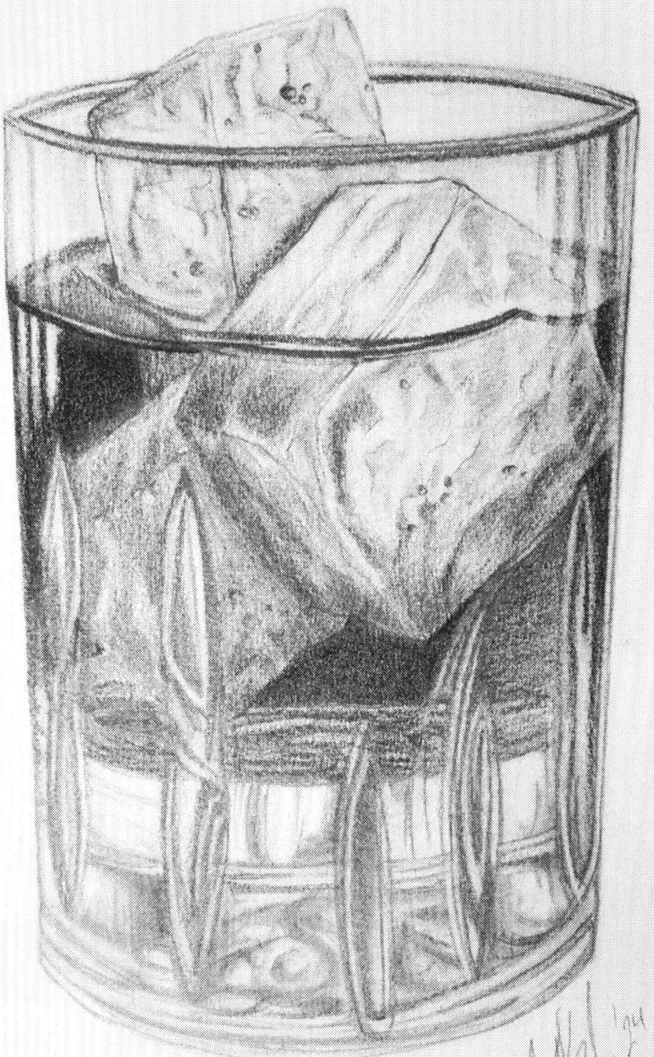

Gathering Data

Chapter Twenty

The expression of absolute incredulity on Maggie's face as Emma and Vespa returned to the table could only have meant one thing.

Maggie leaned forward as Emma and Vespa sat. "Is what Henry's been telling me true?"

Emma didn't know how much the professor had shared in the brief time they were away, but it was clearly enough.

"It is," Emma said.

Liesel set the two still-smoking drinks in front of them. "Enjoy," she said with a playful grin, clearly enjoying the smoke brewing within the glass, then carried on to a nearby table.

"And you." Maggie turned to Vespa. "You're really a . . ." She glanced around as though ensuring nobody was listening in. "A fairy?" She practically whispered the final two words.

"I am," Vespa confirmed.

Maggie's mouth and eyes both hung wide open. Clearly this was a reality she'd never imagined possible. Though Emma had to admit, after a day in Aldrich's world, she had already seen more of what she'd considered magic than she had during nearly a lifetime of hunting magical beings.

"So, it's all real, then? Fairies? Magic? It shouldn't be possible."

"It appears so," Aldrich said. "I wouldn't have believed it myself had I not seen it with my own eyes. I had imagined historical events to have taken different paths when I set out upon this study, but I had never imagined the laws of physics as we know them to be so drastically different."

Maggie rubbed her ear thoughtfully. "Perhaps this could explain some things."

"How so?"

"What if all the stories—fairy tales of magic and elves, ghosts, UFO abductions—what if everything we've written off as superstition and nonsense were somehow slips between our world and another?" Maggie was doing her best to keep her voice down, but Emma could tell the excitement would soon overpower her desire to remain discreet.

Emma didn't know what the penalty in this world would be for possessing magic or being a fairy. In a world where one could produce fire at will, or keep a block of ice under your counter, what did it matter if someone possessed magic?

"That's one theory I've been pondering," Aldrich said. "It would account for a number of folktales and eyewitness accounts of phenomena we haven't been able to explain otherwise."

"Remarkable," Maggie said. "Henry, do you realize what you've done? If that's the case, you'll have explained all sorts of supernatural phenomena! If fairies and magic are just a branch of evolution that never occurred in our world but somehow have slipped into our dimension, then a whole range of things are possible! And you've *proven* that a person—or being—can travel between these worlds! What sorts of stories will turn out to be true? Are aliens simply multi-dimensional beings? The Loch Ness Monster? Vampires? Dragons? If there are weak points between worlds, that would also explain why these beings are seen once and then never again."

"Vampires and dragons?" Aldrich huffed. "Let's not get carried away."

Maggie let out a laugh. "You're sitting across the table from an honest-to-god fairy, and you're worried dragons might be a stretch?"

Aldrich rubbed his mustache as he pondered the statement. "I suppose . . . But maybe it's best not to get ahead of ourselves. There's still a lot of research to be done."

Maggie beamed. "Yes, of course."

"And even if that *is* the case, we still have no idea *how* those creatures would slip through. The accelerator uses far more energy than anything you'd find in nature. We'd have to prove these slips might happen at random."

While the two reminisced about their mutual scientific studies, Emma tried to focus on her old fashioned. The flavors were just as Mia had described. Smoky, sweet, with a hint of orange. It was absolutely delightful. Yet, without her magic to guide her, she couldn't help but lament that it felt like she was missing something. She tried to open her magic, as she had done previously, again and again. But in the end, it was as though she were attempting to talk to a puddle.

She sighed and focused on enjoying the flavors for what they were. It really was incredibly different from anything she'd ever had before. She was happy Mia was willing to write the recipe down for her, and she absently tapped the note she'd placed in her pocket.

She was going to need to find a notebook to keep these recipes in.

Mia continued to work behind the bar, just within Emma's sightline. The woman moved gracefully, pouring drinks and chatting with patrons. Emma couldn't help but smile. That was where she wanted to be. Behind the bar, concocting potions. As she let her eyes scan over the menu, she realized how many more drink possibilities there were than she'd ever imagined possible.

But as incredible as it all was, this wasn't the world for her. As tempting as it was to live in a world with no magic, with nothing tying her to her past, she realized now that she could never thrive in such a place. No, her magic was key to her becoming a bartender.

After another an hour of discussion, Maggie said. "Well, I best be going. It was lovely to catch up with you, Henry, and to meet the both of you, Emma and Vespa." She gave Vespa a knowing wink.

Emma rolled her eyes, but Vespa's cheeks reddened.

"I should probably ask, since you only just returned," Maggie said as she put on her coat. "Have you let your friends and family know you're back?"

A heaviness visibly descended on Aldrich as he took a deep swig of his drink. "It doesn't seem my absence was really noticed."

Maggie's mouth pouted and her forehead crinkled. "I'm sure that's not true."

Aldrich smiled politely. "Yes, of course not. I just . . . it's going to be a bit of an adjustment being back."

"It was good seeing you again, Henry. Keep in touch. I'd love to keep up to date on your research."

"Well, she was delightful!" Vespa said once Maggie had left. "I can see why you liked her so much."

"Yes," Aldrich mumbled. "She's something else." He moved to collect his things. "We should probably go," he said more confidently. "We've been through a lot, and rest would do us good. Tomorrow I'll need to get to work on the accelerator."

"Demon Box," Emma corrected.

"Excuse me?" Aldrich asked. He'd half buttoned his long

coat.

"The device prefers to be called *Demon Box*. It told me when we left the last world."

Aldrich blinked several times and gave his head a slight shake. "My device . . . spoke to you. And told you it wanted to be called . . . Demon Box?"

"Yes." Emma immediately regretted sharing what she had. The professor was definitely going to think she was mad now. "It . . . it told me it did not like being called quantum accelerator."

Aldrich turned to Vespa with a flabbergasted look.

Vespa wore a wide smile and clasped her hands together, seemingly thrilled at the news.

What news isn't she excited about? Emma mused.

"All right, then." Aldrich's mustache twitched. He seemed unsure, but to his credit, he didn't argue. "I've got to get to work on . . . the *Demon Box*."

Emma wasn't quite ready to leave yet, not without knowing one last thing. "Professor, there's something else. You keep saying nobody missed you. That surely can't be true. You were so excited to return here. Maggie couldn't have been the only one you were looking forward to seeing."

Aldrich continued to fasten the last few buttons of his coat, not meeting Emma's gaze. "I don't have any family to speak of. It seems the two friends I thought I had reached out to me a couple times in the first month but never followed up. Even Maggie gave up on me after a time. The university deposited my salary into my bank account, my payments were all automatically withdrawn. Those who noticed me missing assumed I had either taken a sabbatical or took a leave to study elsewhere. I may be back, but I am, it seems, quite alone."

Vespa reached a hand across the table and grabbed

Aldrich's. He absently grasped hers back. Emma wasn't sure if he even realized the lifeline that sat across the table from him.

Over the years, Emma had hardened herself to other people's feelings. Emotions impeded her line of work. But she hadn't realized what it must have been like for the professor to have lived in this world of marvel and not have anyone to share it with.

"Then come with us," she blurted. "You might not have anyone in this world, but you do have us."

Vespa nodded eagerly.

Aldrich shook his head. "But my research . . . I've spent my entire life trying to prove multi-dimensional travel is possible. This needs to be published! My place is here."

Emma considered this for a minute.

"Don't you think your place is with those who care about you?" asked Vespa. "Emma and I can provide you with the help you need to collect more information. Perhaps seeing what other worlds are out there will help your research further."

Emma followed Vespa's line of thinking. "Vespa's right! What better way to enhance your findings than traveling to other worlds and gathering more data? You'll have me with you, so we're less likely to get trapped in another world, and who knows, maybe we'll find another way to jump between worlds. You can try to prove your ideas about dragons and vampires. If your absence will go unnoticed here, there's no reason for you not to ensure your paper is as robust as it can be."

Aldrich's mustache twitched as he pondered Emma's words. "There is some merit to what you're saying . . . If that is something I decide to do—and I'm not saying I'm settled on it —I wouldn't want to be tied to a single world. Don't you want to find a place to stay? Settle down in a world you can call home?"

Warmth overtook her. For a moment she thought her magic had been restored, but then she realized it wasn't that at all. She was getting a grip on what she wanted. Seeing new places had always been the part of being a Hunter that she'd enjoyed most. Now, here was a chance for her to see places that defied her very imagination and to learn a few drink recipes along the way.

But to find a place to settle . . . that wasn't something she wanted—not now, at least.

"Perhaps one day," she said. "But for now, I think my home will be wherever my friends are. Besides, the best part of my old life was that I could travel and explore the kingdom. This world possesses marvels far beyond what I ever could have imagined. Imagine the drink recipes I could learn elsewhere! I could be a bartender between worlds."

"Now that sounds like an adventure!" Vespa clapped her hands together giddily.

"Yes, I do see the value in adding additional research to my studies . . ." Aldrich's eyes met Emma's. His body relaxed as a faint smile crossed his lips. "And I have grown quite fond of the two of you. It *would* be nice if we could spend more time together."

Vespa grabbed Emma's shoulders in an enthusiastic two-handed grip. "Did you hear that, Emma? He's fond of us!"

The words sounded sarcastic to Emma, but she knew the fairy meant them with full sincerity. She couldn't help but laugh. "I heard. And I have to say, in the past two days, I've grown quite fond of the two of you as well."

Aldrich's gaze fell back to Vespa, and he reached across the table with his hand open.

Vespa appeared puzzled but didn't hesitate to reach out and clasp her own hand around Aldrich's.

"If I have learned one thing from all of this,"—his eyes darted from the table to Vespa—"it's that perhaps I shouldn't take what's in front of me for granted."

Emma held her breath. Was this really happening?

"Emma said something to me earlier, and it opened my eyes. I realized, after today, that I have perhaps allowed life to pass me by because I have been too engrossed in my studies. Though, in the end, that probably worked out for the best, because otherwise I might not have met you."

Vespa stared wide-eyed, her grin widening with every word.

Aldrich cleared his throat. "What I'm trying to say, I suppose, is that I don't want to take for granted how important you are to me. If you'd still have me on your journey, I'd love to be given another chance."

Vespa stood, her hand still clasping Aldrich's, and took two steps toward him. Even though Aldrich was sitting, Vespa was barely taller than him.

"I'd like nothing more." Vespa leaned down and placed her lips on Aldrich's.

Emma smiled gently as her two friends embraced. Wherever they were going next, at least they'd be going together.

A World of Magic

Chapter Twenty-One

Aldrich spent the next few days working on Demon Box, getting it ready to take them . . . wherever it was they were about to go. In the evenings, he took Vespa to see the city, to show her the place he called home.

At the beginning of their stay, Emma had taken what time she could exploring Cuanmore on her own. She worked her way outward from Aldrich's flat in concentric circles so she didn't get lost. She prided herself on her navigational abilities, but finding her way through the sprawling city was nothing like tracking in the forest or fields. So much of the landscape looked the same, and there were rules for walking that she was unaccustomed to.

Between the noise and disorienting environment, if she didn't know any better, she would have said the city had been cursed into being as stressful as possible.

As a result, she decided to spend the rest of her time at The Cursed Dragon. Mia got special permission from the tavern owner to give Emma some basic lessons from behind the bar when the pub wasn't busy.

Mostly this involved helping Mia keep the bar clean, but she was able to learn about the different beers, cocktails, and wines Aldrich's world offered. Mia also taught her basic information about barware and techniques that were never part of working in a village tavern as far as Emma was aware.

Nights were spent in Aldrich's flat—mostly pacing the room restlessly while the professor worked on Demon Box, replacing the crystals and fixing the systems that had been broken and depleted over the past six years.

Vespa spent her days reading on the professor's sofa. "I appreciate that Aldrich has taken me out to experience life here. But without my magic, nothing feels right," she had said when Emma asked if she'd wanted to explore with her. "Everyone feels empty and hollow. I can't sense what they need. Like I'm being crushed by the weight of thousands of lifeless souls."

Perhaps a bit dramatic, but Emma somewhat understood. Every drink she made was missing something—a crucial piece of what it was supposed to be.

It was the sixth day since they'd arrived, and Emma was starting to wonder if they'd ever leave this world. The black box sat on the kitchen table, pieces strewn around it. Emma didn't pretend to know how these devices operated, but it looked like the world's most difficult puzzle box with hundreds of tiny pieces, screws, and bolts.

What Aldrich had referred to as "crystals" didn't appear to be crystals at all but small metal tubes. Emma could feel their power from within. The old crystals lay lifeless on the table. They had stopped communicating with her as soon as they'd stepped into Aldrich's world.

There was a brief pang in her chest. Did she actually miss the sarcastic voice rattling in her head?

Suddenly she wondered how it must feel with all of its bits strewn everywhere. "Will taking Demon Box apart like that, hurt it?" she asked.

Aldrich looked at her with a blank expression as he snapped one of the new tubes in place.

Finally. Emma jumped a little as Demon Box spoke into her mind. *There's been a throbbing pain in my neck for six years! Feels like a whole new me. A little airy though, is there a breeze in here?*

"You realize you don't have a neck." Emma spoke the words out loud.

It was hard to determine if she was talking to the crystals or to the rest of the device. From what she could tell, they were one and the same, but swapping out the crystals didn't appear to change the machine's persona.

Aldrich pushed up his glasses with his index finger as he looked up from the box toward Emma. "What's that? What's wrong with my neck?" His hand went to the back of his own neck as though he had to be sure it was, in fact, there.

"No, not you," she said. "Demon Box just woke up and is being cranky again."

"Hmph," said Aldrich.

Hmph, said Demon Box.

Emma had to hold back a laugh.

Vespa glanced up from the book she was reading with a puzzled expression. The book, titled *Peter Pan*, was a dark, leatherbound tome with a silhouetted image of a young boy, a young woman, and of course, a fairy. Emma imagined the image must have been what encouraged Vespa to pick it up.

"I can't say I'm particularly fond of the name Demon Box," said Aldrich.

Like Quantum Accelerator is such a bloody masterpiece? Demon Box retorted.

"It's what I'd been calling it," Emma said. "I had been worried the thing was opening a portal to unleash demons into my world. I guess it liked how it sounded."

Aldrich pursed his lips. "Well, I suppose if I can accept that it was a magical bartender from another world who brought me home, then it only stands to reason that the device I built gained some sort of consciousness and has named itself after a supernatural creature. Though it probably should bother me that we're relinquishing control to something calling itself an instrument of evil."

"Are you saying you believe in demons, Professor?" Vespa said with a smirk.

"It doesn't seem to matter much what I believe. I hadn't believed in fairies, yet you still showed up on my doorstep. If I've learned anything over the past six years, it's that *anything* is within the realm of possibility."

What's he going on about? Demon Box asked. *What have I been named after?*

"Demons are minions of evil," Emma said. "Born of the underworld, hellbent on destroying humanity."

The Hunters often got calls to hunt demons from various parts of the kingdom. Despite their best efforts, the dark creatures were never caught.

Really? Demon Box said. *Now I see why it resonated with me.*

"Don't start with that, or we'll take out those crystals and shove you in the professor's closet."

"Hmm?" Aldrich furrowed his brow with a worried stare. "What's this?"

"Demon Box is being cheeky," Emma said. At least, she hoped so.

That's not fair, it said. *You don't see me threatening to remove your brain. I could, you know.*

"Pfft, you could not!" *Light, could it?* She was sure she didn't want to know.

Oh, trust me you don't!

It was late afternoon by the time the professor had all the pieces off the table and back in their proper places.

"The backup power is ready," Aldrich said. "This should minimize the risk that there'll be another failure that will trap us somewhere."

Good, said Demon Box. *I spent some dark days trapped in the basement.*

"Now, are we ready to test this out?" Aldrich said.

Vespa lowered her book. "Now?" she asked. "I'm just getting to a good part."

"I've got a few more pieces to assemble. But you can bring that with you," Aldrich said. "But for the love of all things science, don't let that . . . Demon Box . . . bring us to a world overrun with pirates."

Emma smirked.

"What about a world where we never grow up?" Vespa giggled as she jumped off the sofa. Emma could imagine she'd be buzzing around the room if her magic could hold her wings for long enough.

"You're a fairy," Aldrich said, straight-faced as he continued to screw a piece onto Demon Box. "You don't age."

"I do too," Vespa said, her tone steadying. "Just not as fast as humans."

Emma resisted the urge to roll her eyes. "Where *are* we going?"

"Well, this world prohibits you and Vespa from reaching the extent of your magical abilities," Aldrich said. "Perhaps you can ask the box to take us someplace where that isn't the case."

A world with more magic. Her first thought was to recoil. She'd been around so much magic throughout her lifetime, and most of her experiences were not good ones, but she eyed the professor's liquor cabinet, and for what seemed like the hundredth time that week, she tried to reach out to the bottles resting inside. There was a faint impression that they were there, but nothing about how to use them or what she could make with them. She yearned to take the lessons she'd learned from Mia and master her craft.

The device sat on the table. It was easier to imagine it being alive now that the yellow lights on its surface pulsed in a slow, steady rhythm. Like breathing. Despite her reservations, Emma understood she could never discover the life she wanted without taking some risks.

"You're right. When I set out on this journey, it was to become a bartender. What I need is a *place* where I can develop my talents to their fullest potential." She turned to Demon Box. "Could you bring us somewhere like that?"

The box's glow shifted subtly. *All right, so let's get something straight. I can't just pull down a directory of every possible world that exists within the multiverse and take you there. I don't have that kind of data storage, and I'm not a bloody genie. What I can do is give it a go based on where I've already been, but I can't guarantee anything.*

"Well, I suppose that's a start. Part of this adventure is venturing into the unknown."

The larger the difference from a world we've already visited, the more difficult it will be for me to control the outcome.

This seemed reasonable to Emma, but she repeated the warning to Aldrich to be sure.

"Yes, well, that makes sense," he said. "The more consequential the change, the more variables are thrown into question. I should have considered implementing that sort of guidance system when I built the device, but I had no idea at the time if it would even work." He lifted his thumb and forefinger to his chin. "Come to think of it, I don't know how I'd make that happen. Perhaps that's something you and . . . Demon Box . . . can do to help me with my research."

Emma paused for a second. "So, since I'm not the power source, I don't need to be the one to ask Demon Box where to go. It could take instruction from any of us. Right?"

Pfft. I'm not taking any orders from that windbag. Demon Box huffed.

Emma lifted a hand to her mouth to contain a laugh.

I'd maybe consider a request from the fairy, but I was stuck in the dark for six years because of that bloke.

That hardly seemed fair. Emma wasn't sure if it was possible, but she tried to conceal the thought from the device. Aldrich hadn't known Demon Box was sentient. How could he? Hell, she didn't even know *how* the device was conscious at all. And the professor had been just as stuck as it had been.

But she didn't think this was the time to bring that detail up.

"I suppose that should be the case," Aldrich said, oblivious to what Demon Box had said. "Although, we couldn't hear it if it had any sort of response. Maybe it prefers to respond to someone it can speak to directly?"

Emma nodded. "That's what it said. It prefers to work with me."

That's a rather loose interpretation of what I said. Go ahead, really let him have it.

Aldrich pursed his lips. Emma swallowed.

I most certainly will not! she thought. *If it weren't for him, you wouldn't even exist.*

Oh, I see how it is, Demon Box quipped. *You're taking his side. Fine, you fleshy beings stick together then. Walking around like you're really something, just because you've got mouths and hands. Just remember which of us can open interdimensional tunnels.*

I am not going to be the one to tell him that his own creation doesn't like him, thought Emma.

Well, don't be surprised if he shoves you in the closet when he's done with you.

"It's nothing personal," Emma said to Aldrich reassuringly.

Hmph, Demon Box grunted.

"Well, you talk to it then. I'm going to finish securing these final few components then I'll start to make preparations. We leave in an hour."

"That will give me enough time to finish my book!" Vespa exclaimed.

The hour passed in a flash. Emma spent most of that time perusing Aldrich's liquor cabinet. She'd enjoyed studying with Mia at The Dragon and until now had seen no point in browsing a cupboard full of bottles that were foreign to her without someone to guide her. But now that she'd had a bit more knowledge, she used the time to inspect what he had on hand.

Recalling Aldrich's bar at the cottage in her own world, Emma wasn't surprised at the selection. It seemed anywhere the professor went, he was well stocked.

She spotted the bourbon bottles straight away. Aldrich, obviously not content with only one, had several from different distilleries.

A few bottles had already been opened. Emma took the corks out of two then quickly decided that wasn't the best decision. Each of them smelled sour and moldy. It shouldn't have surprised her, since they'd likely been open for at least as long as Aldrich had been on her world. But she'd gotten used to being able to tell if a bottle had gone bad just by reaching out to them. Without that ability, she had to use her other senses.

Maybe practice without the use of magic would be helpful, she thought.

She took the spoiled bottles and set them on Aldrich's counter. They'd have to be poured out, but she wouldn't be the one to do it. She contemplated bringing the bottles with her. If they went to a world with magic, she'd perhaps be able to restore them, but it hardly seemed worth the effort.

There were other bottles of liquor besides the bourbon. Some she recognized from her own world: whiskey, gin, vodka; and some Mia had introduced to her: tequila and rum, among others. There was still so much she could learn in this world.

But she also knew she couldn't stay here.

Everyone in this world feels empty.

It wasn't just the drinks. Emma didn't need Vespa's propensity to sense the needs of others. It was palpable in the air as much as the scent of spring danced along the ocean breeze. She could sense it on Aldrich. As magical as this version of Cuanmore felt, the city seemed to suck the life out of its people. Despite Aldrich's insistence, she believed this world possessed a type of magic. Perhaps it took on a different form than what she or Vespa could sense, but it was surely there. And all magic came with a price.

She wasn't sure she could define its toll, but everyone was so tired. Not in the same way as the men who left the fields after a hard day's work, but in a way that demanded the very essence of who they were.

Whatever it was, she couldn't wait to escape it.

"All right, let's get moving," Aldrich said, exiting the bedroom. Besides fresh clothing, he had showered and tidied the edges of his beard. He'd even tamed the wild tufts of hair on his head. "It would be best if we arrived before it gets dark."

"You ready, Demon Box?" Even though the device could read her thoughts, she thought it best to speak out loud to keep both the professor and Vespa informed of what exactly she was saying to the thing. She didn't want any misinterpretations like there had been the first time.

A world full of magic then?

"Yes, I'd like to go to a world where my magic can reach its full potential."

I'll do my best.

World Four

Unfriendly Welcome

Chapter Twenty-Two

The dirt streets of Cuanmore crunched beneath Emma's feet as they landed with a slight hop.

A cloudy sky stretched above them, cast in hues of orange, red, and violet as strands of the sunset tried their best to pierce through the storm rolling in.

Gone were the skyscrapers, cars, and buses, replaced with cottages and quaint buildings that were much closer to resembling those in Emma's world. She hadn't been in Cuanmore long enough to be able to spot any minor differences that would separate this place from her own world. But it had to be close.

If they were going to continue this research journey, they would need some sort of naming system so they could keep them all straight—if Aldrich didn't already have one.

Should she name them after prominent features of what the world contained? She'd have to consult Aldrich later and see what sort of system he'd devised. For now, to keep things simple and straight in her mind, she decided to number them.

Emma inhaled deeply. *Let's see what World Four has to offer.*

She allowed the essence of this fourth world to fill her lungs and rejuvenate her being. The spring air was cool and crisp and punctuated by all the smells that carried in the air before a good Hibernian rain. Gone was any trace of the street traffic and garbage that lined the hard stone streets of Aldrich's world. After a week in the drudge of that city, she'd almost forgotten how clear the air could be.

She wondered how many worlds were filled with those cities and how many were more like hers? Though, at first glance, this very well could have been her world. The village that lay before them was similar in layout and style.

Two youths stood before them with mouths agape—a pair of boys carrying sticks and dressed in sullied clothes, as though they had spent the day in the field with their fathers and were spending their last precious daylight hours playing.

What had they thought of three people stepping out of thin air and onto the road? Emma wasn't sure how much control Demon Box had over the space on which they landed, but the fact that they hadn't exited three stories above the ground was a testament that the device had at least some say on their exit point. It would be best if they could exit in a place where there were no witnesses, but perhaps that was asking for a level of insight the machine couldn't possess.

Regardless, stepping into a world in this way could be dangerous, especially if it were one like hers where magic was outlawed.

The lads took off in a panicked sprint, kicking up dust and pebbles behind them. Thankfully, they were young enough that any reports of three people appearing from midair were likely to be dismissed as imagination.

Though, if this wasn't her world, perhaps they weren't as opposed to the use of magic here. There was no telling, according to what Aldrich and Maggie had suggested, what iterations of reality they might find.

They followed the same path as the boys toward the heart of the village. The buildings on either side of the main street bore a passing resemblance to the world she'd left behind. Emma recognized some of the markets, now winding down for the evening, as well as The Cursed Dragon a few streets over. So far, both the Dragon and O'Sullivan's had been a constant in each of the worlds they'd visited, and it appeared this world was no exception.

"This could be home," she thought out loud. People were staring in their direction . . . at her. But that could have been her imagination.

"The odds are extremely unlikely," Aldrich said. "Unless you directed Demon Box to take us there."

"Maybe that's all it's capable of doing under my influence," she said. "Traveling between a handful of worlds?" Her heart sank at the prospect of that. She could be stuck in either a world where she'd likely never outrun her past, or one with all the technological marvels she could imagine without access to her magic.

Don't be daft. Demon Box piped up. *I was spinning this lunatic to other realities long before you came along.*

"This isn't our world," Vespa whispered. The fairy's wings were visible behind her and slowly pulsed, as though trying to stretch and breathe.

Emma clenched her jaw. Vespa really shouldn't have her wings out in the open in an unfamiliar world. Who knew what the people of this world thought of fairies? If they had them at all.

Emma was about to say something about putting her wings away, but Vespa turned to her with wild eyes. "Can you feel that?"

Her chastisement momentarily forgotten, Emma tried to determine what the fairy meant. There was a chill in the air— winter's bite that lingered into the beginnings of spring, but that was nothing unusual.

Emma's hand went to her dagger even before she realized why. The street before them, which led through the village, held a good dozen people. All of them had their eyes fixed on the newly arrived trio, but Emma was certain none of them had seen the portal. Yet their stares bore a mix of both anger and fear.

"Hide your wings," she said through gritted teeth. It was too late to do any good, as they had already been seen, but even as Emma said the words, Vespa's wings flickered, faded slightly, and reappeared at full strength before creating a final shimmer and disappearing completely.

Vespa inhaled sharply.

More villagers had made their way into the streets, but upon seeing Emma, some hurried away, and others stood, staring, as though frozen in time.

"I don't feel anything," Aldrich said, somehow oblivious to the attention they'd garnered. "There might be a bit more humidity in the air, but . . ."

Then it hit Emma all at once. Like an electrical current surging through her veins and pressing against each of her muscles until they twitched. The sensation of magic coursed through her, filling her so thoroughly that she was sure it would burst out of her pores.

She let out a gasp, interrupting the professor's train of thought, and did her best to stifle it, lest waves of uncontrolled magic escape through her parted lips. The crystals within Demon Box were essentially screaming at her for her magic. It was ten times as powerful as any call she'd felt before, and she'd already had a tough time resisting them in her own world. This was overwhelming, tugging at her from everywhere all at once.

Whoa! Easy there! Demon Box was shouting, its voice breaking through the war raging within her. *The Doc just fixed me! Keep that up and you'll fry my circuits! I might be fixed, but you still can't reactivate these crystals until they've cooled.*

The interruption was enough of a distraction for her to grab the reins of her mind and keep the overwhelm at bay. She used the same technique as she did when on the hunt. If she could escape into her true self, then she could fend off any other stimuli.

Sorry. She directed the apology with her mind rather than speaking it out loud. *The crystals . . . they're practically clawing at my insides. It's like they're desperate to pull any magic they can out of me.*

It may feel that way, but trust me, nothing good will come of it. Now leave me be. I must recharge if I'm to be of any use to you later. The machine's glow darkened, returning to its dormant, black glass state. With it, the call of the crystals returned to a dull hum.

She sucked in a breath as she returned to her senses, realizing nobody had replied to Aldrich. "No, it's not humidity. Professor, there's . . ."

"There's so much magic here!" Vespa finished Emma's sentence, her eyes bugging from her skull. It was clear that she too was struggling to contain it. "I'm sure I will adjust." She swallowed. "As I did in your world. But . . . there is . . . so much of it! If your world was a magical desert, this world is like being thrown into the middle of a vast ocean with the force of a hurricane hovering overhead."

Emma was sure she'd be able to identify every mug of ale that rested within the village and that she could've caused them all to burst from their containers at the same time with little effort. It was such a powerful pull that she feared they might do so on their own, anyway. It was as though the liquids could sense her as much as she could sense them. The same way Demon Box had felt her pull without her trying to channel power into it.

She steadied her breath to gain her bearings. It wasn't just the mugs in the taverns, the bottles on the shelves behind the bars, or the wine being stored in cold storage basements throughout the village. She could also sense . . . people . . .

Emma shuddered as she realized that it was the blood of anyone who'd had so much as a sip of drink.

"It's her!" A voice echoed through the streets before screams erupted from several people who had previously stopped to stare. Others took off, much like the lads had upon their arrival. Doors slammed up and down the street, punctuated by warnings to anyone else who was encountered along the way.

Emma could only make out staccato-pulsed words in the mayhem.

"She's here."
"Get inside."
"Witch."
"Queen."

A bushel of apples rolled along the middle of the street toward Emma, Aldrich, and Vespa, dropped by someone in a moment of panic. One rolled down the path and stopped right in front of Emma. It sat upright as though someone had intentionally placed it there, rather than it having rolled by chance. In less than thirty seconds, the street had cleared, leaving the three alone once again.

"What the bloody blazes is happening?" Aldrich's words disappeared into the night.

"Where have you taken us?" Emma directed her demand to Demon Box, but it remained quiet. She reminded herself that it likely didn't know any more answers than the rest of them.

In a world so saturated in magic, what could have frightened the villagers off in such a manner? A fairy's wings would be concerning, even in her world, but nothing she'd ever known anyone to run in terror from.

"Well, I suppose we should find a place for the night," said Aldrich. "But after that welcome, I don't have my hopes higher than a hayloft. It may be best to assess our situation in the morning."

They made their way through the now quiet streets. Lights in homes had been extinguished, even at this early hour, and Emma could swear she saw curtains pulled back far enough for sets of eyes to peek through. She could *sense* the liquor flowing through at least a dozen people, perhaps more, crouched in O'Sullivan's. But the lights were off, and no music danced from its interior.

Lengthening shadows warned of the rapidly approaching dusk, and Emma couldn't help but feel a sense of unease at what might await them when night fell.

"Is this another world at war with fairy folk?" Emma asked. "Why is everyone hiding?"

Before Vespa could respond, another voice spoke behind them.

"You shouldn't have come here."

Emma recognized the voice immediately. "Liam?" She barely managed to get the word out before everything went dark.

An Old Friend

Chapter Twenty-Three

The damp and musty smell of the sack thrown over her head left little doubt about what had happened. It was a common tactic against witches to prevent them from using any enchantments that required looking at their victim.

"Unhand me!" Aldrich demanded.

Vespa's cries echoed, and Emma recognized the click of iron shackles.

Emma cursed herself for allowing the flow of magic to distract her. From what she could tell, there were at least five Hunters surrounding them. By her count, two held her, and there would have been one each for Vespa and Aldrich. Liam would be thorough, and she expected there were more than a half dozen. Still, she struggled to reach for her blade but found her arms had been restrained by more than just men. Body cuffs had encapsulated her torso and legs and the magic that had been so invasive only moments before was absent, leaving an empty void that was far hollower than she'd have ever believed possible. She'd used the very apparatus herself, against some of the most feared witches who had been especially heinous in their acts. But it wasn't something that would have been used on someone for reverting vinegar back to wine.

"What the bloody hell, Liam? Why are you doing this?"

Anger coursed through her, and she tightened her fists, fighting against the metal clasps held tight against her.

Suddenly, Emma could see again as the hood of the bag was pulled down. It had likely been more for show than fear of her turning them to stone with her stare. The bastard was making a spectacle out of her.

Liam stood before her—at least a version of him. This man held many of Liam's familiar features but was rougher, as though he'd been through hell and back and had aged an additional decade in the process. He possessed a shadow of a beard unshaved for several days, crow's feet clawed around the corners of his eyes, bags darkened his cheeks, and a tinge of premature gray salted his otherwise black hair. The torchlights from his Hunters only amplified the effects.

A spark of knowledge appeared in his eyes—a glint of recognition—before his nose turned up in disgust. "Do not speak my name, witch." He all but spat the words.

Despite knowing this wasn't the man she'd grown up with, the man she'd adored for the past dozen or so years of her life, the remark still stung. He may as well have slapped her with the back side of his hand.

And though this man was not her Liam, she heard the words come out of her mouth before she could stop them. "It's me! We're best friends . . . maybe more . . ."

The words caught even her off guard, a topic they had silently agreed never to broach. But seeing him here, she couldn't help but realize how much she'd missed him. How much it had pained her that she may never see *her* Liam again.

Gasps echoed off the surrounding shops, tearing her from her thoughts, and it was only then that she realized a small crowd had gathered. Dozens of men and women had trickled out of their homes and shops and lined the edges of the streets.

Murmurs wound their way through the crowd, many colored with anger, some tinged with fear.

Liam shook his head, a fiery anger behind his eyes. "You do not know me and have never known me."

The words sunk deep and burned in her chest. This Liam didn't know nor care that his words stung. She straightened her shoulders to keep from wincing and held his steely gaze.

"Do not believe this witch's lies!" Liam yelled over to the crowd. "She means to deceive you with her silver tongue. But fear not. Her spells cannot enchant you as long as she's held by iron."

Liam's dark eyes studied her, calculating. Behind them was burning hatred that carried a heavy burden of pain. A level of disgust she'd only seen when they encountered the evilest beings. What had the Emma of this world done to deserve such ire?

"You will no longer be able to terrorize this kingdom, witch! You will be transported to London where you will be tried and executed for your crimes of witchcraft, heresy, and treason against the true and rightful king of Lancastria. You may call yourself queen, but your reign of terror has ended."

A series of cheers erupted from the crowd.

Emma's mouth moved as she tried to piece together the meaning behind his words.

You may call yourself queen.

"What do you want us to do with these two?" A soldier stood over Aldrich and Vespa who were both now kneeling in the dirt. Their arms had also been bound in iron, their legs with rope. They did not have the full body iron shackle around them as Emma did, though. It was clear Liam viewed Emma as the greatest threat.

"We'll bring them as well. Either they will be found to

have been placed under a compulsion spell and released, or they'll be tried as her accomplices."

"Liam," Emma pleaded. "I promise you, I am not the woman you seek."

"You keep saying my name as though you know me," Liam barked, a little louder than necessary. His gaze wandered the crowd instead of staying on her. These words were meant for them. He reached inside his tunic and pulled out the medallion. It bore the same sigil as the one the Liam of her world wore—its mark meant to ward against any magical enchantments. He held it up to the crowd, sporting a trophy. "Your tricks may have worked on your two companions but not on me. I am immune to your power."

Emma had to refrain from rolling her eyes. Even if she had the ability to do something useful, displaying the medallion was for show—no witch would be able to cast magic through the iron bonds he'd placed on her.

Still her thoughts scrambled for a way to reach him.

"I know things!" she blurted. Emma wasn't sure what she was trying to accomplish, but her mind could not seem to reconcile that this Liam did not know her. "Things only someone close to you would know!"

"You expect that to impress me?"

"Your brother died when a nightfang attacked our camp when we were kids. I sucked the venom from your leg myself when you were struck while trying to save him."

Liam's eyebrow lifted. Likely, he thought she was a madwoman. Emma knew she would have believed so if the events of the past few days hadn't transpired as they had.

He stepped forward and lifted his leg onto a crate that stood on the edge of the street. "This leg?" he asked as he pulled a pant leg up, revealing a finely crafted shaft of wood.

"Like all witches, your tales are full of half-truths and

downright lies. I did lose my brother to a nightfang. That was also the day I swore I'd rid Lancastria of magic. But there was nobody there to tend to me. This leg serves as a reminder that I alone am the decider of my fate."

Seeing the wood where his leg should have been finally quelled the storm within her. In this world, for some reason, she had not been there that day to save his leg. But where did that leave her?

"Your reign of terror across this kingdom has come to an end, witch," Liam continued. "And as long as you are held in iron, your devil words carry no sway. Lock her up. We leave in the morning."

An Unlikely Ally

Chapter Twenty-Four

An angry night sky stretched above Emma and her iron cage. She did what she could to rub the strain from her muscles within its small confines. The guards had removed her body cuff once she was securely inside as the iron of the cage sufficed to keep magic users impotent. All she could do was crouch at the bottom of the structure and watch as the moonlight struggled in a losing battle to push its way through the clouds above. Her other option was to prop herself against a wrought-iron bench that had been mounted to the cage's interior. Either way, comfort wouldn't find her this night.

Perhaps not ever again.

What madness had her double conjured? Emma had been on enough witch hunts to know that this much effort wasn't spent on someone who had altered a few pints of ale. The kingdom was planning on making a spectacle of her, and thus her crimes against it must have been great.

She was set up in a cage wagon close to a set of stables at the edge of town. Close enough to the revelry to hear the villagers continue to celebrate her capture, but even closer to Liam's dozen or so horses and the nauseating smell of their dung.

Two guards had been stationed to watch over her. Even

without access to her ability, she could smell the ale seeping through their pores.

Stupid. Emma thought.

It was all too common within the guard, though. Those who weren't qualified to hunt, but got stuck keeping watch of the home base, were notorious for imbibing too much both on and off their shifts. *That* at least hadn't changed from her own world.

For most witches, warlocks, and sorcerers, the iron cage would be enough of a deterrent, so it rarely mattered. But every once in a while, someone had help from the outside. That was truly what the guard was stationed for.

But Emma held no such advantage.

Lightning flashed overhead, highlighting the bulbous clouds that had masked the stars and now covered the moon. Lanterns flickered from within the stables, their flames shaking in the wind. Wisps of more lanterns traveled across the village square as the townsfolk made their way between The Cursed Dragon and O'Sullivan's Pub.

Their shouts echoed through the crisp evening, punching through the crash of waves slamming into rocks on the nearby shore.

Much like the guards who swayed several meters from her prison, she didn't need to touch her magic to know that most of the townsfolk had imbibed far more than was reasonable.

Fools. There were certain rules that she'd followed as a Hunter, and one of them was to never let her guard down with an excess of drink. Not when there was still a threat of magic.

But they believe they've caught the threat.

Which meant they were out celebrating, when really, if the Emma of World Four was as deadly as they believed, it was very possible they were all making a huge mistake.

The partying continued long into the night. Emma found

herself drifting off to sleep, only to be woken up by some drunk rattling at the bars of her cage with a stick.

"Not so scary now, are ya, witch?" Two young men stood outside her cage; they were barely of age. They staggered and slurred their words like two lost spirits in a whiskey cellar.

Both boys had shaggy, cropped hair. One had a sprinkling of facial hair struggling to make an appearance along his jawline. It would be a couple of years before it filled out. The second lad's baby face wouldn't see a razor any time soon.

"Poke her with the stick, Sam." The lad was trying to keep his voice lowered, in the way that a drunk often does. Harsh on the delivery, but there was no actual decrease in volume.

"I'm not going to poke her, you nitwit!" Sam protested.

"Why not? She's caged in iron. She can't hurt you while she's in there."

"If you want to poke her, you do it yourself!"

"What? Are ya too scared?"

Sam scoffed. "I'm no more afraid than you are!"

The second lad found a hefty stick lying on the ground nearby and gripped it in the self-assured way that a drunkard would pick up a sword. "Come on, she's poked at us enough times. Time to see what she can do without the use of her magic."

It only then occurred to her that the guards were nowhere to be seen. Either they reasoned they were missing out on the celebrations at the pub, or they thought they'd let these two have their bit of fun.

"Markus, don't! She's still dangerous. What if she gets out? Or pulls you in?"

Emma rolled her eyes. She'd had enough of the exchange. "Oh, please," she said. "What do you think I'm going to do? Eat you?"

Sam let out a gasp, revealing that it was exactly what he

had expected. But he caught himself and tried to pass it off as a yawn.

"You d-don't . . . You don't scare me, Witch Queen." Sam spat as an exclamation point on his declaration. But his eyes jerked from the stable to the bushes, as though waiting to be ambushed. He wiped his palm on his trousers.

"You can quit calling her that," said Markus. "She's captured now. Long live King Leopold!"

The entire line of conversation had taken a turn from insults to bizarre revelations about this world. She was in no position to question the lads about what exactly they meant, but pieces were falling into place.

Leopold was King Brampton's son. At least in her world. Something here must have happened to the man she knew as king.

And she'd declared herself . . . Queen? Or was that a nickname the populace had derived for her?

Emma shuddered. It was a bizarre twist, and she wasn't sure if she wanted to find out what it all meant.

Just as Emma had the thought, and just as Markus appeared brave enough to lance her with the stick he'd procured, a shadow crossed between the torchlight and her cell, casting an elongated shadow over Sam and his friend as well as her cage. A silhouette rose before them—an impossibly tall, towering figure.

"You might not be afraid of her . . . but you should definitely be afraid of me."

Reflections

Chapter Twenty-Five

It was like staring into a mirror. Was there anything one could do to prepare for seeing another version of themselves? Emma didn't think so.

She trembled. This strange apparition was, for all intents and purposes, her.

Of course, it wasn't a perfect reflection. This Emma wore a set of black robes, making her all but invisible in the darkness of night. Her lantern illuminated the space around her as she spoke with dramatic effect, reflecting the pale skin of her face. Stark black hair poured out the sides of her dark hood and carried only a hint of Emma's own red.

The youths scrambled off with a yelp, their feet kicking up dirt, tripping over themselves to get away.

The witch version of Emma squinted as she peered into the cage, into Emma's eyes, likely making the same observations Emma had a moment before.

What sort of life had this version of herself led up until now? What sort of assessments was she making about *her*?

"So, the rumors are true." Emma heard her own voice come out of the witch's mouth as the woman pulled back her hood and let her dark hair fall around her shoulders. "What are you, dark spirit? What do I call a specter who bears my own face?"

Dark spirit. Yes, of course. In a world so heavily imbued with magic, what else could another version of herself be except a spirit or magical entity?

But how did one answer that question? Her mind raced for how she would react if she were on the other side. Of course, it might not have mattered. As a Hunter of the Cursed, her reaction would have been the complete opposite from one who had embraced magic so fully as to call herself "Witch Queen." If Emma had come across a doppelgänger or shapeshifter in her world, she'd leave the mirror of herself locked in iron and help Liam haul her to London.

However, while Emma might have shared her face with this woman, they did not share a past. At some point, *this* version of herself ended up embracing magic, rather than fighting it. If she truly was a feared witch in this world, perhaps it lay in Emma's best interest to appeal to her superstitions.

First, she had to get the witch to unlock the cage.

"My name is Emma." Let the witch make of that what she would.

The witch's mouth fell open, and she glanced around sharply as though fearful someone might have overheard.

"How did you learn my true name?" she snapped. A whiff of blue magic sparked at her fingertips, but her eyes widened again, and it disappeared just as quickly. Emma could only imagine the woman realized it might be in her best interest to not cast magic on a potentially powerful spirit.

But Emma had to work hard to mask her own surprise. Whatever blue flame her twin had been about to invoke, it was definitely a power Emma was unable to command. Instead of pointing that out, she simply smirked. "I have my ways."

"Please, spirit, address me as Ravenna." She glanced

around again. "I have kept my identity secret. There are few know who I truly am."

Emma nodded. Ravenna was an interesting choice of name. But she wasn't about to reveal anything that might jeopardize getting Ravenna to help her. She needed to figure a way out of this mess, to find out where Vespa and the professor had been taken, then disappear until Demon Box could take them elsewhere.

"What *are* you?" Ravenna raised an eyebrow.

Emma held her tongue.

Ravenna studied her double apprehensively, searching for her own answer. "Banshees are said to roam the cliffs of Hibernia, but I never thought I'd encounter one. Tell me then, are you here to forewarn of my death?"

Banshee. Of course.

Being fae-creatures associated with death, banshees were said to appear to people as a warning. If they appeared in the person's own form, it was always a bad omen.

Good, this could work to my benefit.

She had many questions for Ravenna, but none of them mattered as much as getting free of her cage and finding her friends—and hopefully getting off this world.

She had two options. Play along or tell Ravenna the truth.

Emma wrestled with how much she believed she could trust herself. As difficult as it was to wrap her brain around, Ravenna was not Emma. The townsfolk here downright feared her. Even Liam had held up his guard around her.

The witch might see her as a threat and decide to end her right there. Or worse, what if this version of herself could pull the truth from her using magic as the fairies had in World Two? Ravenna could decide that declaring herself queen of one world wasn't enough and force her to reveal how to travel between other worlds. If Emma could do it with her limited ability, Ravenna would certainly have the capability.

Other worlds . . .

That gave Emma an idea. If this plan worked, not only would she be able to help herself and her friends, but she could save this world from her other self.

First, she had to convince Ravenna that she was indeed a banshee as she feared.

"Can you get me out of here?" Emma intentionally avoided answering Ravenna's question. It's what any fae creature would have done, after all. "The villagers of this place took me by surprise and locked me in iron."

A smirk crossed Ravenna's mouth as she studied her doppelgänger. She raised a thumb to the edge of her chin. "And they did so thinking you were me. Perhaps this works in my favor. With you locked away, it perhaps means I've escaped my fate."

Emma resisted reacting. She'd worked her way out of situations worse than this before, and it all hinged on how confidently and calmly she could handle herself. But then again, this was *herself* she was dealing with.

"Do you really want to take that chance?" Emma put a subtle sneer behind her voice. "I alone have the power to spare you from your fate. If I'm trapped in this box, my hands are literally tied."

Emma watched her own face still. Watched herself considering her options, weighing the value of her own words.

She thought about how she would react if the roles were reversed. If it was her on the other side of the cage wall, talking to her twin, trying to decipher whether her double was trying to deceive her or not.

What would she be able to tell herself that she'd believe?

Was there anything she could say? Was there enough of an overlap in Ravenna's past and her own to draw from?

"It was Liam Connor who locked me in here." Emma held her breath. There was every possibility that Liam had been truthful and merely been assigned the hunt for Ravenna, the same as any other. But Emma liked her odds, so she rolled the dice. "Not only that, he claimed not to know you. Denied he'd ever been part of your life in front of all of Cuanmore. The wound you dealt him must have cut deep."

Ravenna flinched. Her blade had struck true. While Emma's version of Liam allowed her to go through the portal, despite her crimes, this Liam had no such grace for Ravenna.

Perhaps he never felt the way her Liam had felt for *her*.

A sharp pain twisted in Emma's chest as a blade of realization landed and pierced through her heart. She had to stop herself from releasing a gasp as waves of understanding came crashing down on her.

Oh, Liam.

Liam, *her* Liam, had traveled to the edge of the kingdom—not to hunt her down and lock her in an iron cage—but to ensure she was okay. And when the truth was revealed, he showed her he cared in one of the most meaningful ways he knew how.

He had let her go.

She forced herself not to lose her grip on what was at stake in the present, but for a fleeting moment it all disappeared, and she was free falling with nothing around her for support.

Instead of pursuing her arrest, Liam had released her to an unknown fate, but it was a better chance than what would have been waiting for her in London. Emma dampened the shock of her own revelation as Ravenna cringed.

Regardless of the feelings it stirred in her, Emma had clearly pushed the right buttons.

"My only crime was being born *Cursed*." Ravenna spat the word with more venom than Emma believed herself to have ever possessed. "And Liam believed the kingdom's lies enough to try and see me slain for that and that alone. How could I let that stand? How could I not take up arms and protect myself? Liam can choke on his own blood. If he's the fiend who did this to you, don't worry, spirit—you and I will have our revenge."

Ravenna held up a set of keys. They were dull, but they still reflected light from the lanterns posted nearby. Emma didn't want to ask how she'd obtained them.

She swallowed. Perhaps the guards hadn't snuck off for a pint after all.

Emma took a steadying breath as her counterpart inserted the key into the cage door and the lock clicked open. As it opened, Emma startled for a moment but held her composure. Magic rushed into the cage and enveloped her.

How would her life look if her world had been filled with this much magic? What if her Liam had sought to destroy her instead of allowing her to flee—would she seek vengeance as well?

"All right, banshee, tell me, what must I do to avoid my fatal fate?"

Emma had to think fast. But first she needed to get the professor and Vespa.

"Liam's also captured a fairy and a sorcerer," she said. "We need to set them free as well, or our mission will fail."

"A fairy?" Ravenna cocked her head. "Who knew Liam could be so cunning?"

"We were unprepared," Emma repeated. "But this sorcerer has a device that will protect you. With the four of us working together, we'll be unstoppable, and you'll escape your fate."

Emma held her breath. This felt like the longest of long shots.

Ravenna stepped back from the door of the cage, leaving it open just a crack. Her fingers fidgeted. Emma recognized the subtle movement. It was the same sequence she would have performed over top of her blades if she were untrusting of someone. Except Ravenna appeared to be powerful enough to not need the blades.

Emma swallowed and tried not to think of the magic her alter ego might have at her disposal.

It took a moment, but Ravenna's fingers did stop. "Okay. Let's do this. But I warn you, spirit, no tricks. If I sense you're up to something, I won't hesitate to use every ounce of my magic to rain fury upon your head. If that happens, you'll wish for whatever tortures Liam and Lancastria would have performed on you."

A Different Life

Chapter Twenty-Six

Emma slipped into the night through the back streets of Cuanmore along with her counterpart from World Four.

The Witch Queen.

Her senses hadn't stopped tingling since she'd departed her prison, and she had to resist answering the calls of the ale, wine, and spirits that flowed freely throughout the village. There was hardly a grown man or woman awake who didn't have a hefty amount of alcohol pulsing through their veins, and there was no shortage of liquor being carried about or poured at the town's two taverns.

Emma hadn't seen where Aldrich and Vespa were being held, but she knew where the second set of cage wagons would be parked—on the backside of The Cursed Dragon.

Wet dirt squelched and sunk beneath their feet, leaving deep impressions. It must have rained while she dozed off in the cage.

They carried no lantern and stuck to the alleys and lesser traveled roads. Most of the townsfolk were at one of the two pubs, so it wasn't as difficult as it might have been on another night.

Emma still couldn't get over how strange it was to watch herself skulk along the village streets. Despite what Liam had said to the contrary, Ravenna's movements betrayed her training. She had served as a Hunter—at least for a time—and Liam had bloody well known this woman.

"I must ask you something," Emma whispered as they assessed their next move.

"What is it, spirit?" Ravenna replied.

"How long have you known?"

Ravenna turned to her with a puzzled look. "Known what?"

"That you possessed magic. When did you first discover it?"

Ravenna studied her. "If you *are* indeed a banshee, I can only assume you already know. If you wish to test me in order to spare my life, I'll answer your questions. I know secrets are seldom hidden from the spirit realm." Her face, which until now had mostly shown as much emotional expression as a stone, softened. "In a way, I suppose I've always known. Though I kept it hidden."

"And what of Liam?" Emma ventured. "He wasn't so understanding?"

"Liam is the man the kingdom raised him to be. Hate and all."

Even in Emma's own world, Liam's dedication to his duty reigned supreme. But to turn so vehemently against Ravenna . . . She supposed there had always been the chance he'd react in the way his position demanded.

She thought about Liam's wooden leg. "Do you remember the nightfang attack on the village where Liam's brother stayed? Were you there the night it happened?"

The daggers in Ravenna's glare were enough to send her own skin crawling. Did she ever look that way when annoyed? No wonder the village had been terrified.

"You know right well I wasn't, spirit."

Emma darkened her voice as best she could, lowering it to a growl. "It doesn't matter what I know. I want to hear your account."

The venom didn't leave Ravenna's glare, but she answered. "That was the day I discovered this gift," she said through gritted teeth. "If that man hadn't been so pigheaded, I would have been there. Even if I'd been unable to save Liam's brother, perhaps I could have saved his leg."

It would have done more than that, Emma thought. She realized saving his leg that day had been the bond that had cemented their friendship.

"I was glad for it," Ravenna continued. "Glad that after he tried to capture me, he lost his leg instead. Glad that the night-fang brought havoc and destruction down on their encampment. I knew that day this was the order of things. The king had started the war on magic. I was going to end it. If it they wanted a fight, they'd see what magic could do at its full potential."

Full potential. The words she'd spoken to Demon Box came crashing down over her head and she momentarily fought to breathe.

This was what would become of her possessing magic? Was this the inevitable fight between mortals and magic users? She'd seen it on varying levels in three worlds now. In fact, the only world she hadn't seen it in was the one with no magic at all.

She steadied her breath, slowed her heart rate. If Ravenna possessed the fullest potential of her magic . . . perhaps it *was* a curse after all. She didn't want to believe it, yet the evidence stood before her and bore her own face.

"So you've taken it upon yourself to fight back against the mortals?"

"I didn't start this war." Ravenna's voice hardened. Any

vulnerability that had been there disappeared as she strengthened her resolve. "Why should I be the one who hides?"

And there was the difference between the two of them. Where Emma had decided to remove herself from the rest of the kingdom, to disappear and live a simple life, Ravenna chose to stand up and fight back.

"It would be an easier life," Emma suggested. "Why not become a bartender? Use your magic to do something less destructive."

Ravenna was partially illuminated by a lantern hung from the building above them. Emma worried for a moment that if someone were to walk by, their cover would be revealed. But her counterpart didn't seem to share her concern.

"Do you know how many magic users the kingdom has killed?" she hissed. "Do you know how many *I* have killed?"

Emma knew—at least, she knew how many she had killed in her own world. More than she wanted to think of.

"They had no right to take me in as a child! They could have let me die in my sleep, and I would have been better off. But instead, they brainwashed me—turned me into this... this monster! I will not sit idle while they hunt me! While they rob others of a full life in order to satisfy their bigotry. This injustice must stop, and they will not listen to reason."

Emma swallowed. She couldn't say the same thoughts hadn't raced through her head. But she knew not all humans were to blame for the actions of the king's guard. "How many innocents will die because you seek vengeance?"

Witch Emma snorted. "Innocent? The mortal who locked you up once had feelings for me. He turned on me the second he discovered magic coursed through my veins. Don't think any of these mortals wouldn't do the same."

The witch moved on, her point made, and it was clear she

was finished speaking on the subject. Emma knew herself well enough to know that if she tried to push further, all hope of rescuing her friends would be lost.

The Rescue

Chapter Twenty-Seven

As if they were spirits, Emma and Ravenna danced toward The Cursed Dragon under the shadows of night.

Even at this late hour, the Hunters would still be drinking, and those townsfolk still standing would be trying to keep up. By this point, the wiser among them would have given up on drinking but refused to go home, afraid they'd miss a moment of the celebration.

Emma crouched next to Ravenna as they arrived, out of sight from the backside of the pub. Through the darkness, Emma couldn't make out the cages that held her friends, but lantern light reflected off the faces of guards who stood protecting their captives.

These guards were completely sober—Emma couldn't detect any alcohol in their systems. Being on duty so close to the Dragon meant they were closer to Liam, who was likely inside. Even though he was no doubt enjoying the evening, he'd have their heads if he caught them drinking on the job. Close proximity meant a better chance of him catching them if they did.

"Wait here, spirit," Ravenna whispered then disappeared before Emma could argue.

One by one, the guards' lanterns winked out. There was

no sound of struggle, no cry for help. They simply vanished, leaving the back alley in complete darkness.

Ravenna appeared again at Emma's side.

"What did you do with them?" Emma asked, trying to keep the horror from her voice. She had killed before. Assassination came with being part of the king's service, but these had been Hunters. They had done nothing but follow orders to stand guard and may have had families back home who awaited their return.

It wasn't just because of her magic that she'd left her days as a Hunter behind her; each day it became clearer how much she longed for a simpler life.

"What needed to be done," Ravenna replied. "Don't pretend they wouldn't have done the same to you and your friends if given the chance. Come, we must free them before more arrive."

The two had only taken a few steps before Vespa's voice echoed into the night. "Emma?" There was no way Emma could make out Vespa's face in the darkness, but fairy eyes would see much better in the dark.

"Quiet, fairy! You'll give us away." The witch cast a small flame above them so they would not have to continue on blind. The flickering light was unlike any fire Emma had seen or the electric lights from World Three. A glowing blue orb that appeared to be made of nothing but magic fire floated over their heads.

"There are two of them!" Aldrich's voice was low, but the sound still reached Emma's ears.

"Twice the fun?" Vespa's voice was a half whisper, but Emma could almost hear the smirk.

"This is the sorcerer, spirit?" The witch's face was nearly hidden in the dark, but the intonation implied she was skeptical.

"He possesses a talisman with magic far more powerful than anything you've seen." Emma wasn't completely sure that was true in this world. "It is this item that will be your salvation."

"Sorcerer!" Ravenna demanded, ignoring her own request for silence. "What is this talisman you possess?"

With a flick of her wrist, the witch conjured a second ball of flame. No lantern contained it, yet it didn't appear to be hot. The faces of her friends glowed in its light, the bars of the iron cages holding them casting shadows across their faces.

Despite being imprisoned, Vespa still bore a delighted smile. Apparently, the prospect of not just one but two Emmas coming to her rescue was more thrilling than the threat of Ravenna's wrath.

However, the little color in Aldrich's off-white complexion had drained. Emma wasn't sure if he was more terrified of being captured, of a second Emma being present, or of the fireballs that glowed from nothing, hovering both above them and in Ravenna's hand.

Emma held her breath. For this to work, they were going to have to play along with her ploy, and she had no way of conveying to them what that was or what was at stake without drawing suspicion from the witch.

None of them would leave this world if Ravenna turned on them—at least not through the portal.

"Er . . . yes . . ." Aldrich stumbled, but he at least caught on that he shouldn't argue. So much hinged on what she couldn't control.

"There's two of you!" Vespa said, clapping. "Now we'll have twice as much fun! Or . . ." She paused, lifting her finger to her chin in a thoughtful pose. "Perhaps twice as many drinks?"

"Drinks?" Ravenna questioned, and Emma realized this

was the point where she'd need to step in or risk everything going horribly wrong.

"Yes!" Emma cut in. "As I mentioned, Vespa is a fairy. She prefers to use food and drinks to play tricks on the mortals. You know, fairies being fairies and all."

"Ah, I see. Well, I'm not a stranger to a good drink myself. As you probably know, it was through drink that I discovered my own magical ability."

Emma's heart dropped through her gut and to the dirt below. Air failed to enter her lungs as she struggled to catch her breath and compose herself.

Were drinks only the beginning of what she could do? And if that were the case . . . would her future inevitably mirror that of the woman who stood before her? Drunk on power and a sworn enemy of the mortal realm?

She couldn't think of that now. Too much was at stake. There remained an unasked question in Vespa's eyes, which she needed to address before something couldn't be unsaid.

"As you've likely realized, Ravenna is the witch whose form I've embodied. It is her death I have foretold unless we combine our forces and use the talisman to assist in her quest."

Vespa's smile transformed into another puzzled look, and Emma braced herself as the fairy spoke.

"Talisman?" Vespa asked.

There were worse questions Vespa could have asked at that moment, but for a fairy whose aim was to be helpful, she wasn't doing a particularly good job of it at the moment.

"Demon Box," Emma said through gritted teeth.

"Ah! Yes! Demon Box! Where has that little rascal gotten off to?"

What is that? Demon Box's voice cut in. *The voice of a winged creature? Perhaps an angel? Am I at death's door? Sing to me, sweet cherubim, I await my name at the pearly gates.*

Good grief, Emma thought. *With a name like Demon Box, there will be no pearly gates for you.*

The flame Ravenna held erupted from dull orange into heated red. She lifted both arms, poised to strike, but her eyes darted around, unsure of where the threat was. "Who was that?" she demanded. "Show yourself, fiend!"

"Easy!" Emma raised her hand and cautiously grabbed Ravenna's arm. Despite the tension, she couldn't shake how much it felt like her own. A strange sensation, but it worked to break Ravenna out of her trance. "That's the talisman. We call it Demon Box."

"Fascinating," Aldrich whispered.

"Both of them can hear it!" Vespa said, grasping the professor's hand.

Yes, both of us can hear it. One more way this could all turn out badly. Emma hoped Ravenna wasn't powerful enough to hear *her* thoughts.

Emma could feel the pulse of the crystals calling to her from an iron chest on the back of one of the wagons. Liam might not have known what it was capable of, but he'd figured out enough to lock it away. Thankfully, he hadn't destroyed it.

You're thankful? said Demon Box. *Imagine how I feel!*

Emma rolled her eyes. Whether it was fortuitous or not, she was still able to communicate with the device through, what appeared to be, solid iron. Despite its quips, she was glad the device was unharmed, but it would have to watch what it said if this was going to work out.

Demon Box, you're going to have to play along. We need to bring Ravenna under control, but she can hear anything you say, same as me. If she figures out what you can actually do, she'll spread her hate to other worlds.

Emma waited a beat for the device to acknowledge her words, but it couldn't, not without Ravenna hearing it as well.

"It can communicate with you?" Ravenna asked. If she had heard Emma's words for the device, she hid it well.

"With us, it seems," Emma stated. "Others cannot hear it."

Ravenna flicked her wrist. In one swift motion, the flame in her hand returned to its placid blue form and the iron chest on the wagon opened with as much ease as the lock on her cage had.

Light, was there anything this version of herself couldn't do?

Out of the chest, a familiar black bag rose as though being pulled upward on a string. It rotated, and the bag fell away, revealing Demon Box. Its facade lit up; blue and gold danced along its surface in a frantic pattern.

What's happening! Demon Box called out. *Why am I flying? Put me down! I just had my paneling replaced!*

"You are right, spirit!" Ravenna said as she drew Demon Box toward her along the invisible string. "This talisman possesses a great magic! I have never felt a pull to magic quite like this one! What does it do with so much power? Sorcerer! Explain!"

"Er . . ." Aldrich began. Emma silently willed him not to say too much. "It opens a doorway to control time and space."

Emma winced. That was too close to the truth.

Ravenna cackled. "You don't say. A most excellent gift, spirit. I'll follow your plan if it means my salvation from this fate you've predicted. Plus an opportunity to control this vessel."

Emma nodded. As long as she maintained control of the situation, her plan had a chance to work. "Let's free them, then. There's bound to be more guards making their rounds soon. It wouldn't do for them to raise the alarm now."

"A couple of guards won't be any trouble." The witch closed her palm around the blue flame, and when she opened it again, a small ball of something Emma could only describe as a contained lightning storm materialized. "Let them come. This village will burn to the ground one way or another."

Ravenna closed her fist and the lightning stopped. Then she snapped her fingers and the locks on the cage doors clicked open and fell to the ground.

The locks were solid iron, and they still couldn't repel the strength of Ravenna's magic.

"You cannot set the village ablaze," Emma said. "Not yet. We need to activate and direct Demon Box with discretion. You asked what it would take to avoid your fate. If we make a stand to fight too early, you will fail."

I will fail.

Ravenna rolled her eyes in an all-to-familiar way. "Even though I admire that face of yours, you are really grating on my nerves, spirit."

"I know the feeling." Emma strained the words through gritted teeth.

"You there! What are you doing?" a male voice boomed through the night.

They were already too late.

With Great Power

Chapter Twenty-Eight

Two guards approached. Their dark blue uniforms reflected the light of the lanterns held above their heads.

"Quick!" Emma directed her attention to Aldrich. "Bring Demon Box to the front of The Dragon. We'll meet you there." She motioned Ravenna to hand the device back to Aldrich.

Ravenna almost looked bored by the directive, but surprisingly, she complied without hesitation.

Aldrich's mustache twitched as he took hold of the device again, and he raised an eyebrow.

Trust me. She mouthed the words and intensified her stare in as much earnestness as she could muster. "Once we're there, Ravenna will activate the device. Set it up to fire at the entrance of the pub. Go!"

Aldrich's expression screamed that he was still unconvinced, that this was not a plan he wished to follow. But with one look at the guards, he took Vespa by the hand and steered her toward the front of the building.

Vespa nodded and her face hardened. Her wings appeared as she followed the professor.

"Fae!" one of the guards cried. The sound of metal scraping resounded as they unsheathed their weapons. The two held their swords in front of them, shaking as though they'd never fought a day in their life. For all the magic in this world, fairy creatures, it seemed, still primarily kept out of sight.

A lightning ball formed in the witch's palm. The damned woman was hellbent on killing mortals. No threat of imminent death was going to deter that.

Emma reached out to the men with her magic, to the alcohol in their veins. They'd had more than a few pints over the course of the past few hours.

Stupid guards. But today it would save their lives.

Emma thought back to the night she had unintentionally lightened Liam's mood with his ale. Here the alcohol was already within these men, which should have made it harder to pinpoint, but the current of magic in this world was so strong she could sense the very part of each blood vessel that carried it.

Her counterpart, it seemed, had a flair for the theatrical, as Ravenna could have inflicted more harm upon these men from the inside out. Or perhaps, as she'd gained control of more violent magics, it hadn't occurred to her that she could still influence the properties of the drink after it had been consumed. Either way, Emma poured herself into the two men as she would have into Demon Box, and with it, she issued one simple command:

Run! Run like you've never run before!

There was barely a pause as the two men glanced at each other and then took off in the opposite direction. Ravenna cackled again. Instead of releasing the lightning, or casting it at the men, she unleashed it above her head and into the air. It crackled and snapped, causing a chain reaction in the dark clouds above them. A cascade of lightning rippled through the sky, unleashing one bolt after another into the distance and out over the sea. The result charged the air around them with electricity. Emma's hair stood out on end, strands of it drifting upward as though gravity had relinquished its hold.

All the while, she resisted the urge to glance at her own hands.

Is that what I'm capable of?

It was unnerving enough that she could impart her will upon two other human beings, regardless of it saving their lives. No person should possess that level of power. Should one be allowed to grow so powerful that they could control the skies?

"Leave them," Emma said. "If others don't realize what caused that bolt of lightning to fly upward from the ground, they will certainly take it as a bad omen."

"They're all too drunk to notice." Ravenna was rubbing her hands together, like she was trying to get the electric feel off of them. "Is there no way for you to take another form, spirit? I grow tired of my own voice telling me what to do."

Emma nearly laughed. "You know the lore. Appease the banshee and avoid your fate. Once that's occurred, this will all be over."

As long as this works.

"Tell me more of this talisman. The sorcerer spoke of the ability to control space and time." Ravenna adjusted her robes as though the magic she'd expelled was causing her insides to itch. "But what exactly does it do? How will this help me avoid this fate you've foretold?"

Emma smiled. "It opens a door of infinite possibilities."

Patrons stumbled out of The Cursed Dragon, but they didn't notice either Emma or Ravenna standing near the doorway. Most of them appeared to be heading down the road to O'Sullivan's. Some were making the opposite trip back to The Dragon. Neither tavern would want for coin this evening.

Emma fought the overwhelm of alcohol calling out to her from within the stone walls of the bar. It was a tidal wave threatening to crash down upon her and drown her in an ocean of magic she'd be unable to contain.

"Do you hear it too?" she asked.

"Hear what?" Ravenna huffed as she tore her eyes from the position where Aldrich and Vespa had set up. Demon Box was there, being shifted into position.

"The call of magic from within the pub's walls? Does it sing to you still?"

Ravenna's shoulders and chest relaxed only slightly. "Not as strongly as it once did. Now, other, more basic elements call to me. Fire, electricity, even the Earth itself. Each of these I can use to face my enemies. Drinks? Why waste my time on the stupidity of mortals?"

Emma steeled herself. It might not affect Ravenna, but Emma feared if she let her guard down the call might overtake her. She had to save her focus for Demon Box.

"The sorcerer will have aimed the talisman toward the entrance," Emma explained. "Once I activate it, you head through, and the course of your fate will be altered."

"And with this talisman activated, I'll be able to control the minds of those inside?"

Yeah, sure. Emma thought. What she said was, "Exactly."

"Why would you share this magic with me, spirit? Why not leave me to my fate?"

"You think the mortals' quest stops with witches?" Emma knew the answer to this—it was the very mission of the Hunters. But now she was staring at it from the other side. "Witches, monsters, and otherworldly creatures are just the easy ones to find. What do you think the Hunters will do once they've rid the kingdom of those? Soon fae, banshees, sprites, and all manner of magical creatures will be targets. I've seen what that future would bring, and despite our advantage, a war between men and magic would not end well. You are a great witch, one like the world has never seen. There is a reason they call you queen—you have the power to stop such a fight before it even starts."

It was partially true. The second world they'd visited had seen such a war. She also knew the king and the Hunters would not stop in their quest until all magic had been eradicated. Ravenna would know those things as well. Emma hoped it would be enough to convince her. But she had no doubt that allowing Ravenna to control so much power wouldn't prevent a war—only tip the balance so that those without magic would suffer instead.

Ravenna maintained a steady gaze, but her eyes betrayed the satisfaction she felt at having a spirit compliment her.

Light, am I that vain?

"I can feel the magic contained within that thing from here." Ravenna's lips curled upward. "Such great power within it waiting to be unleashed! I'd ask where you found such a device, spirit, but I doubt you'd tell me."

Emma nodded. She could feel it too. It was almost unbearable with the amplified magic coursing through the air. Sparks danced around the witch's fingers in anticipation.

Are you ready, Demon Box? She wasn't sure if the device would hear her at a distance, but almost immediately, it replied.

Awaiting your direction, madam.

Madam? Who are you trying to impress? Even as she thought the words, she realized the answer was Ravenna. She smirked. Demon Box understood the assignment.

When I give the word, she thought, *I want you to open the gateway to Aldrich's world. And remember, Ravenna can hear what you say. Don't repeat my instructions.*

There was a moment of silence. Emma wasn't sure if the device hadn't heard her or was trying not to give the plan away.

Are you sure that's wise? Came the reply.

Ravenna looked at Emma with distrust for the first time since she'd met her twin.

Yes, thought Emma, *and may I remind you, Ravenna can hear you as well as I can.*

Understood . . . it's just that it will provide Ravenna with an extraordinary amount of power.

Emma let out a sigh of relief and closed her eyes to collect herself.

Thank you.

"That's the plan," she said aloud as she opened her eyes to witness Ravenna beaming with a self-assured grin.

Light, she hoped this was a good idea.

Magic Corrupts

Chapter Twenty-Nine

Emma could have had Ravenna channel into the device, but there was no way for her to know if the witch's intent would override Demon Box's. The device said it set the destination based on her request, but she didn't want to risk the magic weaver having the final say.

She stepped with Ravenna into the lantern light of the street. There were a few drunks walking the street still, but they were so far gone they either didn't recognize the two women or didn't care. In their minds, Ravenna had been caught. There was nothing to concern themselves with.

"The plan is to center ourselves with the doorway. Once the talisman is active, you'll rush through. On the other side everything will change."

Ravenna cackled again, and Emma cringed. It was unnerving hearing herself react in this way. Now she just had to get Ravenna through the gateway and pray this wasn't a gigantic mistake.

Two scruffy-faced men exited the pub and locked their eyes with the pair of women.

"Am I seeing double, Marshal?" One of them asked the other. "Or do we have here a set of twins?"

"If it is twins, it's one for the both of us, Kenneth," the second man guffawed.

"Not . . ." Kenneth drunkenly stumbled over his words. "Not on your life . . . I'm taking . . . them both . . . home."

"We'll see what your missus says about that!"

Both men doubled over in fits of laughter and carried on along their way. The joke had been forgotten, but they were still quite absorbed in their own amusement.

Their appearance raised an interesting question, and Ravenna apparently had the same thought. "What if someone exits the pub while I'm on my way in?" the witch asked. "If they get in the way of the magic before it's finished?"

They'll be vaporized. Demon Box's words cut into her mind.

Emma tugged at her jacket. That hadn't been what she was expecting. She could have asked Ravenna to erect some sort of barrier to prevent them from leaving until the gateway closed, but judging by the wide smile on the witch's face, that wouldn't be happening anytime soon. The thought of the townsfolk disappearing into oblivion delighted the witch.

The door of the pub opened once again, and two men stepped out. One she recognized instantly.

"Activate it now!" Ravenna cried.

Emma was relieved the mirror version of herself hadn't realized that she could have activated Demon Box herself.

"You!" Liam growled at Ravenna as his hand reached for his dagger. Then he saw Emma, and his face contorted in confusion. Liam took three steps forward before pillars of earth rose from the ground before him, blocking his path. He was close enough to the pub that he'd be in the way of the portal's stream.

Even though this wasn't her version of Liam, Emma still didn't want harm to come to the man. She had to think of something.

"Liam . . ." Ravenna's voice was mockingly sweet. "I had high hopes for you."

"Let me go, Emma!" Liam spat the words through gaps in the stone pillars holding him prisoner.

"You know I'm Ravenna now," she said, pulling her hands behind her back with an exaggerated pout. "Emma was a Hunter and that simply wouldn't do. I went from becoming an oppressor to a vigilante for those who can't fight for themselves."

"You're a terror," Liam snarled. "A prime example of how magic corrupts."

Ravenna snorted. "You think magic set me on this path? You think magic is the reason I've worked so hard to fight for those whom you and your Hunters seek out and execute?"

The wind picked up around them, and Emma struggled to keep her hair in place. She lifted her hood so she wouldn't have to fuss with it.

Not a single strand of Ravenna's hair so much as twitched. It was as though her anger was manifesting in the elements around her.

Emma had to do something. She allowed her magic to probe for anything she could use. Demon Box sat ready to go, but that wasn't helpful. Not while Liam was in the way.

Unlike Ravenna, even with this world's increased magic, she was unable to control elements other than drink. She could sense the ale from the pub in front of her. Could she use that to her advantage? She didn't see how.

She could also sense, somewhere behind her, that the ale in O'Sullivan's desperately wanted her power as well. But it was too far away to be of use.

"Magic corrupts." Liam reiterated. "You are the proof."

Lightning balls formed around Ravenna's hands. Emma was going to have to do something soon if she didn't want to watch this version of her friend fry. The wind howled, tugging at tree branches until they were bent over from the strain. Shingles from nearby rooftops peeled off before being tossed down the roadway.

"You think I wanted this, Liam?" Ravenna didn't appear to be shouting, but her voice amplified over the wind with ease. "What did you expect the result to be of having your best friend—your only friend—abandon you because of something you couldn't control? I *loved* you, Liam, and you tossed me away like scraps to a dog."

"You think I didn't *care* about you?" Liam pressed his face against the dirt cage. He had to strain to be heard but there was no passion behind the volume. "I loved you enough to see that you shouldn't have to live with this *curse*." The word spat from his mouth like venom.

Ravenna screamed and lifted her hands, as though intending to pull lightning from the clouds above her.

It was now or never.

Emma reached out, allowing all the magic she could find to flow through her. It was overwhelming, like trying to breathe in a windstorm—which she was also trying to do. The energy nearly flattened her on her back, but she held firm, allowing herself to swim with the current instead of against it.

She reached out to every available unconsumed ounce of alcohol in The Cursed Dragon and yanked on it as one would a rip cord.

Screams filled the pub, but there was no time for any of the patrons to react as a wall of ale came crashing through the door and streaming into the street like a violent river. A wall of yellow liquid shattered glass as it erupted through the window, funneling around the doorway before it rushed toward Ravenna.

As Ravenna looked up, distracted by this new development, the lightning arcing toward her reduced to a simmer. But she couldn't get her hands up in time to stop the brewed flow coming straight toward her.

Liam tensed as the beer passed him, and Emma used the force of the liquid to crash through his dirt cage and knock him down. He grunted as he hit the ground.

Combined into one mass, the beer became one collective entity. Which worked in her favor, since she was going to need to use every bit of concentration she could muster.

She pushed the beer toward Ravenna, whose eyes had gone wide. The witch had still not let go of her lightning completely, and she pushed a wave of electrical current into the mass coming right for her. Emma managed to instruct the wall to rubberize, and the charge harmlessly deflected into the air.

Perhaps there was more she could do with this force than she'd realized.

Emma spun the liquid, forming a cylinder that encased Ravenna within the empty space at its center. It was all Emma could do to disorient her twin, but she knew it wouldn't take long for Ravenna to break through it once she gained her bearings.

Okay Demon Box, your time to shine.

The reply was sarcastic. *Oh, yippee!*

Emma mentally rolled her eyes.

Out of the corner of her eye, Emma caught a glimpse of Aldrich steadfastly watching the entire scene play out but helpless to do anything about it. Vespa was using her magic to keep an array of guards at bay. Nearly a dozen stood shouting, outlining a perfectly formed perimeter. The fairy had trapped anyone who crossed the boundary in a gelatinous mass.

Fool. Emma berated herself. She'd completely ignored the

fact that other Hunters and guards might swarm to try and stop her. She'd need to thank Vespa later.

If it hadn't been for the abundance of magic on this world, Emma had no doubt that what she was about to do would have been impossible. Even as it was, she wasn't entirely sure she'd be able to pull it off.

She tugged on the magic flowing from her into the beer cylinder and pushed a piece toward Demon Box.

Ah! It burns! It burns! Demon Box's cries rattled around in her head.

Sorry!

It was a strain on both her and her magic, trying to accomplish two things at once. Sort of like the childhood game of tapping your head with one hand while rubbing a circle on your belly with the other. If she mixed the intent of either stream, the result could be disastrous. Fortunately, as a Hunter, she'd trained to concentrate under duress and despite any distractions around her.

Emma could already feel Ravenna's push on the cylinder. At first, she assumed she could walk through it, but the beer adapted and pushed back.

Waves of power coursed through Emma's body, and the now-familiar flame of the magic channeling into Demon Box had lit up within her. Except, with the beer magic flowing through her at the same time, it felt like a volcano had erupted from within and would surely burn her alive.

Every part of her wanted to feed into Demon Box. Not just her magic, but her being as well. She had to control the flow, for she feared its full potential would burn out both her and Demon Box as well.

The swirl of colors and darkness that generated in front of The Cursed Dragon called to her, making promises that within its grasp she'd be home.

Except she knew where this portal led. And it wasn't home.

Around the circle, Vespa and Aldrich still stood steadfast. Her senses heightened, Emma could see the beads of sweat rolling down Vespa's face, and the sheer horror reflected on Aldrich's.

These two, who were the most unlikely friends she could have imagined, were her home now. The ones who didn't care whether she possessed magic or not. The ones who were willing to travel to other worlds with her as she realized her dreams. And she'd do the same for either of them.

A wave of dizziness followed, but she steadied her stance. She only had once shot at this.

The wind picked up once again as the portal opened in front of The Cursed Dragon. By this point, she hoped all the patrons had made their escape so the chance of someone running into its backside was minimal.

"You *fool*!" Ravenna cursed as she broke free of the cylinder's grasp. An invisible hand parted it like a curtain, and Ravenna merely stepped through. "What trick is this, spirit?"

Emma didn't have any energy or attention left to respond. Instead, she pushed whatever intent she could muster back into the beer.

It reformed again, transforming from cylinder to the shape of a giant hand. Six-foot tall fingers dripped ale onto the ground below. A Ravenna-sized palm flexed, giving it the odd appearance of having muscle stretched across its liquid form.

With all her strength, Emma pushed a final shove of magic into the beer hand and willed it to force Ravenna toward The Cursed Dragon and into the portal's maw.

Ravenna screamed as lightning bolts flashed around the pub before she disappeared into the spinning disk.

All at once, Emma let go of everything. The portal winked

out, and what beer hadn't followed Ravenna through fell to the dirt, splashing against Emma's cloak and Vespa's gelatinous barrier. The wind that had been responding to Ravenna's magic dissipated, and all fell silent.

Emma's magic didn't dissipate as much as it was sucked out of her, leaving her breathless and hollow.

She collapsed into the beer-soaked mud, and everything went black.

Greatest Adventure

Chapter Thirty

Liam Connor was the first thing Emma saw when she opened her eyes. His brow was furrowed, though Emma couldn't tell whether it was with concern or contempt. She had to admit those graying brows did make him seem perpetually angry.

Her vision cleared, and the smell of dank beer overwhelmed her; she still lay in a mucky swamp of it. She groaned and fought to move. Liam's arm was pointing toward her, and for a moment, Emma feared that after all she'd just been through, he was still going to toss her in irons and haul her and her friends off to London.

However, as she blinked away the dirt and beer, she realized his hand was empty, and his palm was outstretched to help her stand. Hesitantly, she took it. His hand was familiar to the touch. The same size as her Liam's, the same calluses built up from relentlessly handling a sword against monster after monster.

As he pulled her upright, Liam quickly broke contact, ending the magic. He wiped his hand on his dark Hunter's jacket in a smooth movement. She tried not to take it personally; she was covered in dirt and ale, after all.

She's alive! Demon Box shouted.

Emma lifted a hand to her temple. *You realize I'm the only one who can hear you, right?*

Yes . . . right. In that case: You're alive!

Emma stretched her aching joints as she stood. The pounding in the back of her skull was a rude reminder that she was indeed.

It would seem so, she thought.

Seemingly satisfied, Demon Box powered down, its lights dimming and leaving the space around it dark.

Holding the box was Aldrich, who stood beside Vespa. They were several meters back at the edge of the guard-enforced perimeter, hand in hand.

Nobody moved. The Hunter guards remained encased, from the shoulders down, in Vespa's gelatinous goo, and the townsfolk stood fearful that they might meet the same fate if they tried to get too close.

Aldrich's face was a medley of relief and concern. He hurriedly set Demon Box back in his bag, all the while muttering something to himself that Emma couldn't hear.

Vespa's eyes were alight, and her trademark smile broke across her face. Emma half expected her to echo Demon Box's proclamation of her survival, but the fairy seemed content to hold her position, and the guards, for the moment.

Liam discarded his jacket, his dark tunic nearly invisible in the night, save for his light-colored flesh that stuck out from its neck and armholes.

"You saved my life." His eyes maintained their intensity while their dark colors danced, reflecting the light of the surrounding torches and the moon, which had broken free of the cloud cover. "I suppose I owe you yours."

He surveyed her with a gaze that sent shivers through her, causing her flesh to break out with goose bumps. She tried to recall the last time Liam looked at her in that manner and came up short.

"It's remarkable," he said. "You look just like her. How is

that possible? Are you a spirit? Or some benevolent fairy creature brought to rid us of this great evil?"

"I wouldn't have thought you'd believe such a being could ever be benevolent," she snipped.

Liam stood steadfast, neither cracking a smile nor offering a rebuke.

Emma brushed off her hands on her own cloak, trying to mask her hesitation. "I'm not either of those. Ravenna and I are the same. Our choices and circumstances altered who we turned out to be."

Questions reflected on Liam's face, and his mouth moved as he struggled to find the words to voice them.

"Don't worry about the how," Emma said, anticipating his thoughts. "The difference between her and me was the result of how you had treated her. Just because you don't understand something, Liam Connor, does not make it inherently evil. But how we treat others? Showing kindness to someone you don't agree with can be the difference in how the rest of their life plays out."

He paused as if unsure what to make of her words. "Will she be back?" he asked, eyeing the entrance to The Cursed Dragon.

"It's unlikely," Emma said. "Though, at this point, I must admit nothing is impossible."

Liam tightened his lips until they whitened and nearly disappeared from his face. "And you? Now that you've defeated her, do you mean to claim the title of 'queen' for yourself?" He annunciated the word with harsh disdain. "Or do you have other plans?"

Emma smiled. "My plan is to become a bartender, but not here. We will be leaving the kingdom as soon as we are able."

Liam nodded, though his expression didn't change. "Well, in that case, since you saved my life from that witch, I'll let you and your friends free. But I expect you never to show your faces in Lancastria again."

A myriad of responses floated through her head. Most of them quips that would not help her situation. But at the heart of it all, she was tired. Tired of fighting, tired of this war between magic and mortal. She just wanted to leave it all behind. Surely one of these worlds would allow her the rest she desired.

"I have no plans on returning," she said. "All I ask is for a place to sleep tonight, and to be able to leave with my friends in the morning."

Liam pursed his lips in an annoyed glare, but after a moment of contemplation, he nodded.

"Very well," he said. "Now, if you don't mind . . . could you have your fairy release my guards?"

Emma turned to face the crowd after giving Vespa the word to let the guards loose. Each guard grabbed a sword or knife from its sheath and took two steps forward. Liam stopped their advance with a simple raised hand.

The villagers remained where they were. It was likely none but the closest could have heard the exchange that had occurred between Liam and her. She had been in this place many times before. A village, terrified of some influence that had been haunting them for days, weeks, sometimes years.

How many villages had she saved from such a threat in the past? How many of those threats, like Ravenna, had only turned on mortals because of how they'd been treated?

She'd thought she had addressed the last of these crowds, but all they saw was a woman with the same face as their aggressor who'd just defeated that witch by using magic. Provoked by the Hunters or not, Ravenna had terrorized these people. She owed them something.

"The witch, Ravenna, is gone now." Emma naturally

amplified her voice toward the crowd as she had done addressing so many villages in the past.

Despite the familiar position, it felt strange. She'd spent her life removing those accused of performing magic, but this needed to be different. She was no longer a Hunter—she'd performed magic in front of these people—and though she conjured ale instead of lightning, it was still magic. These villagers were like so many she had stood before—their eyes wide, lips and limbs trembling in the light of the torches and lanterns they carried. Each of them was terrified of the magic that had threatened to ruin them and their town. But having seen one magic pitted against another? They wouldn't know what to think.

"Your village is safe from her. As some of you saw, I used magic to banish her to another realm. Despite what you have been told—despite what even I've believed and lived for my entire life—I've come to learn that magic is neither good nor evil but simply a tool. You will never be rid of magic completely—it washes over this world like a tidal wave. It's guaranteed that some will be caught in its wake, as it is as much a part of this world as each of you are. Ravenna did not start out evil, but she was backed into a corner by those who wished to do her harm. Don't use her as an excuse to persecute those who can touch the fabric of magic. Use her as an example of how you failed a human who has the same needs as any of us. Love and kindness."

Emma didn't know what she expected. Applause? Cheers of celebration? What she received instead was stony silence. The only noise came from the distant roar of the waves crashing against the cliffs on the shoreline. The evening's natural breeze had returned, gently caressing the skin of her face and hands.

The Hunters stood firm, swords in hands. Their glares moved from Emma and her party to their leader for direction.

"That's enough for tonight." Liam's voice was flat and hollow. She'd expected anger, but if this Liam were anything like hers, she would swear he was considering the words of her speech. He would have performed much the same routine as she had from village to village—without the plea for magic users, of course. Whether it was Emma's performance or her message, the townsfolk were rattled enough that they failed to be as eager to break off to the pubs as they had been earlier. They simply stopped and stared at each other as though unsure what to do next.

"Everyone return to your homes," he continued. "The threat has waned. At least for now."

It took some convincing—especially after Emma had cleared The Cursed Dragon of ale—but Mr. O'Malley eventually agreed to allow Emma, Vespa, and Aldrich to rent rooms above the pub. It turned out that King Leopold had placed quite the bounty on Ravenna's head, and since Emma did rid the world of the witch, the prize was technically hers.

Even if she were sticking around, Emma wasn't in any position to accept such a reward. It would be awkward to show up in London with Ravenna's face and request it—though she had to admit, she would have loved to have seen the king's expression. So, instead, Liam promised he'd return with the news and forward the appropriate sum to Mr. O'Malley to compensate for damages.

Liam provided O'Malley with a Warrant of Entitlement on the king's behalf that appeased him enough that he opened the few rooms he had to his strange new guests.

"What I wouldn't give for a hot Hibernian cider right now," Aldrich said as he alternated between sipping the wine from his glass and holding it up with one eye open as though he might learn something from its color.

Emma forcefully swallowed as she took her own sip. The wine *was* awful. She'd wanted desperately to speak to it, but even with the abundance of magic that still hummed around her, she was too tired. The evening's duel had drained her of all energy, and even sitting at the table demanded a monumental effort.

Nearly the entire village had gone home for the night. There would be no celebrations to mark the departure of Ravenna, not as long as Emma remained in Cuanmore.

Vespa seemed indifferent to the wine. Instead, she spent her time studying the pub that was almost the same as the one where she and Emma had first met.

Only a few guards lingered at the tables, begrudgingly sipping on wine that hadn't been used in the assault. They took a particular interest in her, glaring daggers at her when they thought she wasn't looking. Most of them were still dripping with the goo they'd been encased in. Emma couldn't help but smile. Other than ordering drinks and a few indiscriminate grumbles, none of them had spoken more than a few words since the portal had opened.

Aldrich also appeared rattled by the entire encounter. The color was still absent from his face, and his eyes darted around the room as though unable to focus. It was easy to forget that he had come from a world without magic. Even in her own world, her position had ensured she'd dealt with magic users frequently, where most people would encounter one, maybe two magical beings throughout their entire lifetime. So even though Ravenna was the first one she'd actively used magic *against,* it wasn't as much of a shock to her.

Vespa had cuddled up next to the professor, her head resting on his shoulder.

It was the fairy who broke the silence after sitting up briefly and lifting her own glass of wine to her lips. "You haven't told us yet, Emma, where did you send the other version of yourself?"

"The only place that made sense."

Vespa looked confused as did Aldrich.

Emma gave the professor a knowing nod. "I sent her back to the professor's world."

Vespa's mouth opened in horror. "What! Why?"

Aldrich tilted his head as he put the pieces together. "Because there's no magic there."

"Exactly," said Emma. "And with no magic users to help her out, she won't be able to leave either. Hopefully, she'll be able to discover who she is without her powers."

Vespa grinned. "Maybe she'll get a job with Mia as a bartender!"

"It's possible," Emma laughed. "But we won't know for certain unless we decide to go back to Aldrich's world."

"That could be awhile," Aldrich said, nodding. His complexion had returned as the conversation pulled him out of whatever thoughts he'd been having. "Your fight has made me realize the potential of what could be added to my research. The possibilities are terrifying, but what a scientific treasure trove! When we return to my world, I'll have detailed notes and research that my colleagues will be able to test."

"You haven't given up on returning to your world, then?"

Aldrich raised his hands, palms facing Emma. "Heavens, no! Not by a long shot. I'll travel with you as long as I can, but these findings must be shared with my world. Granted, I won't need to stay long once I do." He rubbed Vespa's hand reassuringly.

"Well, I hope not every world is as adventurous as this one," Emma said as she surveyed the bar. Liam's guards had finally tired of staring them down and were now talking and laughing among themselves. For a moment, things in the bar seemed almost normal. If she closed her eyes and imagined she was back in her home world, she could pretend she was just another patron, enjoying . . . er . . . at least sipping on a glass of wine.

She inhaled deeply.

"I hope it *is* as adventurous!" Vespa clapped.

"Vespa! Are you serious?" Emma laughed. "We just were imprisoned! Liam could have executed us on the spot! Never mind that Ravenna was incredibly powerful! We're lucky I was able to convince her I was a banshee."

"You didn't want to save the world, but you at least saved this town! Think of all the people you could help with your giant beer hand!"

That remark turned a few heads.

"I'm not interested in saving the world," Emma said. "You were the one who convinced me that there's value in seeking a quieter life. I have already saved hundreds of villages. Do you know how many monsters roam our lands? It's exhausting. Aside from my magic, there was a reason I wanted to work at the bar. *This* is a refuge for people. A place they can go where they don't have to think about monsters, or witches, or the expansionary wars of the kingdom."

"But look at how many people we helped!" Vespa said. "Plus, they might not be as scared of magic now."

Emma shook her head. "If anything, I might have made them more afraid. People are scared of what they don't understand."

"I must admit,"—Aldrich nodded—"as fascinating as it was

to witness this shift in reality, I, too, would prefer something a little less . . . dangerous."

Emma smiled and lifted her glass to her two friends across the table. "I am happy the two of you are safe."

They lifted their glasses in return, and warmth flowed through Emma. This time, it wasn't magic, not in the way she had thought of it. Instead, it came from knowing she'd found where she belonged.

Despite not knowing which world they might end up in, Emma had a home with these two and even Demon Box. Emma had never imagined she'd be one to possess any sort of magic, but the power that existed between these friends was perhaps the greatest surprise of all.

Vespa beamed, her fairy glow pulsing around her. "So, where to next?"

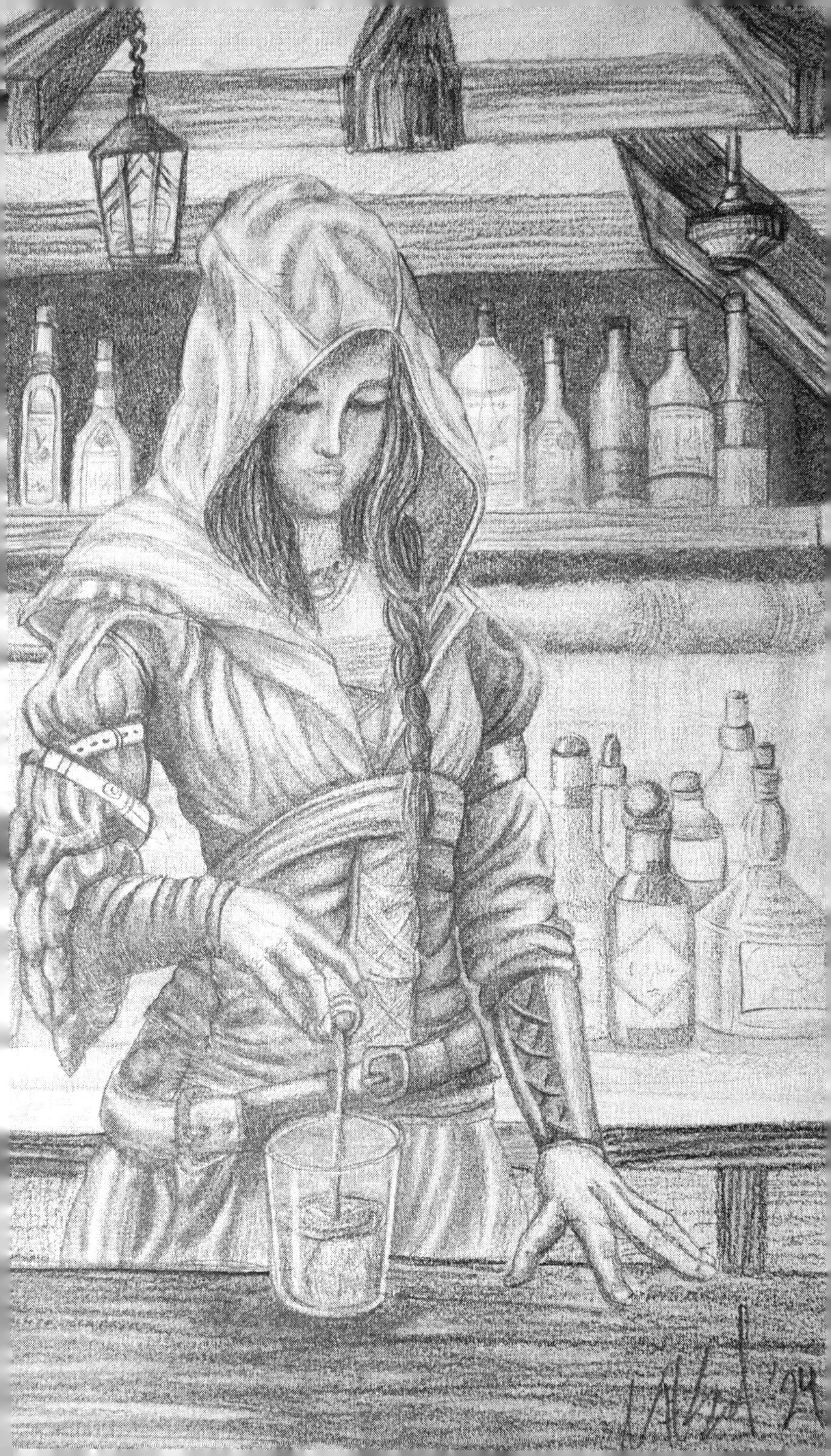

Epilogue

World Five

Emma set down the glass she'd been cleaning on the bar and smiled as a new patron approached. She was so engrossed in her thoughts that she hadn't noticed who the man was until she looked up.

Emma swallowed, forcing down any outward reaction to the violent storm of emotion that surged through her insides. Her stomach tied itself in knots, but she put on her calmest face. This shouldn't have been more difficult than facing a legion of magical creatures, but somehow it was.

"What are you having?" she asked.

The traveler smiled, and Emma struggled to maintain her composure. She wondered if she'd ever get used to seeing Liam's face on someone who was not her Liam. She doubted it.

He was different here, of course. The world they'd traveled to after her fight with Ravenna was nearly as technologically advanced as Aldrich's but had enough magical residue that she could still sense the alcohol she worked with. It was a place, they'd decided, where they could stop and catch their breath for a while. It seemed the people here were unaware of magic's existence and, according to Vespa, the fae hadn't bothered themselves with humankind for centuries and were happy to keep to their own realm.

This version of Liam had the youthful face she remembered from her own world. Gone were the gray hairs and worry lines of World Four Liam. He was dressed from head to toe in a slim-fitting charcoal suit that emphasized the bulk of his shoulders and athletic shape of his torso. His hair had been styled neatly, in a way that was fitting for this world, but the Liam she knew would never have worn it like this. Like much of what she'd encountered in World Five, this Liam was a cleaner version of himself.

"I'll take the best ale you've got," he said.

"Well, that's a matter of preference," Emma replied steadily. "We've got a few on tap right now. Do you want me to list them for you?"

"Dealer's choice," Liam said with a familiar boyish smirk as he tapped his payment card on the bar top absently. "Say, do I know you from somewhere? You look awfully familiar."

Emma inhaled deeply. Over the course of the past few weeks in World Five, she had tried not to think too hard about where her counterpart might be—if she'd existed in this place at all. It had been difficult, but she had resigned herself to the fact that she might never know. Now, Liam stood before her, and if they had ever met here, it hadn't been more than in passing.

She could accept that a flow of events might cause a rift between them, but to never have met? She struggled to wrap her head around that fact.

But Aldrich had gone over this with her a dozen times. She possibly didn't even exist in this world. The probability of a person being born at all was infinitely small. There would be many worlds with Liam in them, but not her, and many with her and not him, and infinitely more without either of them. The similarities in worlds they had already encountered was a testament to how much easier it was for Demon Box to open gateways to worlds similar to ones it had already been to.

She'd tried not to think about it too much. But Liam's

sudden appearance as a patron of The Cursed Dragon threw her head into a spin.

"I don't know," Emma answered truthfully as she pulled on the tap for a fresh, hazy pale ale. It was the seasonal rotation, and its notes of citrus and apricot made her mouth water every time she poured it. "Do you come out to Cuanmore often?"

Liam shook his head. "This is the first time I've been out this way, actually. It's a beautiful city."

"Did you come in from London?" Emma finished the pour and set the pint on the counter before sliding it over to the man with her friend's face.

"Is it that obvious?" Liam ran a hand through his hair.

"The accent gives it away." Emma smirked.

Liam held her gaze thoughtfully. The smile faded into something more nervous.

"Your accent isn't Irish either. You're from England as well, aren't you? London?"

"Close enough," Emma replied.

"Listen," he said. "I'm only in town for a couple of days, and I rarely do this, but . . . is there a chance you'd want to grab a coffee? Maybe you could tell me more about Cuanmore—things I shouldn't miss while I'm here, that sort of thing?"

Emma let her gaze slide across the floor of The Cursed Dragon to where Vespa and Aldrich sat. They were engrossed in their own conversation, hands clasped across the table, and weren't paying attention to her or the man who was not-Liam trying to ask her out.

"Are you asking me out?" She knew he was, but she was stuck for what to say.

"What if I am?"

"As lovely as that sounds." Emma bit her lip. "This is not

really the best time for me to start a relationship. Especially something that would be long distance."

Long distance—that was an understatement. They hadn't put a time limit on their stay here, but she knew Aldrich would be eager to catalog new worlds soon.

"From coffee to relationship?" Liam chuckled. "Just like that?"

"What, are you just looking for some fun tonight? If you are, maybe I've misread you."

"Who said it needed to be casual? You could come with me to London," Liam said without missing a beat. "I'm sure there would be an interesting bar where you could pour drinks."

Emma smiled. That *was* something her Liam would have said—cocky and obliviously foolish.

"Ah!" he said, without giving her a chance to respond. "I knew that would pique your interest. You don't look like someone who would be content to stay in one spot."

As much as she knew this wasn't her Liam, his boyish charm was hard to resist. He was being ridiculous, but she understood his sense of humor, and knew he was trying to get a laugh out of her.

It worked. "Why don't we start with a cup of coffee," she said. "Maybe I could get to know you more. *Then* maybe we can discuss whether I'd move back to London or not."

"Great!" He rapped on the bartop again. "It's a date. Where should I meet you?"

"There's a place down the street called Rudy's Bakery. Meet me there at eight tomorrow morning."

He took a swig of his drink and his eyes lit up as he studied his glass like he couldn't believe what he'd just tasted. "You weren't kidding. This is fantastic."

Emma nodded. "This one's on the house. I'll see you tomorrow."

With a self-satisfied grin, Liam took his drink and made his way to an empty seat at the far side of the bar.

The airy tapping of Vespa's feet announced she had approached before Emma had even turned around.

"I know what you're going to say," Emma said.

"You do?" Vespa replied lightly. "Can you read minds now too?"

Emma picked up a cloth and wiped at an already clean spot on the bar. "I know we're not staying here. I know it's probably a bad idea. But it's just coffee."

"Your psychic abilities aren't as good as you thought," Vespa said. "I wasn't going to say you shouldn't meet with him."

"You weren't?" Emma lifted an eyebrow as she grabbed the next glass that needed a polish.

"There are likely millions of versions of Liam out there," Vespa said. "But I still believe there's only one version you're meant to be with. Despite each of them having similarities, each of them will be unique in some way. Just like the version of you in the last world might have shared many things with you, she wasn't you."

"But what if I'm meant to be with the version of Liam I left behind?"

"If that's the case, Aldrich has the coordinates for your world. But you know how things will end if you return there."

"Probably tied to a spit and lit on fire."

Vespa paused, maybe to consider whether Emma was being serious or not, then continued. "My point is, you've spent your entire life living under the expectations of someone else—of who the kingdom said you should be. Take some time to figure out who you are along the way, but that doesn't mean you need to shrug off possibilities. Just don't hold on too tight until you're ready. Aldrich is mapping all of these worlds. You can always return someday."

"You don't think I'm setting myself up for heartbreak?"

Vespa puckered her lips as she thought. "Heartbreak is part of being human. But without a little risk, you might miss out on something grander than you could have ever expected."

Emma smiled. "Thank you, Vespa. And if it makes you feel better, I have no intentions of starting anything serious anytime soon. Right now, all I want to do is practice mixing drinks and explore new places."

"When you've found where you're meant to be," Vespa said with a wink, "you'll know. Besides, I don't think this is the end of our story just yet. I don't think Liam's part is done either."

Emma smiled. "For the first time, I have friends who care about me. I can explore as I like, and,"—she nodded to the glass she was holding—"I get to do something I've always wanted to try. I know where I'm meant to be—at least in this moment. And for right now, that's all that matters."

"I agree," Vespa said. "Now how about you mix me a drink?"

The Greatest Pub In The Multiverse

ACKNOWLEDGMENTS

If you had asked me four years ago if I thought I'd be sending out my tenth book into the world I might have laughed at you. Publishing a novel has been a dream of mine ever since I was a kid, but until a few years ago it was something I had always thought was out of reach. As I grew older that dream seemed more and more like something that I'd never actually get to.

The Bartender Between Worlds holds a special place in my publishing journey. Not only for being my tenth work, but already, as I write these notes pre-launch, it has defied my expectations and shaped the path that the rest of my writing career is sure to follow. The support has been overwhelming, and there is not enough thanks in the world for those who have stood alongside me during this journey.

First and foremost I need to send a huge thank you to my wife, Nettie Steuernagel, for the amazing illustrations included in this book. I literally couldn't do this without your support and belief in me and my writing.

I also need to send out a huge thank you to Natalie Cammarata for the developmental edits and the fun commentary you provided in your notes. It made the editing process that much more enjoyable and I appreciate the time you spent on it (in the midst of a move and your own book launch no less)!

Aime Lund, I appreciate the Copy Editing & Proofreading that you do. Thank you for diving into the details and going above and beyond in what you do.

To the Miblart team. You exceeded my expectations with this cover. Thank you for the work you continue to do to help bring more readers to my books.

Joshua Del Toro, I'm so glad I stumbled onto your TikTok account. Thank you so much for the TikTok launch party that you hosted with me and the recipes you provided for the special edition. You helped the Kickstarter build that initial momentum that set the trajectory for the entire campaign.

I can not possibly try to name each and every person here as I'm sure to forget someone. Please know, if you have been in conversation with me, supported me, interviewed me, been interviewed by me, retweeted, reposted, rethreaded, reviewed, or given a long-distance high-five in this direction, you are appreciated and I thank you for the positive energy and vibes.

Last, but by no means least, I need to thank the incredible 381 backers of the Kickstarter campaign for this book. With the help of these amazing readers I was able to not only fund this book entirely, but also create a phenomenal limited special edition in addition to producing the audiobook version. These supporters showed me that this author dream is something I can make a reality and I thank you from the bottom of my heart. You'll never truly know what your support has meant to me.

Listed in alphabetical order of first name:

A. Martinez, A. Muhovich, Aaron K, Abigail Santos, Abigail Spears, Ace T B, Adam Arvidsson, Adrian Keen, Adva Shaviv, Alex Grade, Alex Lewis, Alex Wrigglesworth, Alexandra Corrsin, Alexandre Pirot, Alice Blette, Alison Finn, Allee Snyder, Allie McDermott, Alpaca, Amanda Balter, Amanda Corbin, Amber Toro, Amy Nguyen, Andrew Haug, Angela Haas, Anja Peerdeman, Anna Desouza, Anna Kensing, Annie Kavanagh, AnnMarie Aho, Ariane Beauparlant, ArkRoTan, Aruktai, Arwyn Cunningham, Ashara N. Taylor, Astridd, Ayla Walker, B Davies, Benjamin Port, Bet Zyx, Big Bad John, Bill Kohn, Billie J. Davis, Boe Kelley, Book traveler, Bram H-W, Brieane Shanahan, Bruno San Agustin, Bryan Geddes, C Villasenor, Caleb Christensen, Caledonia, Camilla Vavruch, Cara Blaine, Caranam, Carol Gonzales, Carolee S, Cassie Newell, Cat, Catherine Holmes, Catherine McPherson, Chance, Chanting Darner, Charlotte E. English, Charlotte Pleym, Chelsea Wehn, Cherelle H, Cheyenne P., Chris Roeszler, Christa Concannon, Christina Baclawski, Christine Andres, Clare Van Eede, Clarissa, Colleen Boyd, Cori Ander, Corinne Brucks, Cortney Babcock, Crohnic Gamer, CrookedAnchors (Craig), CrystalLakeManagement, Cyndi Taylor, Damon Morton, Dan Kenner, Daniel E. Coolbaugh, Dave Litsky, David DeHaan, David Holzborn, David Van De Kop, Dead Fish Books, Dean Lambert, Dean Randolph, Debra Lynn May, Dee Rooney, Deidre Downs, Denise Jaden, Diane Hansebout, Diego Riley, Dinsy Johns, Dion Doege, DJ, Dominic Chiavassa, Dominique Declerck, Donna Bull, Eddie Joo, Elizabeth Simpson, Emma Adams, Emma Brown, Emma F., Enconto, EphemeralDreamer, Eric R. Asher, Esteban, Fallenzap, Eun-byeol Kim, Fay, Felicitas Odemer, Fernanda S., Figmentsdreams, Fira Richardson, Frank Rosellen, Frederick Nace, Frejs, Gaby van Halteren, Gary Olsen, GASIWAC, Glitch in Normality, Grae, Haleigh Kirch, Haven Currie,

Holger, Horatio Astor, Hugo Essink, Izaak, J A Mortimore, J Mills, J. Mead, Jacob joseph, Jan B, Jason Pulham, Jax Naylor, JED, Jen Morton, Jenna Levitski, Jeramie Vens, Jesper Kaudern, Jessica Armstrong, Jessica Hoyal, Jessica Rae, Jessica Staub, Jessica West, Jessie Gary, JHMcKeen, Joakim Pramanik-Jonsson, John Fritz, John Idlor, John Ladley, John O, John P Curtin, John W. Mahaney, Jon Jordan, Jonathan and Tara Martens, Jordan M, Jordan Stiles, Jorick, Josh Syl Wyant, Joshua Duncan Gibson, Joshua Magady, Judy McClain, K. V. Sentinel, Kaitlyn Sexton, Kaitlyn VanderPloeg, Karen Bulgarelli, Kasey, Katalin Laczina, Katelyn Mason, Kayla Stonecypher, Kelly, Kelly McMahon, kellygreengold, Kellyn Stinnett, Kelsey Stenberg, Ken Seed, Kent M. Smith, Kenyon Wensing, Keric, Kevin Scott, Kimberly, Kris M, Kristen Altmann, Kristie, Krystal Bohannan, Kurt Beyerl, Kyle G Wilkinson, Kylee Reed, L Brochu, L Gase, Laura Pomerantz, Lauren, LC, Lee Butler, Lianne Watkins, Lilith Sylvia Daisy Mühlberg, Liz Shipton, Lizzy Grohmann, Louise Margareta Josefa Raudzus, Lovis Geier, Lucas C. Kascher, Luke Lorah, Luna Sky, M Oritz, Magda, Maggie Laigaie, Manja Engel, Margaret Menzies, Margie, Marie Cordalis, Mark Geier, Marko S, Martin Carpenter, Mary Crauderueff, MaryAnne Armstrong, Marybeth Martin, Matthew Goodall, Maya H, McKenna Hubbard, Megan O'Rusell, Megyn "Sapphi" MacDougall, Melissa T, Meredith Carstens, Michael Johnson, Michelle LaCrosse, Mighty Taco, Mik, Mike H., Miranda Forner, Mirthys_Law, Misha R Pantoja, Momo, Mordechai Gofman, Nadine Britt, Nat, Natalie Munford, Natasha Hanold, Natasha Rueschhoff, Nava Starling, Nicolas Mandujano, Nicholas Ryan, Nicholas W Fuller, Niki Kuhlman, Nikki Malakoff, Oliver Butwell, Oneirica, Or'El, Paul Smith, Paula Roszina, Per M. Jensen, Peter Allen, Philip H., Phoenix, pjk, Rachel Lowe, Rachel

McGill, Rae Moore, RainbowKitty, Raven, Ray, Raychel Kill, Rebecca Chasen, Rebekah, Renee Denison, Renske, Richard Sawyer, Riot Blake, Risa Scranton, Rob Cifaldi, Rob Steinberger, Robby E Haentze, Robert E Creed, Robyn Moore, Rosa Thill, Ross H Pitman, Rowan Stone, Russell, Ryan H., Ryan Todd, Sam Errakis, Samantha Bartell, Samantha Newberry, Sarah Munsil, Sarah Niebergall, Sarah S., Sarah VP, Scott R., Seaken, Sean Elliott, Sentrosi7, Shane Millar, Sharon Lawrence, Shay Dinur, Shelby Tubbs, Sherry Mock, Shirley Stenabaugh, Silvia Amber, Simon Mark de Wolfe, Sissel Rasmussen, Sneaky_Bacon, Sonya M., Starflakes13, Starr Z Davies, Stephanie, Stephanie Meredith, Steven Byrd, Stevie Rose, Stine-Mari, Susan Wilson, SushiMango, Suzanne & Puck, SwordFirey, Tania, Tania Rocha, Tanja Blette, Tanya Young, Tara de Jong, Taylor D., Thaddeus Stokes, The Wimmers, TheMightyKitsune, Thomas Belanger, Thorrikk, Tiffany C, Tilly Wallace, Toby Sellwood, Tom Fowler, Tommye Rozee, Twinneko, Tyler Cheek, Vel, Vicki Hsu, Vincent Saint Vincent, Vulpes, Will, Windingsea, Wizard Flight, Wyngarde, Z.S. Diamanti, Zaqueen, Zephyr Mini, & zoe.

Thank you all once again. M

Made in the USA
Middletown, DE
24 July 2024